For Edgar

For Edgar

Sheldon Rusch

BERKLEY PRIME CRIME, NEW YORK

THE BERKLEY PUBLISHING GROUP
Published by the Penguin Group
Penguin Group (USA) Inc.
375 Hudson Street, New York, New York 10014, USA
Penguin Group (Canada), 90 Eglinton Avenue East, Suite 700, Toronto, Ontario M4P 2Y3, Canada
(a division of Pearson Penguin Canada Inc.)
Penguin Books Ltd., 80 Strand, London WC2R 0RL, England
Penguin Group Ireland, 25 St. Stephen's Green, Dublin 2, Ireland (a division of Penguin Books Ltd.)
Penguin Group (Australia), 250 Camberwell Road, Camberwell, Victoria 3124, Australia
(a division of Pearson Australia Group Pty. Ltd.)
Penguin Books India Pvt. Ltd., 11 Community Centre, Panchsheel Park, New Delhi–110 017, India
Penguin Group (NZ), Cnr. Airborne and Rosedale Roads, Albany, Auckland 1310, New Zealand
(a division of Pearson New Zealand Ltd.)
Penguin Books (South Africa) (Pty.) Ltd., 24 Sturdee Avenue, Rosebank, Johannesburg 2196, South Africa

Penguin Books Ltd., Registered Offices: 80 Strand, London WC2R 0RL, England

This book is an original publication of The Berkley Publishing Group.

This is a work of fiction. Names, characters, places, and incidents either are the product of the author's imagination or are used fictitiously, and any resemblance to actual persons, living or dead, business establishments, events, or locales is entirely coincidental. The publisher does not assume any responsibility for author or third-party websites or their content.

First edition: August 2005

Library of Congress Cataloging-in-Publication Data

Rusch, Sheldon.
    For Edgar / Sheldon Rusch.—1st ed.
        p. cm.
    ISBN 0-425-20409-X
    1. Poe, Edgar Allan, 1809–1849—Influence—Fiction. 2. Police—Illinois—Henry
County—Fiction. 3. McHenry County (Ill.)—Fiction. 4. College teachers—Fiction. 5. Serial
murders—Fiction. 6. Policewomen—Fiction. I. Title.

PS3618.U74F68 2005
813'.6—dc22   2005041137

PRINTED IN THE UNITED STATES OF AMERICA

10 9 8 7 6 5 4 3 2 1

For Edgar

O N E

On a Tuesday morning in mid-September, the last thing Elizabeth Taylor Hewitt needed was a dying crow at the edge of the road she walked each day to give her mind a respite from the subject of death. And the worst thing she could have done in violation of her morning routine was to stop and observe the creature in its waning moments of earthly existence. But stop she did, her black trainers scraping to a halt on the pockmarked asphalt, her overworked eyes coming to a rest on the gleaming black plumage of the bird.

West-freaking-Nile. Textbook example.

It wasn't enough that the summer had been filled with media reports of the latest human case of the disease and the running count of the poor, immuno-compromised souls who had succumbed to the awful thing. But then to have these hellish lawn-ornament-reminders of the peril—regardless of the data that downplayed the threat to the general population—it was almost as if nature was playing some twisted version of Truth or Dare with the human species, some backyard barbecue game of mosquito roulette.

Hewitt looked for a sign that the thing was, in fact, still alive. Some movement of its breast. Some flinch of its beak. Some shudder of its tucked and silent wings. But a minute passed and there was nothing. Which left Hewitt to wonder if the thing had already died, standing up, just like that. It struck her that the bird appeared nothing like a creature that had recently been capable of taking to the skies, but rather like a carcass that had already been invested with taxidermy, the sheen of the body already vibrant in a fresh coat of shellac.

She assumed, however, that a dead crow couldn't stand straight up. Not this long anyway. So the wet veneer had to be something else. Something not applied, but expressed. Did crows sweat? Or maybe it was the bird's way of doing something else altogether. Absent the ducts necessary for such expression, maybe this was the way a dying bird wept.

Christ it was a freaking crow. A nasty, arrogant, squawking, pain-in-the-ass crow. Hell, she hated crows, hated everything about them. She also knew it was harder to hate a dying thing than a living one—even in the extreme, when applied to the most demonic purveyors of homicide. Whether the killers lay dying on a sanitized gurney in the death cell at State Prison, or at her feet—in one instance in her arms—from a bullet administered by her own service revolver, death was never something to celebrate. Death was always a bad ending.

It was an unseasonably cold morning for late September in the Midwest. Hewitt was glad she'd grabbed the barn coat on the way out. If she could have done anything to help the godforsaken crow, she would have. She told herself, promised herself that. But between the earth below and the heaven that existed somewhere beyond the bubble of the silver-blue sky, there wasn't a Goddamn thing she could do.

It moved. A heave of its chest and an angling upward of its beak. Enough to send a shiver through Hewitt's nervous system. She reached back and turned up the collar of her coat, felt the reassurance of a little extra warmth at the back of her neck. She felt her feet moving, her legs and hips turning. And then she was no longer looking at it, was, in fact, walking away, walking home.

It was about a half-mile back to the condo. And once she got there, the exact same distance back to the dying crow. One difference in her approach to the bird the second time was that she wouldn't be surprised by it. The other difference was the weight of her service revolver in the right side pocket of the barn coat.

It was a really idiotic thing to be doing. To any sane onlooker. And definitely in the eyes of State of Illinois firearms law. But counting present company, there were no particularly sane onlookers to be found. And the one State of Illinois law enforcement official present had already decided to look the other way.

Her eyes read the roadside. Goldenrod dominating. With pockets of expired tiger lilies. The barbed branches of a wild rose bush, its pink flowers long since gone to floral dust.

She fingered the revolver in her pocket, liked, as she always did, the no-nonsense hardness of it, its ability to always feel several degrees cooler than the temperature of the rest of the world.

She felt the safety. On.

Less than a hundred yards now to where the crow stood waiting. Waiting, as fate had decided, for her, her resolution to its plight. Hewitt was surprised by the rigid purposefulness to her walk, the way her body had become so geared up for her use of the weapon. Crow or not, her adrenals were up and pumping.

Thirty yards to the terminal bird. Twenty. Ten . . .

Jesus. The crow was down. Of all the damn things, the ungrateful bird had gone ahead and died without her. In her mid-back she felt a flutter. Her adrenals bailing on her.

She'd underestimated the West Nile. It was more efficient than she'd figured.

Screw you, sweet cheeks. This bird is mine.

She retrieved her hand from the pocket of her coat, forcing her fingers to abandon the cold metal foreplay.

THE IMAGE OF the glistening black bird stayed with her through her breakfast and shower. It even reanimated long enough to hop up into the front passenger seat of her blue Mazda for the commute into headquarters. In fact, it didn't leave her alone until the third cut on her John Coltrane/Johnny Hartman CD—*My One and Only Love.*

Chicks Who Like Jazz. She was a card-carrying member of the association. It was always a little comical, how the jazz thing could be intimidating to men. Especially on a first date. The first time the opening measures of "So What" came humping and bumping their way out of her living room stereo. To the inevitable question, with one or two exceptions, her answer was always short but helpful—in a music store kind of way. "Miles Davis. *Kind of Blue*."

Funny too, how quickly a man could override his initial intimidation. Usually in the same evening. Jazz and tits, cool. Jazz with a pussy chaser, good to go.

Anything to make the evening special.

Hearing the deep crooning voice of Johnny Hartman with the smoky-lung genius of the Coltrane sax made Hewitt's mind ache for a special evening. Now that she was shaded to the far side of thirty-five, she experienced these occasional pangs, these quickenings, and the suggestion that it wasn't just standard issue horniness but was more of a little pink Post-It note from her reproductive system—that if she was ever going to use it for what it was ultimately intended, time was definitely a-wasting. And beyond that, in a deeper aspect of life's long-range planning, was the notion that whether she used the love equipment to bear children or simply to make her day-to-day struggle a little more bearable, there was no sense wasting it. Because the day would arrive when the dying bird would come to roost on her own lawn.

Her cell phone rang, and she clicked on to the voice of her supervisor, Captain Ed Spangler. She didn't bother to turn the volume down on Coltrane/Hartman. Spangler was well aware of her little jazz problem.

"En route, Hewitt?"

"Ten minutes out."

"I was wondering if your vehicle has a valid sticker for the Illinois state park system," Spangler barked in his day-after-attending-a-football-game voice.

"Which park, and what did they find?"

"Chain-O-Lakes. A mom and her little girl out hiking. Found a human skull nailed to a tree. I guess the kid is actually the one who found it."

Hewitt flashed the thought of herself as a child, what it would have been like, poking around the bushes and trees and looking up to see a freaking skull staring back. "Well, at least she'll always have the scariest story when she goes to camp."

"County sheriff's already there with techs," Spangler said. "But because of the location, it's our jurisdiction. I'd like you to head up there and have a look."

"A day in the park with some new friends," Hewitt said. "How could I say no?"

TWO

The little girl stood at her mother's side, her right hand in the pocket of her powder-blue sweatshirt. If not for the official outfit of the McHenry County sheriff's deputy with them, the child might have been waiting dutifully while her mother discussed wing bars with an ornithologist on a morning bird walk.

Hewitt had the girl square in her sights as she walked toward the taped-off oak tree that had now become a state landmark for the sorriest of reasons. Off Hewitt's shoulder, the McHenry County sheriff, Dave Mangen, was filling her ears with his personal twist to the discovery.

"I mean of all the damn things. Hell, my only daughter delivers her first child last night. My first grandchild. A boy yet. And seven-thirty this morning I get the call to come out here to see this God-damn thing. Not exactly the way you want to spend your first day as a grandfather."

"You're the sheriff," Hewitt said. "When bad things happen, you're the one they call. From my experience, bad things don't take a lot of days off."

"Hell, no one knows that better'n I do," Mangen half-spat as they ducked under the tape. "It's just that it'll be hard not to remember the one with the other . . ."

His voice trailed off as the oak tree greeted them. Hewitt's eyes climbed the tree, followed a low branch outward to see the skull affixed there, a long strand of gift-wrap ribbon hanging from an eye socket and dancing in the wind.

"Hell of a thing," Mangen muttered.

Hewitt didn't respond. She was instantly absorbed by the condition and appearance of the skull. Pure white. As if blanched, cleaned, polished. Prepared for its unveiling. And, as she followed the gold ribbon to where the loose end twitched just a few feet off the ground, the skull had been marked for easy discovery in that way, too.

"Quite the artist," Hewitt said, more to herself than the lawman.

"There's a nail driven in the tree, and a hole in the back of the bone."

"That's the way Martha Stewart always insisted on hanging a skull," Hewitt said, her tone about as flat as it got.

"Ladder's there if you want to go up and have a look," Mangen offered.

Hewitt accepted. A young deputy with bronze hair and hazel eyes and a little too much Calvin Klein Obsession held the ladder for her as she climbed. With Mangen hanging out a little too close for comfort as well, Hewitt was glad she'd picked her black jeans and not the black DKNY skirt.

A little more than two lengths of her body and she was eye-to-eye with the thing. Her initial thought was confirmed. This was no classroom piece that had been sitting around staring at anatomy students. This was a human skull that until quite recently had been covered with a human face. With eyes of a special color, a distinctive nose and mouth, each favoring one or the other of the parents that had brought this individual into the world. To end up here.

Peering behind the skull, she saw the nail and the hole in the parietal bone—as advertised. Returning her attention to the front, she observed the way the gold ribbon ran into the eye socket, how it was affixed to the orbit by duct tape. And down below, the way the ribbon fell so close to the ground—almost as if it had been intended for a child to find it.

It was time to talk to the little girl. The mother, too. But definitely the girl.

"There's a campsite about a half-mile up the trail," she heard Mangen say as she made her way down the official McHenry County ladder. "I've got a man over there asking if anybody heard or saw anything."

"Nobody did," Hewitt said as her feet hit the ground. "This guy didn't go to all the trouble of preparing a scene like this so some camper could catch him in the act. My guess is he didn't leave a lot of breadcrumbs."

Hewitt turned her focus to the gold ribbon, took a moment to examine the end of it. She saw it was flat, unbent. If anything had been tied to it, there was no indication.

Hewitt left Mangen there with his deputy and the techs who continued to document the scene with the taciturn industry of a hotel cleaning crew.

"I'm Special Agent Hewitt with the State Police," she said as she approached the mother and daughter. The deputy who'd been attending to them receded professionally.

"If you like," Hewitt continued, shifting her eyes and attitude to the girl, "you can call me Liz. What can I call you?"

The girl didn't understand, looked to her mom.

"What's your name, sweetie?" Hewitt clarified.

Her mom gave her a nod and a little squeeze at the nape of her neck.

"Maddy," the girl said in an elfin voice.

"Pretty name," Hewitt said.

"It's really Madison," the child volunteered.

Hewitt gave the girl her best disarming smile, not totally disingenuous—there was, after all, the topspin of coincidence. "You know something, Maddy? I went to college in a town called Madison. In Wisconsin."

"Is that where you learned to be a police lady?"

The girl's question took her by surprise. The mom stepped into the empty space of Hewitt's reaction.

"When she saw you walking up, she asked who you were. I told her a police lady. I'm sorry if that's professionally insulting."

Midwesterners. Hewitt smiled at the notion, the connection. Always so damn accommodating. Apologetic as an avocation. Hoping desperately not to offend. Or to stand out from all the other brightly polished apples in the barrel.

"I'll be happy to answer to police lady," Hewitt said.

She began the interview with the mom, Montgomery Krier, but she kept her body language with the child. As the questioning progressed, she began to focus her attention on the little girl's right hand, specifically how it remained inside the right pocket of her sweatshirt, the forearm muscles tensed, as if whatever she was holding inside was something she wouldn't give up easily.

The questions to the mom yielded little. No, she hadn't seen anyone on the grounds acting suspiciously. Nor had she heard anything during the night at the campsite. A few interesting personal things had spilled over into her responses. She and her husband had been separated since June, and this was their traditional last camping weekend of the season. She was determined to make it a nice experience. She'd kept Maddy out of her kindergarten class a couple of extra days so they could share some really nice mother-daughter time.

A county sheriff's first full day as a grandfather forever tainted. A separated wife and her daughter, their brave camping trip irretrievably marred. A skull in a tree had a way of messing up the world.

Hewitt had succeeded in pulling one useful bit of information from the mother, however. In the moments before she found the skull, the little girl had run up ahead on the hiking trail and had been out of her mother's sight. When pressed, the mother calculated that about a minute had passed before she heard Maddy call out. But it was definitely enough time for the girl to have been alone with the skull and, more important, the gold ribbon.

"Maddy, now I have a few real simple questions for you."

The girl looked away from Hewitt to her mother, received affirmation that the police lady was okay.

"How old are you Maddy?" Hewitt asked in a voice much closer to a Nickelodeon announcer than a police lady.

"Five and a half."

"Let me guess your favorite color."

Another look from the girl to her mother. Another permission slip signed.

"Is it green?"

The girl shook her head.

"Pink?"

Another no.

"Purple?"

A reluctant grin. An acquiescent nod.

"Just one more question, Maddy," Hewitt said. "When you first saw the gold ribbon on the tree, was there anything else there? Like maybe a piece of paper. A little note. Anything like that, Maddy?"

Halfway through her question, Hewitt saw the reaction she'd anticipated. A slight ripple in the petite band of muscles in the child's right forearm. It also drew an uncomfortable hesitation from her, into which the mother quickly asserted herself.

"Honey, did you find anything else?" she asked before shooting Hewitt a look that apologized for her interference, if that's what Hewitt judged it to be. Hewitt smiled patiently.

On to her now, the mother forced the issue with her daughter a little sooner than Hewitt would have liked. "Maddy, do you have something in your pocket?"

Another tremor of nerves and sinew in the girl's arm as she slowly withdrew her hand. Hewitt's insides fluttered at the prospect of a personal signature, a potential calling card from the bad brain who'd brought them all together.

But instead of that, she was treated to a big fat nothing. Or, a big fat nothing in the shape of a pine cone.

"I found it before," Maddy Krier explained in a voice she saved for apologies to grown-ups. "I found it before I found the skull. I wish I didn't find the skull. Every time when I close my eyes, I see it."

Hewitt understood. When her own head hit the pillow, and she closed her eyes at night, there was almost no end to the kinds of pictures that could appear in her brain's home theater.

"I know, sweetie," she said. "I've seen lots of scary things, too."

"Do they ever go away?"

"Yes," Hewitt told her. "Yes, they go away. And then you get back to seeing nice things when you close your eyes. Like your mommy's smile."

She turned to the mom who was smiling as if cued by a studio photographer. She handed the woman her card. "I'll be in touch, Mrs. Krier. If anything happens—Maddy remembers something—please call me right away."

Montgomery Krier gave Hewitt a look that said she appreciated how Hewitt had dealt with her little girl.

"Thank you," she said—in that sincere Midwestern way that made you feel guilty you couldn't do just a little bit more to help. "Is it okay if we go back to our campsite now? With all the attention around here, I think we'll gather up our things and go home."

"Sure," Hewitt said. She glanced over at the media contingent. "I'll have a deputy escort you. You gonna be okay?"

The woman moved her hands behind her daughter's head and positioned them, in a practiced manner, to shield the little girl's ears.

"As long as we keep our eyes open, we'll be all right."

THREE

For the life of her, Genevieve Bohannon couldn't imagine how the cat had gotten inside her house. And while she slept. Well, that part she had determined to be impossible. The doors were locked. The windows showed no evidence of tampering. She'd checked them all. Twice. And that had taken some doing. With the rambling, three-year-new Cape Cod and its overabundance of glass panels from which to smile at the outside world.

There was only one conclusion she could draw—that the pathetic furry thing had been waiting outside her door the night before and, when she'd come home half-drunk and about as carefree as a woman her age could be, the cat had slipped past her in the darkness and found a place to hide until morning.

Not that she minded having a houseguest. Although it did have to be a black cat, didn't it? It was still a hell of a lot better to wake up to the mystery cat than the Latino guy who had once again tried so hard to talk his way into her life and her pants in the smoke and neon of the bar at Outrage.

That the son of a bitch had come as close as he had made her shudder. He wasn't totally detestable or anything. It just wasn't what she was looking for. So instead, this. A black cat in the corner of her kitchen. At least she wouldn't have to make it bacon and eggs.

Damn thing just standing there looking at her. Like she was the interloper. Boy, that was rich. After she'd worked her ass off sideways to end up with the whole damn house as partial proceeds from the divorce.

"It ain't easy being single, is it?" she said to her visitor.

More staring from the cat. And when it turned to her now and its eyes caught a beam from the overhead track light, she could see that the poor freak was missing one of its eyes. It didn't gross her out really. If anything, it made her feel sorry for the thing. She wondered if it was hungry. When she took a couple of steps toward it, the cat did nothing in response. Shouldn't it at least flinch? Maybe it was some kind of retarded cat. Or maybe the missing eye was part of some head thing, some brain injury. It had gotten in the house though. It had been smart enough to figure that out.

"You want a bowl of milk or something?" she asked, a little surprised by the compassion in her voice.

Damn, she was out of milk. She did have some half-and-half.

"Would you settle for cream?"

She was looking now to see if the thing had a collar. None she could detect. She took another couple of steps toward the animal, to get to the fridge. "Don't mind me."

The cat finally moved then, seeking the corner between the cupboard and the sliding door. Genevieve Bohannon fetched the carton of half-and-half and poured most of it into the worst soup bowl she had, saving enough for her own coffee needs. She set the bowl down in front of her guest and stepped back to give it some space. *"Bon appétit,"* she said.

The cat looked back at her with its single eye, unsure.

"Trust me. The expiration date's good."

And with that, Genevieve Bohannon proceeded to make her own morning beverage—Starbucks house blend—in her hundred-fifty-dollar Krups brewer, the second one she'd owned since the divorce. The first one she had given to the Purple Heart people. She supposed she could have tried to clean the damn thing of its six months of hard water and coffee stains. But even if she had followed the owner's manual to a tee, the coffee would've never tasted as good again as when the thing was new. So she'd put herself on the six-month plan. A brand-new Krups every half-year. She figured it was the least her husband owed her. The asshole.

The cat had its face in the bowl. When it paused to look up at her, the cream on its face glistened against the black fur in a way that was at first comical and then, by turns, a little depressing.

"Go ahead, indulge," Genevieve Bohannon said. "Whoever you are, whatever you've been through, however the hell you got here, I'm sure you've earned it."

FOUR

By noon, Hewitt and the skull had gone their separate ways—the skull to the State Crime Lab, Hewitt to ISP Headquarters, a cryptic brick citadel of a building of late-1960s design. In an inescapable way, however, the special agent and the skull had now become inseparable. And because of that, she and the little Krier girl had something in common. Sitting at her desk, looking out the second-floor window of her office in Homicide Special Section, Hewitt found that if she closed her eyes, she could see the skull, too.

So she left them open, let them drift to the sketch pad on her desk, still open to the last drawings she'd made. It was one of her processing tools. The sketching, noodling, mapping. Her way of visualizing the crime scenes and the criminals that became her live-in partners whenever the game was on.

At the top of the page were two sketches of the crow that had fallen into her life. The first image depicted the bird in its stiff stance as the last minutes of its life scattered to the wind. The second image showed the crow lying on the ground, with a thin outline of the ethereal bird beginning to take wing, to fly wherever crow souls flew.

On the lower half of the same sketchbook page was Hewitt's rendition of the state-park crime scene from, as fate had dictated, a bird's-eye view. There was the trail, the tree, the little figures of Montgomery Krier and her daughter. And in the tree, on the special limb, the skull, drawn to scale. In Hewitt's big world, about the size a skull would have to be to fit into an empty diamond ring setting.

A dying crow in the grass. A skull in a tree. What would be next on her sign-of-the-apocalypse hit parade? Would her boss, Captain Spangler, come walking into her office shoeless, sockless, and sporting a pair of freshly transmogrified cloven hooves?

Well, that much she already knew from the sound approaching her semi-closed door. Not the uneven clip-clop of the beast. But the scuff and squeal of a pair of black oxfords.

"So what do we know?" Spangler asked before he and his shoes were all the way inside the room. He plunked himself down in the visitor's chair. It was always odd how his perpetually pleasant wrinkle lines and constantly slipping bifocals made the captain look more like someone you'd chat up at a bridal registry than an authority on the darkest aspects of humanity.

"The skull's at the state lab. We canvassed every hiker and camper in the park. I interviewed the mom and girl. All I can say at this point is that we need the skull to do some talking."

"Well, the reason I stopped in is because Zoeller wants to be the one to make it talk."

Zoeller. As in Dr. Carlton Zoeller, the state medical examiner. Hewitt visualized Zoeller's nervous coyote eyes, his thin nose, his expensive caps smiling condescendingly. A better image than the tree skull, but barely.

"Why am I not in shock?" Hewitt said. "A big visible case with lots of lights, cameras, and action. Not to mention female reporters with above-average intelligence and top-shelf perfume."

"He'll be overseeing it. Which means I'd like to have you oversee him."

"Shit, and I was planning to go to the Shedd aquarium this afternoon and take in a dolphin show."

"The dolphins will still be there when you close the case," Spangler said, his face pulling in tight enough to negate all but the last of his wrinkle-line pleasantness. "I don't want to overplay this. But I also received a call from the governor. He's not real fond of skulls showing up like ornaments in his state parks. For some reason he feels it might be bad for tourism."

"Noted," Hewitt said. "And thanks for not overplaying the governor's concerns."

"I figured you probably have enough on your mind as it is," Spangler added as he lifted himself out of the visitor's chair with a quickness that mirrored the way he'd dropped in.

Thirty minutes later Hewitt was at the state crime lab, taking the elevator to the basement for her impromptu meeting with Carlton Zoeller. She found him in one of the lab rooms adjacent to the autopsy suite where the usual victims—the ones that came with heads attached to their bodies—were examined.

Zoeller was alone, seated in a chair, looking at the skull where it sat looking back at him from a tray alongside a computer terminal. The way Zoeller sat there, hunched and quizzical, made Hewitt think of the poster of the ape contemplating the human skull—the Darwin in reverse send-up.

Without turning to look at her, Zoeller spoke into the antiseptic air. "And that would be Special Agent Hewitt coming to make sure no one was doing anything untoward with her discovery."

He turned now to face her, offered a protracted and, in its way, dismissive blink of affirmation.

"I thought you might appreciate this," Hewitt said, approaching with a file and withdrawing the single sheet of information she'd compiled during her brief visit to the ISP mothership. "It's a short list from Missing Persons. I culled the names of some missing women. Dental records are in the ISP database. All you have to do is go in and start digging."

Zoeller set the sheet down beside the skull. "Oh, I've been digging already. And you're right on the female."

He was already tapping the keys of the computer with his long, bony, and typically well-manicured fingers. "When we have a positive ID, I'd like to represent the forensic establishment at the news conference."

"I've already marked a spot for you on the podium," Hewitt said. "In masking tape. Yours is the one marked with the initials CZ. And the little smiley face."

FIVE

The victim was Brandi Kaczmarek, a thirty-six-year-old Caucasian female who had disappeared from the face of the earth six weeks earlier. Her name had been included on Hewitt's short list of potentials. But when Hewitt got the news via phone from Captain Spangler, she didn't feel any sense of accomplishment. All she felt was the adrenaline level spike in her body and her game face mold itself into place as she looked at herself in the rearview mirror of the Mazda. The victim was, after all, thirty-six. Which made her, in Hewitt's book, an honorary sorority sister.

Hewitt thanked Spangler for the information, told him she wanted to hold off on the news conference until the following morning, asked that he use his influence to keep Zoeller at bay until the proper time had been determined.

"So you think this is going to be serial?" Spangler asked.

"My mind tells me it's possible."

"What does your gut say?"

"Yes."

She gave him her reasons. She'd been giving them to herself all afternoon. The skull wasn't just some schizophrenic art project. It was a trophy. A prize to be displayed not just for the person who discovered it, but for every pair of blinking eyes on the planet. And history informed her that prize-takers weren't usually satisfied with just one.

"Obviously, I hope you're wrong," Spangler offered.

"No one hopes that more than me," Hewitt said.

She was heading north on the Tri-State, moving considerably faster than the rest of the traffic, seeing the mental image of Brandi Kaczmarek's skull without having to close her eyes.

"Next of kin is a Victor Kaczmarek of Elk Grove Village," Spangler rattled in her ear. "It's all in the Missing Persons file."

"Victor Kaczmarek is the father?"

"Yeah. Mother's deceased."

"So her dad's the lucky one to get his heart ripped out when the uniforms show up at the front door."

"She's been missing six weeks, Hewitt. It's not like he hasn't thought about worst-case scenarios by now. I know that won't help. But tell me something that will."

Dads disconnected from their daughters. And vice versa. The theme that played its loud refrain over Hewitt's life. Included in that, of course, was her police work. It was a weakness, it was a strength. Depending on how she used it.

"Hewitt?" Spangler's voice like a hypnotherapist bringing her back.

"I'm here."

She caught herself just in time to make a quick exit from the Tri-State so she could head northwest toward McHenry County. Someone behind her laid on a horn. She didn't bother to check the mirror.

"Sounded like a good move, Hewitt," Spangler chided. "Mind if I ask what the hell you're up to?"

"I'm going back to Chain-O-Lakes," she told him. "I've talked myself into believing I missed something there today. So I'm going back to see if I can scare it up."

"In another hour you'll be scaring it up in the dark."

"The record shows that's where I do some of my best work."

HEWITT SAT ON the blanket she had taken from the trunk of her car, her back leaning against the base of the oak tree. Though it looked like just another oak tree again, Hewitt knew it would never be allowed to be that. It was now a local legend. A place where the curious would gather, where teenagers would come to drink their parents' booze and smoke pot on Halloweens for as long as it was celebrated.

In just a few weeks they would have their first chance. Who knew? Maybe she would join them for the inaugural. Catch a buzz on some

Southern Comfort. Grab a couple hits off a joint. Maybe she'd arrest herself and let all the horny little pre-adults go.

She had nothing. When her thoughts would fishtail wildly like this, she knew she was up against it. Or, in this case up against an old oak tree that was in no particular hurry to start giving up its secrets. *A skull in a tree. A skull in a freaking tree.* There was something about it. Something on the tip of her mind. Something that was dying to whisper the secret to her. But all she heard in the ways of whispers was the wind skimming through the trees.

True to Spangler's prediction, she was doing her contemplating in the dark. *The skull. The ribbon.* She closed her eyes, saw the bright ribbon blowing in the breeze. It had been the thing that had caught the Krier girl's attention. The skull alone, given its positioning, might have gone unnoticed for the better part of a day, or days. No, the ribbon had been put there to attract attention.

She visualized it again. Dancing in the wind. Dancing . . .

It was like a photograph flashing in her head then. A single frame of her memory's imagination frozen in a flash of light. She saw the skull on the limb of the tree again. *That limb.* In her mind's eye, she followed the ribbon downward, to where it would have touched the ground had it been afforded enough length.

She reached out, touched the ground in that spot with her fingers.

It seemed wildly implausible, to imagine what the girl might have found there, what she might have concealed and taken away. Hewitt lifted herself from the blanket, then positioned it so she could kneel on it as she turned to face the tree—at about the same height where Maddy Krier had been little more than a half-day earlier.

If it had been herself—if it had been little Lizzy Hewitt three decades ago—she would've been smart enough to switch, to substitute the pine cone for the real prize. Especially once her mother had started freaking out over the whole thing right before her eyes. And especially when an army of police began showing up because of something *you did*.

So little Maddy Krier could have hidden whatever she found somewhere else. Pants pocket. Hell, maybe as simple as sticking it in the left pocket of the powder blue sweatshirt.

If Maddy Krier had found something, Hewitt had to get her hands on it. If she hoped to intervene before another white-bone trophy was nailed to some otherwise unsuspecting tree. That's where her intuition told her this was going. If it was serial. And she was solid on that. As solid as the trunk of the oak tree which she now used to pull her grown-up body up and out of her six-year-old self.

S I X

Montgomery Krier met Hewitt at the front door of her modest suburban saltbox as if she was encountering a trick-or-treater on Christmas Eve.

"Mrs. Krier, I'm sorry to trouble you at this hour. But I believe it's possible your daughter might have some information we might've missed earlier today."

"Information?"

"I think there's a chance she has some evidence—physical evidence—that could help us."

Montgomery Krier opened the door and allowed Hewitt inside. In front of the carpeted staircase, Hewitt explained what she was looking for.

"Well, I didn't see her with anything unusual," her host offered. "She was upstairs in her room a lot. So . . ."

"So maybe it's possible," Hewitt helped. "You know what they say—when the kids are quiet . . ."

If there was actually an aphorism like that, Hewitt had no idea what the finish was. But it didn't matter. Montgomery Krier understood.

"She's asleep. But we can go look. Just so we're quiet. I had a heck of a time getting her to go down. If she wakes up again, she might be up for a long time."

The way she said it suggested that if the little girl did wake up, it would be partly Hewitt's responsibility to get her back to sleep. With that implication hanging in the foyer, Montgomery Krier turned and led Hewitt up the staircase.

The little girl's bedroom was at the end of the hallway upstairs. The door was half-open and the dim glow of a night light escaped from the room.

Following the mom's lead, Hewitt entered the bedroom and reentered a part of herself, where the child she had once been would always be sleeping. Her eyes were instantly drawn to the chest of drawers and the butterfly lamp and its glowing night light. The lamp was surrounded by a gallery of child's trinkets, knickknacks and figurines, many of which cast large shadows against the opposite wall in a cacophony of shapes that suggested the skyline of a Byzantine city.

"If Maddy had found something really special to her, where would she put it?"

"Where any kid would," the mom answered as she nodded toward the head of the bed.

Hewitt took a half-step back from the path she would need to take to the bed if she was going to check under the pillow, which her host was clearly suggesting she should do.

"I haven't had much tooth fairy experience," Hewitt said, her voice fuzzily self-conscious.

When the mom didn't respond, Hewitt knew she was on her own. She crossed the floor, her feet suddenly heavy against the creaking wood. Compared to her, the tooth fairy had it made—that petite body, the gossamer wings, the pixie dust to sprinkle on the kid if he or she started to stir from their dreams of white ponies and golden bears.

Approaching the side of the bed, Hewitt began to lean forward when she caught the smell of the sleeping child—a mix of graham crackers, grape juice, and naturally scented little-girl hair.

"I can get you a flashlight," Montgomery Krier said behind her.

Hewitt reached into her coat pocket, took out her penlight, held it out for the mom to see, said nothing. The little girl's head rested heavily in the middle of the pillow. Hewitt reached out, took the loose end of the pillowcase, lifted it. She bent her knees, lowering herself for a look as she switched on the penlight.

Nothing there.

So now Hewitt had to lean in and, in effect, contort her body so she could reach around to the other side of the pillow and work her hand in from that side without waking the child.

Bizarre. How she was investigating a head-chopping killer, but the thing she feared most in the world was waking up this kid. No sooner had she thought it, when the sleeve of her car coat brushed Maddy Krier's slumbering forehead.

The child stirred, said something that sounded like "man in the moon," then turned onto her side, facing Hewitt and giving her access to the far side of the pillow. More critically, she stayed asleep.

Hewitt's hand was under the pillow now, feeling nothing but one-hundred-percent cotton until her fingernails clicked against something solid. Her fingers found it then. Cool to the touch. Metal. With a definite shape.

She pulled the object into the beam of the penlight. The gasp she heard upon the movement of her mind, and its confirmation of the object, sounded like it had come from someone else in the room. But the child continued to sleep. And Montgomery Krier was the only other one there.

SEVEN

"How did you know?" she asked her new friend.

She was pouring herself a glass of private-label Napa Valley chardonnay. All the better to complement the game hens she'd prepared. All the better because it was a good bottle of wine from her ex-husband's collection, from the cellar she padlocked after he filed the first papers.

And all the better because she had company for dinner. A male friend. Quiet type. Dark. Mysterious. Sensitive. Most important, the kind who would leave her in one piece the morning after. Or twelve years down the matrimonial road.

"How did you know?"

The cat sat on the chair opposite her at the glass table in the kitchen. The recessed lights above had been set to the lowest dimmer setting. A tall white candle flickered on the table between them, freshly lit, the first bead of wax yet to form.

How had he known?—she asked herself as the first taste of wine crackled over her tongue and tumbled against the back of her throat. Of all the things she needed in this her fourteenth month of liberation. An animal. An animal other than a human male. An animal with absolutely no interest in depositing himself in the safe box between her thighs.

But what did she expect? She was a DWF, and a rich one. The suitors came salivating. Like a stray cat to a bowl of half-and-half. Not that she had been stingy in putting out the bowls. Her cream-letting had taken her through the wonders of the Chicago nightclub circuit. And she'd pretty much run the gamut. Starting with the trendy clubs, with their DKNY and Kenneth Cole devotees. Then eventually finding her way to the raunchier side of the tracks. Arm and leg wrestling with

the leather-pants and muscle-shirt legion. And in between those mag-
netic poles, her recent foray into the karaoke clubs. To get up there on-
stage, with the proper amount of alcohol in her veins, and sing for them
like a canary in a pet shop, just hoping to attract an owner to feed it,
to change its newspaper periodically, and not torture it too badly on
crazy nights.

The timer was beeping on the counter. Genevieve Bohannon went
to turn it off. Looking back, she saw that her dinner guest hadn't
moved. As she went to the oven, the cat turned its head, followed her
movements, seeming to know that the treasure of the baked bird was
about to be revealed.

The oven door swung open with its customary squeal. The sizzling
essence of the basted birds filled Genevieve Bohannon's nostrils. She
looked at her guest, her friend. Lifting and shifting his little black feet
on the chair. Like a dancer warming up before the curtain rose.

There were four of them—the game hens. Neatly, symmetrically
laid out in the square pan. More than a year out, and she was still in
the habit of making larger meals than a single person—a DWF—
needed. Then again, it never hurt to have leftover meat in the house for
the overnight guests in her life. Cold meat in the fridge. After a night of
pelvic wrestling. A basic but well-received perk.

Donning the oven mitt, she lifted the pan out of the oven and
placed it on the Niagara Falls hot pad she'd been given as a gag gift. In
any event, she would have the extra poultry for something to gnaw on
later, and as something with which to reward and entertain her latest
overnight guest.

She made a plate. A whole bird, the stuffing that came with it. Some
sweet potato with butter. And the first nonbagged salad she'd made
herself in months. Her plate.

For her guest, the preparation was easier. From the Chicago Cutlery stand on the counter she took a serrated knife. With the tip she
punctured the papery skin of the bird, then sliced away a nice opening.
From there, she proceeded to cut thin strips of meat from the breast.
These she laid out on the table before her guest, one at a time, delight-

ing in his carnivorous twitchings as each strip was offered and summarily dispatched.

"I'd give you some wine. But I'm not sure the Humane Society
would approve."

She was seated at her place setting now. After a dozen or so strips
of game hen, her guest had begun to show some fatigue for his gluttony.
The two-and-a-half glasses of wine had warmed and anesthetized
Genevieve Bohannon's throat and esophagus. Her heart being on the
same downward track, she assumed it had warmed as well. And sitting
there sipping a little more, she was further warmed by the impression
that her heart wasn't dead yet. Confused perhaps in her emotional connection with a vagabond one-eyed cat. But alive nonetheless.

For the first time, in the candlelight, she allowed herself a good look
at the missing eye. Not pretty, but what the hell? She drew herself away
from the empty socket and went to the surviving eye. The clear focus of
this one. The intelligence. The message it seemed to be sending.

I'm more important than you think.

"Isn't it pretty to think so," she said aloud. "That's always been a
pet line of mine—from Hemingway. A pet line." She laughed. "No pun
intended."

Another laugh. She was getting drunk now, and she was delighted.
To be back in the arms of the mysterious stranger—intoxication. Mysterious yet undeniably welcome. The warm comfort of slipping into an
escapable danger.

Escapable. That was they key. If she had ever been able to successfully concoct the belief—that she could have actually gotten away with
it—she would have had him killed. Using his own money to consum-
mate the deal. But dead husbands in the wake of an ugly-ass divorce . . .

The cat was purring. Purring to her. Not just to itself. That was her
take anyway. Wine-addled as she was. No, definitely. It was purring to her.

I'm more important than you think. I know it. You know it, too.

Ah, shit, she was drunk. But maybe—nah, it couldn't be. Sure. Why
the hell not? Maybe some of the purring was escaping, escaping outward, through that thinly veiled hole in its head.

Shit, she was nuts. The point was the damn thing was purring. And if she stopped letting her mind run around like a rabid animal, she could probably cooperate with the alcohol until she began to purr herself.

She took her fork and lanced the golden-brown parchment that covered her game hen's breast. And she was halfway through the delicious bird, having already finished her sweet potato and salad, when the sound of the doorbell filled the big house. As she crossed the floor and made her way to the front door, the cat went with her. A nice little comfort. The man of the house.

Looking through the lattice of the front-door window, she saw another man, the dark tone of his overcoat a perfect fit with the shadows of her porch. His body language appeared unthreatening. And the eyes that reflected the foyer light felt sincere enough. Even hopeful. As if the man behind them was looking for the answer to a puzzle.

EIGHT

With the object of her discovery in an evidence bag on the kitchen table upstairs, Hewitt was busy in the basement of her condo unit, moving storage boxes from the cache of them in the corner, looking for the one box that would allow it all to make an insane kind of sense.

As stored personal history went, this container was pretty well buried. But after working her way through the years of accumulated stuff, she finally got to it. An old brown box that had, in its original incarnation, housed products for the A. Gagliano Produce Company. For its reincarnation in Hewitt's life, it had been marked "EH UIC Stuff" on the front panel.

There was dust on the box, dust on her hands, dust unloosed in her thoughts as she carried the heaviness of it all to the better light above the old card table. It was like removing the lid of a coffin then—more that than a cardboard box of college books, papers, and records she'd been unwilling to remit to a rummage sale or a dumpster over the course of all those years.

The lid was off and the musty smell of old paper and book bindings puffed against her face. Once again, this part of her archaeological mission required her to do a little digging. And it was when she got to the bottom right side of the box that she found what she was looking for. An old book, thick as a Bible.

She lifted it from the box, set it on the card table. As she did, her eyes caught the light that reflected up from the large white envelope toward the bottom of the box. A white envelope with the initials "SLH" written in Hewitt's own script. This artifact she would leave in the reliquary, along with the accordion file of papers and lesson plans that lay beneath it. At least for now.

Hewitt returned the lid to the box, snuffed out the brief light that had illuminated the white envelope. She returned the box to the stack of them, switched off the overhead light, and went upstairs.

When she got to the kitchen, the evidence bag was exactly where she had left it. Which meant the object inside hadn't attempted to crawl away. As bizarre as the whole damn thing was turning out, crawling didn't seem beyond the realm of possibility. She took a tissue from the box on the counter and set it on the table. After pulling on a pair of latex gloves, she reached inside the evidence bag and procured the insect.

It was a gold scarab beetle, about three inches long and two inches wide at the center. The body was made of metal and appeared to have been hand-painted to its lustrous tone. Oddest of all, the top of the thing—the bug's back—had been further painted with black markings to suggest the shape of a human skull.

To Hewitt's mind, the probability of coincidence was absolute zero. She set the beetle down on the tissue and opened the book to the table of contents. The book was a collection of everything ever published by, some would argue, the greatest of American writers, in the chronological order in which the works had been written. But before she paged ahead to the story in question, "The Gold Bug," Hewitt stopped at the picture of Edgar Allan Poe that preceded the editor's introduction.

She looked at the stress lines on his face, the dry riverbeds of his genius and anguish. She considered his hair, unkempt, on the edge of wild, like some lower furry life form that had attached itself there, never to leave, even in death. Last, she looked at the eyes. So near in their gaze that she could have been, just then, clinking aperitif glasses with him in a toast. And at the same time, so far away that he could have been in the throes of any number of unimaginable fantasies in the very same moment.

But that was just it. He could imagine such things. While the rest of the world could never enter such private rooms, Edgar could. Edgar did. And the proof was in the Bible-thick volume in her hands.

Hewitt left the photograph, paged her way to the story, "The Gold Bug," and began to scan the pages for the directions she needed to initiate a court-sanctioned dig in the sandy soil of Chain-O-Lakes State Park.

NINE

She awoke to a burning smell. Not a bad burning smell. The smell was almost pleasant. It was hot wax. Candle wax.

As much as she tried, she was having trouble opening her eyes. Through the circulating fog of her mind, her brain managed to locate her hands and, with the intricate pulley system inside, she was able to finally lift them near her face.

God, what the hell had hit her? The chardonnay? The way she was feeling, it was like she'd been hit over the head with the bottle.

She felt her eyelids, worked her fingers to lift them open. And just before she succeeded in raising the lids, she felt the pressing of something alive against the side of her hip, exploring the side of her body.

She lifted her head from its passed-out position on the floor, focused her eyes. And there, in a crouching silhouette, backlit by a candle was the cat. It poked its forehead against her reclining body again, this time just off the side of her breast. Nudging her, with its soft dark face, to keep her from drifting back to sleep.

Where the fuck was she?

Fear flooded her nervous system as she forced her way up and onto her elbows. The cat must have felt it too because it let out a confused, forlorn cry as it backed up against the brick wall.

Oh, my God. Oh, my God. Oh, my God.

She forced herself up into a sitting position, ran her fingers against the brick, ran her eyes in all directions over the candlelit wall. She couldn't find any openings. And upon that realization, her heart exploded in her chest. Her mind rushed into the vacuum the detonation created—to fill it with the last things she remembered.

As she raced through her thoughts, the cat nuzzled her again. It was looking for answers, too. She reached down, felt its warm face, the wet adhesion of its tongue against her hand.

The visitor. The man who owned the cat, asking if she'd seen a stray black one with a missing eye. Looking so sincere, so sad on her doorstep. He'd lost his cat—a cat so unpleasant to look at only someone who truly loved it would come looking when it ran away.

"I'm so sorry to trouble you," he'd said in a voice she trusted instantly.

She had let him come in, showed him the cat. They'd talked. Right there at the kitchen table. She remembered his reluctance, her insistence. Declining a portion of game hen, he had instead accepted a glass of wine. She'd gone to the dining room to get a goblet from the hutch. The only time she'd left the room. The only time she had left him alone. Alone with the cat. The table. The meal. The wine.

He'd put something in the wine.

Her eyes fell to the floor. The way the candle lit the floor. The parquet floor. *Her floor.* She saw the old cigarette burn on the tile she'd never replaced.

He'd put something in the wine.

And then . . . then he'd built this thing. This brick-walled cell in the corner of her living room. There was no question. She was still in her house. She was home. Imprisoned with a black cat. A candle. Her body. Her mind.

And somehow in the frantic spinning of her brain, she was able to delineate the thought that this predicament was something she had known before. This place. These two creatures, human and cat, entombed together by some demonic entity.

"Welcome home, Genevieve."

The sound of his voice, the way it felt like it was coming from inside the bricks, made her know the space wasn't completely sealed. A cold hardness of will came to her, and she raised her woozy legs to stand, with the help of the wall. When her eyes found their way to eye level, she saw the opening. A single brick space.

"Yes, I see your eyes now Genevieve," the voice on the outside said. Not evil, not mocking. Unchanged from the way it had sounded mak-

ing conversation at the table. As if the voice wasn't troubled by what the mind that controlled it was in the process of carrying out.

"What are you doing to me?"

The voice was hers but sounded like someone she didn't know. The response came quickly, easily from the visitor. As if he had anticipated the question for some time.

"Giving you relevance. Giving you meaning. Giving you . . . voice."

"Please," she gasped, raising her head, pressing her face into the space between the blocks. "Why are you doing this? You don't even know who I am."

In the silence that followed, the cat bumped her leg with its fist of a head. The candle flickered at the slow whipping motion of the creature's tail.

"I know all that I need to know. And for that, for revealing that to me, I will always thank you. You will never know the depth of my appreciation."

In his voice, Genevieve Bohannon heard the ruffling sound of a curtain closing. She lowered her eyes to the slot, straining for some glimpse of him. But the view revealed no aspect of the visitor until, suddenly, his own wild eyes rose to the space to mirror hers. And the shriek that came from deep in her pelvis and radiated upward through the great conduit of bone and tissue only made his eyes grow wilder with pleasure, with a white-hot burning joy.

"I'll do anything you want," she managed through her numb lips, her cold teeth. And having said that, she recognized having thought it before. At the kitchen table, in his presence as he sat there so innocently—so innocent it had attracted her to him.

"Of that I have no doubt," he said. And with those words, his eyes, his face withdrew from her sight. Breathlessly, she waited for his return, felt the panic pooling like blood from a rip in her brain when he did not.

"Won't you take me? Please . . . I'll be the best fuck you ever had."

Her voice higher now, ballooning with adrenaline as she called to him through the opening. She felt the searing pressure of her eyes straining for another glimpse of him.

"Please! I want you to make love to me."

Her voice nearly an animal cry now. And she couldn't control it, couldn't keep her brain from pouring out its self-preserving contents.

"Please. Let me have a chance. I'm an amazing fuck. I'm wet. And soft. And tight." Her voice caterwauling now, on the verge of howling. "And I'm loud. I'm really loud."

She stopped, waiting again for his response. And when her waiting had run its course, her brain bade her voice to continue. But the voice mechanism was unable to unscramble the cacophony of messages. And the throat was only able to open and offer, to the shocked ears of the black cat, the first full scream of the night.

TEN

Her roommate's body falls in slow motion through the darkness of the autumn night. The gauzy layers of her black costume ripple against the achingly slow breezes of her descent.

On the last night of her life, she is wearing the costume of a witch. It had only added to the spectacle, the stories, and, as Hewitt had always believed, the coroner's conclusion. The conclusion that her roommate at UIC, a girl from the little town of Black Earth in southwestern Wisconsin, had taken her own life.

Her college roommate. Sarah Lee Hooker.

If ever there was a girl who didn't fit her name, it was Sarah Lee Hooker. On local radio and TV the next day, the words *Sarah Lee Hooker* had saturated the airwaves and a cold first-of-November rain had begun to fall by midmorning. All those little droplets pelting the campus. All those little drops of Sarah Lee Hooker.

Still clinging to her waking state, Hewitt rolled over in bed, felt the glow of the clock-radio light, kept her eyes closed. She had experienced the dream so many times that she no longer had to be asleep to see the image, to feel the falling. It would come to her like this, on the outer edge of her first sleep cycle of the night. It would come to her. And then she would force herself to let it go.

She felt a downshift in her breathing. She began to drift.

Falling . . .

Falling . . .

3:17. SHE WAS awake again. Sarah Lee Hooker was long gone.

Again.

The freaking phone was ringing. She reached to the nightstand, her hand scraping the side of the Poe anthology. Her hand slow-crawling over the fatness of the book, finding the phone.

"Hewitt."

It was Spangler, calling with the news that he'd been successful in pushing through her request for a dig on state grounds.

"Judge Terlach just called," he rattled in her ear. "She's faxing over the order right now."

"Any push-back from her?" Hewitt managed.

"No. I submitted what you gave me. The elements of the Poe story. All that. The odds of it being a coincidence, you know, like you said. Bottom line is she bought it. You'll have a state crew up there at first light. Once you find what you're looking for—or not—we need to hold a news conference. At HQ. I've got local and now some national media humping my leg like a cocker spaniel on Viagra."

"Thanks for that lovely image," Hewitt said. "If I want to see horrifying pictures, I'll go back to my dreams."

"Well since I've got you up, I want to say how impressed I was with your ability to put this Edgar Allan Poe thing together. Anything you want to tell me about that?"

"As far as?"

"As far as most people who work for me wouldn't have been able to connect those dots."

"At UIC," Hewitt said, "I was an English major. My junior year, I took a course on Poe."

"And I assume you handled the material well."

"I believe I managed to inveigle an A from the professor."

"I would've expected nothing less," Spangler said in his fatherly voice, which at that hour felt strangely comforting. "Anything else from your college days you'd like to tell me about?"

"I could probably scare up a couple of stories," Hewitt told him. "Over drinks sometime. It is—last time I checked—the middle of the night."

Spangler agreed to the rain check. They signed off. That was one of the things about Spangler. Unlike normal people who typically sounded like they were coming out of anesthesia in a middle-of-the-night call, Spangler could sound like he was up on his exercise bike sipping a glass of freshly squeezed.

Hewitt set the phone back on the nightstand, her hand grazing the book as she did. She laid down, let her head be swallowed by the pillow. When she closed her eyes, she finally acknowledged the rain that had been beating against the roof all the while. The rain. The little drops of Sarah Lee. Shit. She was back there again. Beginning to see the falling witch all over again.

She sat up, turned on the light.

The Poe book stared back at her from the nightstand. Maybe it was a bad idea to have the book so close to her head while she slept. That entire lifetime of thoughts, dreams, mystery, magic, hallucinations, atrocities. Maybe all that writing had an energy of its own that could venture out of the pages and stir up a nearby brain. Hewitt knew that the words and images of at least one of the stories had already stirred up one bad brain out there in the world.

She picked up the book, opened it to the marked pages, her eyes getting hooked on a barb of prose here and there. In the second half of the story she began to see the parts she'd highlighted in yellow. The skull placement in the tree. *Main branch, seventh limb, east side.*

From the crime scene photos she now knew the skull had been positioned in the Chain-O-Lakes tree to emulate the position in the Poe story. In the original tale, the dropping of the weird gold bug from the left eye of the death's head would provide the pirates the first coordinate from which to determine the exact spot to dig for the hidden treasure.

In the lonely incandescence of her bedroom, Hewitt tried not to imagine the atrocious treasure that awaited her in the cold, desecrated sand.

ELEVEN

First light came grudgingly to Chain-O-Lakes State Park. The night rain had persisted, and the pissing overcast had turned the rising sun into little more than a rumor.

By the time the first shovels hit the wet sandy loam, there appeared to be more media members than state of Illinois personnel on the grounds. The media were kept back behind the police line. And when the shovels began to liberate the first objects from the burial site, many in the digging party wished they were back behind the line, too.

Hewitt stood at the head of the dig site in her yellow state-police rain poncho, her eyes narrowed, her face creased with anticipation. The rain, though appropriately dismal, actually made the work of the state crew easier. The sandy ground was tending to clump and pack for easier removal.

It was at about ten minutes and four-and-a-half feet into the dig when they liberated the first object. A black trash bag wrapped and taped around its contents. With the predictable smell of a decaying body. Well beyond the most fetid necrotic stage, but bad enough. Definitely bad enough.

There was a forensic pathologist she knew—a woman about her age—who, when Hewitt asked how she dealt with the smells, put it in a simple perspective. "It just smells bad," she told her. There was absolutely no point, no benefit to be derived in breaking it down into degrees or categories.

It just smells bad.

A second black plastic bag was uncovered, wrapped in similar fashion. The pieces were set on the plastic tarp at the edge of the grave beneath a portable awning that had been set up to keep things dry. It was clearly that—a grave. Unmarked, untended, and undetected for some time. Why the bad brain behind it had chosen now to reveal its location—and why in such a twisted fashion—were the things that would skitter through Hewitt's head like mice in a maze until she found a way to make the skittering stop.

The third bag was on the tarp. A fourth would soon join it.

"Got yourself a seriously sick puppy, Hewitt."

It was the voice of Sheriff Mangen, behind Hewitt's right ear.

Hewitt shrugged, felt the stiffness of her government raincoat. "Hate to admit it, but I've seen worse."

"Why the hell would the son of a bitch go to all that work?"

Hewitt let enough time pass, allowed enough rain to fall that it seemed she was going to let Mangen's question pass as well.

"Because it makes perfect sense," she finally answered. "Maybe not to any other mind on earth. But to the one mind that matters, it makes all the sense in the world."

Hewitt left Mangen standing there with a stumped game-show contestant look on his face. Under the awning, she got another hit of the bad smell as she pulled on a pair of latex gloves.

She wouldn't open any of the parcels now, these cryptic gifts of the bad brain who soon enough would be getting his desired ya-yas. The media, his media, was on full alert now. All there. In full regalia. The reporters in their nice Gore-Tex. The cameras poised with their death-seeking lights cutting through the atmospheric sponge. And in the air, two news choppers with electronic eyes more powerful than the most highly evolved raptor.

Hewitt would leave the unwrapping to the dry, sterile environment of the lab. She already knew what was there to be found. But she couldn't stop herself from reaching down to the first of the packages anyway, wanting to gauge, for starters, the weight of the contents. She picked it up carefully, felt the radius and ulna bones, still held together by the ligaments, sheathed in a layer of desiccated flesh.

She started to ease the package back down to the tarp, letting it slide through her palm and fingers, feeling the forearm bones giving way to the wrist. And then the hand, which caught hers. Almost as if it had tried. She held onto it for a moment. Held the petrified thing. What had once been its grasp. And she felt from the hand a message that reverberated into her own hand, her spine, her brain.

Help me.

TWELVE

Hewitt made an indelible mental note to do everything in her power to honor the request from Brandi Kaczmarek's bones. Confirming who the bones belonged to would call for the requisite pathology. But Hewitt's own bones had already given her the only report she needed.

By eight-thirty the circus had begun to clear its way out of the park, and Hewitt was on her way back to ISP headquarters. The news conference was scheduled for 9:00, with an internal briefing at 8:00 in Captain Spangler's office. After soothing herself through the freeway jam with more Coltrane/Hartman, Hewitt walked into Spangler's office at state police headquarters at 8:04.

Spangler was on the phone. Occupying one of Spangler's two visitors' chairs was Public Information Officer, Ms. Minerva Vann, all sixty-one years of her, in a pert gray suit June Cleaver might have worn to one of Beaver's parent-teacher conferences.

Minerva Vann insisted on her full first name. There was some talk that, as a younger woman, she had answered to Minnie. But given the popularity of a certain gas-powered suburban transport vehicle, she'd reverted to Minerva in the early 1980s. In any event, she was a fixture at briefings like this, odd name history or not.

Ms. Vann handed Ms. Hewitt a copy of Spangler's prepared statement. Hewitt read through the double-spaced single page of the typically just-the-facts copy as Spangler finished up his call. A personal call. He had a daughter in college—a pregnant daughter in college who was planning a December wedding.

Hewitt finished reading the statement. Standard stuff. Spangler was the emcee. Hewitt would be the entertainment. Sitting there, she could feel Minerva Vann's stare, the way the woman always waited like an over-trained poodle for acknowledgement.

"Nice," Hewitt told her, rattling the paper. "This nails it."

Minerva Vann nodded. Hewitt felt like she should toss her a little treat or something. Maybe a Milk-Bone. With those sixty-one-year-old teeth, it wouldn't have hurt.

"So I'm the *what,*" Spangler said. "Hewitt, you're the million dollar question. *Why?*"

He said it to Minerva Vann, but he quickly shifted his focus to his special agent. "Anything fresh on that front?"

"Developing," Hewitt said. "Not quite ready to collect that million. I'll let you know when I am."

"Good. I'll be expecting at least one prime rib dinner."

It got a smile out of Hewitt, but Ms. Vann wasn't playing along.

"I know we've been through this before," she addressed Hewitt. "But I really believe you and the department would be best served if we worked together to craft a statement. Or at the least talking points."

You and me working together—Hewitt thought. And after that, maybe we could exchange bundt cake recipes.

Hewitt reached in the pocket of her leather car coat, produced a 3x5 note card with her scribblings.

"Talking points," she said. "After Captain's setup, I come in with some details. I talk about what we found. How, after analyzing the way the skull was placed in the tree and finding the bug, we made the connection to the Poe story, to the buried treasure—so to speak—as measured off from the tree. Just like in the story. All of which led to the dig. To Brandi Kaczmarek's body. The other parts of it anyway. I've had a scan made of the bug, and we'll be providing it in an e-file or hard copy. I'm not expecting much from that. State lab is looking at it. Other than the little girl's, it was clean of prints. It looks to be handmade. So I'm not anticipating there'll be a credit card record at ugly-freaking-bugs.com. I'll proceed to inform the media that the state medical ex-

aminer will, to the degree he can, answer questions related to pathology after my remarks. So Zoeller gets his requisite face time. And from
there, I'll give them a very muted indication of what we're looking for
in the way of a suspect."

Hewitt stopped there, but it was clear that Captain Spangler was
looking forward to being the first one to hear exactly how Hewitt
planned to serve the last of it up for public consumption.

"Until we get deeper into the forensic psychology and build a profile, I'm not going to offer up conjecture just to keep people enter-
tained," Hewitt said. "I believe we're looking for a well-organized,
intelligent white male who fancies himself an intellectual and enjoys
disappearing into his own little fantasy world. And he's probably not a
man who respects women a hell of a lot. But I don't know all that. Not
yet. I don't even know for certain it's a man. Which means it could be
almost anybody."

Ms. Vann shifted her shoulders and pushed out her chin at the suggestion.

"Minerva, I'm fairly sure it isn't you," Hewitt told her as she returned the note card to the pocket of her jacket.

An hour and a half later, the news conference had been entered
into the historical record, and Hewitt's 3x5 thoughts and the image
of the ugly-freaking-bug had been disseminated to the local media
and, in a matter of cyber moments, the planet. It was a hell of a
story. If you liked your homicide sensational and hideous. It was the
kind of thing that would sink its hooks deep into the public psyche.
To that end, it would be only a matter of time until some enterprising media member branded the killer with a special moniker for
franchising the story.

The fastidious little fucks were no doubt already looking for just
the right handle, the right kind of titillatingly clever references for
their bylines. Somewhere some bottom-feeding T-shirt maker was having the brainstorm of putting the gold bug on a Hanes Beefy-T. Hell,
Letterman and Leno's writers were probably already cooking up
monologue jokes.

It would be a phenomenal amount of attention suddenly focused on one bad brain in one little corner of the world. Hewitt was fine with that. For as much insanity as it would generate, there was one perfect reason for opening this trapdoor to hell and turning on the floodlights.

It was exactly what the bad brain wanted.

THIRTEEN

Unfortunately, the person who would have to shoulder the heaviest load from the immediate media crush was Brandi Kaczmarek's closest next of kin.

Her father.

Already there were news vans parked curbside under the giant willow trees when the Mazda pulled into the driveway and crept its way to the back patio where Hewitt parked as prearranged by phone with the homeowner.

Hewitt got out of the car, walked the flagstone path to the back door, wrapped on the glass. She noted a crack in one of the panes, attributed it to the portable basketball hoop adjacent to the driveway. It made her wonder if Brandi Kaczmarek had played hoops. If that had been the case, she hadn't shot any baskets there in a long time. The old net looked so brittle that the next ball that went through would likely vaporize it.

She could hear the sound of heavy feet padding on the breezeway floor. Moving too slowly. As if they wished they didn't have to go where they were going.

He appeared at the door then, not so much a live human being as a life-sized, man-shaped balloon created in his likeness to recall the man he once had been. Hewitt was showing her badge, but it was already clear he recognized her from TV. He put his big hand on the door latch, gestured with his head for her to step back on the stoop so he could swing it open. As he did so, Hewitt couldn't ignore the thought that his movements were like that of a drugged bear.

"I'm Agent Hewitt," she said as he made room for her to step into the breezeway. "Elizabeth."

"Vic Kaczmarek," he said—and if a drugged bear had a human voice, it would have sounded like that, too. "Drink coffee?"

"I'm afraid I'm the only detective in the world who doesn't," Hewitt said. She was following him through the real back door and into the kitchen now. He went to the Mr. Coffee on the counter and poured himself a cup.

"I'm more of a hot chocolate person," Hewitt said.

She could practically hear the zing of the nerve she'd hit with him. She sensed what it was, hoped she was wrong.

The big bear turned away from her, padded across the kitchen to the little pantry closet. After some digging, he turned with a box of powdered sweetness that made Hewitt shiver. From the case file, she had already learned that Vic Kaczmarek lived alone, that his wife had passed away several years earlier. She now knew he was a coffee drinker. So the presence of the Swiss Miss meant only one thing. The way he gingerly opened the box and removed a packet with those big paws made Hewitt know he'd performed exactly this same sequence of actions when his daughter had come to visit. Where they might've been sorority sisters before, Liz Hewitt and Brandi Kaczmarek were soul sisters now.

"Would you like the water heated on the stove or the microwave?" she heard him ask.

"Microwave's fine," she said. "I'm sorry to put you to so much—"

He cut her off with a wave of his paw. "Hell, don't be sorry about that." He went to the sink, drew a cup of water, put it in the microwave and pressed BEVERAGE.

Two minutes later they were sitting at the kitchen table, she with her steaming Swiss Miss, he with his black Eight O'Clock Bean. Hewitt set the case file on the blue-and-white checkered place mat, opened her notebook.

"Mr. Kaczmarek, I know you've answered a lot of questions since your daughter first disappeared. What I'd like to do today is discuss a few things based on what we know now."

He had his face down, his eyes reading the changing surface of his coffee as he tapped the side of the cup with his index finger.

"They call it a 'Missing Persons'," he said in a voice as dark as the grounds at the bottom of his cup. "I knew damn well after the first day Brandi was no missing person. She was working at her job. She was planning to go back to school. She wanted to go into nursing. She had plans. She'd finally gotten away from the jackass she married. At first I thought maybe him. But they said his story always checked out. And the truth is, he was a jackass, but he was no Goddamn killer. I . . . I used to pray she would give me a couple of grandchildren. Now I thank God she never did."

He lifted his cup, sipped what he needed to steady his thoughts.

Hewitt was paging through the file. "I understand she was divorced about a year at the time."

Vic Kaczmarek nodded, resumed his cup-tapping.

"I know she dated some men after the divorce," Hewitt continued. "And I know you've been asked about them. The detectives from Missing Persons did a good job of running that down. But given what we know—you saw the news conference . . ."

He nodded again, his gaze adrift in the dark roasted sea.

"Did she ever mention anyone who was either interested in writing or literature? Or someone who did a lot of reading? Someone who might've talked about an interest in Edgar Allan Poe?"

He shook his head at all of it. "After the officers came and told me what the son of a bitch did to Brandi, I thought through all that. I thought who would she know? Who would know her? And . . . And I knew it couldn't be somebody she knew. It was something from hell. Something . . ."

His voice broke. And with it, his face, his body—from what Hewitt could see, his remaining spirit. Or whatever it was inside that he had trusted as a source of strength and inspiration and survival.

It was time for Hewitt to do a little soul-searching sipping of her own. She sat quietly, letting Vic Kaczmarek have the time he needed. In the interim, she drew from her own cup of memory, not exactly being the model of recovery after loss herself. Within moments, she was reconnecting with the archive of kitchen-table talks she'd had with her own father. And in the dark context of the well-lit kitchen, her memory lens darkened, too, irising down to the worst of those table talks.

"Lizzy, honey. Your mother went to heaven last night."

She could feel an energy shift from Vic Kaczmarek. He was looking up now, was reading her face and the emotions that danced there like shadowy creatures in a dark ballet.

"It ain't easy is it?"

"No," Hewitt said, pulling her face back together, getting her mind out of her chest and back into her head. "No, none of it is ever easy."

"That's why there's no contract to sign the day you're born. Life is pretty much sold as is."

It was eerily like something her father would've said. And it gave Hewitt pause, made her consider the valences of the two living entities sitting there at the table, and those of the two departed ones who were never more than the firing of a synapse away. Was there some kind of metaphysical overlap? Or were the departed ones such a part of the living that they still had a voice?

"Mr. Kaczmarek, if I'm going to help find the person responsible for what happened to your daughter, I'm going to need to understand everything I possibly can about her. The things about her that really defined her as a person. The things she liked to do. The places she liked to go. The things she loved. The things she was afraid of. Is there anything you have—writings, letters, anything—that would help me get to know her?"

While she waited for his response, she unclipped the photo of the victim from the file bio. A wallet photo from a studio session. She had her dad's deep, liquid eyes. And, Hewitt assumed, her mother's thin nose and ample smile. Nice-enough looking. But not pretty enough for that to have been the sole source of attraction, the flag that flapped in the sick fuck's brain.

"There's no letters really. Maybe some postcards somewhere in the basement. She was a caller. She loved to talk on the phone."

He paused, the fingers of both hands coming together and tightening into a single balled fist on the place mat in front of him.

"That's one of the things I miss most. Just picking up the phone and hearing her voice. Her laugh. The way she breathed . . ."

Hewitt had no trouble getting that. She remembered how, in the weeks and months after her father's death, she would start for the phone, sometimes even pick it up with the ingrained impulse to call her dad at her mind's slightest provocation. Even now, five years down the road, there were still moments and sensations that would trigger the response.

"So is there anything?" Hewitt said. "Anything you can think of?"

"There is—if you want to see it—there is one thing I could show you. We'd have to go to the front room."

She followed him through the floral-print wallpaper and Euro knickknack motif of the house, to the living room. He went to his La-Z-Boy, offered her a seat on the afghan-draped couch. With his remote, Vic Kaczmarek turned on his TV and VCR. He quickly rewound the tape that was already there and hit PLAY.

"Last summer they had a sixtieth birthday party for me. And the highlight . . ." His voice broke. "Well, you'll see it."

And there it was. Careening in from the opening static. A home video camera in search of a subject. It steadied a little. Summer day. People outside. A patio get-together. Balloons. Decorations. A card table with gifts. And at the head of the proceedings, Vic Kaczmarek, sitting in the same La-Z-Boy he was sitting in now.

"Okay, here goes."—a voice from off-camera, rising over the buzzing party ambiance. An amplified voice. The camera swiveled to the source. Brandi Kaczmarek. In her best party dress, a little tight from the twenty pounds or so of extra weight she carried, a shy smile on her face, but a look of resolve in her eyes.

"Happy birthday, daddy," she said into her handheld microphone. The mike fed back a little then, and she pulled it away from her face, gave it a couple of swishes in front of her as if she was shooing away a fly. "Of all the songs I love, this is the one that always makes me think of you . . ."

She nodded to someone off-camera. In seconds, the fully orchestrated intro to a standard, special-occasion DJ song began to wash over the party, its guests, and, especially, its honoree. And at the point when Bette Midler should have entered, Brandi Kaczmarek began to belt out her own version of "The Wind Beneath My Wings." With an air of evangelical conviction. In a strong, sweet voice.

There was really only one word to describe it. And that was *beautiful*. The way the song seemed to flow so purely from her heart—even with the canned accompaniment. And the way the camera operator panned back and forth between Brandi and her father gave it a poignancy that wasn't lost on Hewitt's tear ducts. That this particular tape had been parked in the VCR suggested the even more heart-crushing notion that Vic Kaczmarek had been watching it regularly—trying in some way to keep his communion with his daughter alive.

She was in the refrain now, holding nothing back, face beaming, heart and lungs surging. Then it was back to the karaoke band, to set up the next verse while Brandi waited, the smile never wavering as she looked across the patio at her dad.

"This is Brandi," the live version of Vic Kaczmarek said from the edge of his recliner, his eyes locked on the screen. But even in profile, Hewitt could see that the look on his face was almost the same as his recorded expression. And hard as it was to find a positive side to any of it, Hewitt found herself feeling heartened by the notion that this one perfect moment between father and daughter had not only been captured but immortalized.

"Such a beautiful voice," Hewitt offered.

"All her life she sang," Vic Kaczmarek said. "She sang for the love of it. This was a birthday party. But Brandi never needed a special reason. She'd be off doing something, and you'd just hear her start singing. Now whenever I see a bird sitting alone in a tree or on the windowsill, I think that's Brandi. That's her spirit singing to me."

He returned his focus to the video as his daughter took the song to its crescendo. Hewitt couldn't help but think of the dark bird that had recently appeared in her own life. And it made her wonder, as Brandi Kaczmarek surrendered the last notes of "The Wind Beneath My Wings," why God had never allowed crows to sing.

FOURTEEN

Denver Slaughter had a couple of bills to mail. One to the phone company, the other to the power company. He checked the thermometer outside the mudroom window, saw it was fifty-two. A little chilly for this time of September, especially this late in the morning. Given that, and the drizzle, he selected his waterproof Chicago Bears windbreaker from the coat tree.

It was a long walk to his mailbox. Longer still since his hip replacement. So even though it was just a trip to a mailbox at the end of a long driveway, Denver Slaughter was in the habit of calling to his wife before he exited the house for any reason. Just in case the damn hip locked up on him. Just so she'd know where to go look for him.

"Mailbox, Helen," he called through the house. "Mailbox!"

He was out the door then, not waiting for her response. Sometimes they came, sometimes they didn't. So he always yelled loud enough that she'd hear him the first time.

Chilly. The damn rain. But clearing to the west where a couple of dozen Canada geese formed a V in the sky. It was coming. No doubt about that. The first hard frost of autumn, followed soon enough by the big wool blanket of winter. He wasn't looking forward to what the winter cold would do to his hip, to all his damn joints for that matter. But he was looking forward to the one thing about Midwestern winter he'd come to savor over his seventy-one years.

The quiet.

The quiet of stepping out of the house on a fresh snow morning and listening to the perfect winter silence. They called it the dead of winter. But to Denver Slaughter's mind, it was a good dead, a dead to be savored.

He had managed to limp about halfway down the driveway when

he slowed and stopped. The sound of his shoes on the asphalt and the rustle of his nylon jacket ceased too. For a man his age, he had very good hearing. Bad joints, but good ears. So he stopped to take in the sounds of the early fall morning.

Cocking his head to the east, he listened for the sound of the geese. Those high honks, with no real sense of order, yet in their own way coming across as almost musical. And he heard it all right. Rising across the landscape. But something in his ears recoiled at the sound of it. It wasn't right. It wasn't geese. Couldn't be them. The sound was high like that. But too high. It wasn't the sound of many. It was the sound of one. And what it was, what Denver Slaughter's ears made it out to be, made no sense at all.

It was a cry, a feral cry, coming from a distance. As his ears calculated that distance, it was also clear it was much too loud a sound for the creature that was making it. As if—but it couldn't be—as if the sound of the animal was coming from a loudspeaker. A *loud* loudspeaker.

He thought of going back to the house. To tell his wife. But he was already more than halfway down the long driveway. Whatever the hell it was, he would go see for himself.

It was a quirky subdivision. Quirky not just by the way it was zoned for parcels of at least five acres. But quirky in the types of residences that existed on those lots. For that matter, quirky in the residents. There were the older country homes, like his. Those that had come before the development. And then there were the bigger stone-and-cedar homes. *The new places.*

Denver Slaughter was at the end of the driveway when he stopped to listen again. The crazy sound seemed to be coming from one of the new places. The Zimbricks'. Or the Bohannons'. Both enjoyed the thick roadside foliage that offered the kind of privacy that seemed to attract people to the subdivision. Enough that they were willing to pay the ridiculous prices the developer asked for the lots alone.

It was between an eighth and a quarter-mile to the first driveway—the Bohannons'. Unfortunate what had happened there. With the couple split up now and just the wife living there. The *ex-wife*. Genevieve. The handful of times he'd talked to her, he'd wondered if she ever let herself be a Genny. She'd made it pretty damn clear, though, that she was a Genevieve.

The sound getting louder now. No question what it was. And his ears now pointing to the Bohannon property as the origin.

At the Bohannon driveway, he limped to a stop. What the hell was Genevieve Bohannon up to? What the hell would you have to do to make a thing sound like that? Hard to figure as it all was, but now at least knowing where it was coming from, he could walk back home and call Genevieve Bohannon and ask her what was going on at her place for God's sake. But no, he couldn't do that now. The way the thing was crying out, he found himself walking up the Bohannon driveway, step by painful step.

Halfway up the drive, he got a real cold feeling. Not just the chill wind on his face and hands. But the feeling of cold metal up and down his back, as if his spine had turned into the same surgical metal that held his hip together. A few more yards now and he would at least be able to see the house, to get his first sense of what the hell was going on.

His feet heavy against the asphalt. His nylon jacket sounding spastic against the outside wind and the inner struggles of his body. His breathing—way too heavy for his seventy-one-year-old lungs.

There. The Bohannon house. In all its stone-and-cedar glory. And coming from it, from somewhere, was the insanely loud sound of a cat in heat.

At the cobblestone walk to the front entrance, he stopped, saw the side casements to the front picture window were open to the screens. He felt his voice well up inside his chest.

"Hello?" he called, trying to make it loud enough to penetrate the cat sounds. He knew if he tried, he could make his voice louder. He also knew it wouldn't make a difference.

The closer he got to the house now, the more he regretted having those good-for-his-age ears. Making his way across the porch step, he pressed his finger hard into the doorbell. He listened for the sound of the bell, but it didn't have a chance against the volume of the crazy cat. By now he knew the sound was being made by some reproduced means. Some recording of it. But who on God's green earth would have such a thing?

He tried the front door. Locked. He saw the flash of his own balled fist strike the face of the front door. So hard it actually made the door move. The pounding continued. Five, six, seven, eight times. Until the bones in his hand shot back enough pain to make him stop.

Bad hip and all, Denver Slaughter stepped down from the porch and navigated his way through the well-manicured flower bed in front of the picture window. He moved through the flowers carefully, putting strain on the new hip he wouldn't have normally done. But crazy cat sounds or not, it was still a neighbor's flower bed.

Sticking his foot between two bee balms, his instep caught an edge of flagstone and rolled, rolling the ankle with it and reverberating up the leg all the way to the hip—*that hip*. He felt himself falling, but managed to catch the window sill with his hand. With the pain ringing in his ankle, leg, and pelvis, he lifted himself to the window, cupped his hand to shield his eyes and looked in.

He had been inside the Bohannon house only once—when he had come to welcome them to the neighborhood with a bottle of inexpensive sparkling wine. He never knew if they had been offended by his cheapness. But he had never been invited back. Yet in that one visit he had managed to get a good look at the interior. His recollection of the living room was pretty damn good. And peering now into that same living room, he knew damn well that the black block structure in the corner of the room hadn't been there before. Nor would it have occurred to anyone in their right mind to build such a monstrosity.

Denver Slaughter stood there staring, his leg and hip throbbing, his head pounding with the horrible cat cries. And as he turned away from the window, with the impulse to seek help, a human figure against the gray sky nearly stopped his heart.

Disoriented as he was by the cat screams, the brick structure, the pain, he was still able to recognize, with enormous relief, the shape of his wife's body.

"Denny, what is it?"

He stepped toward her through a patch of bleeding heart.

"I came looking," his wife called over the wailing. "I thought maybe you fell."

He could see she'd brought the cell phone in anticipation of a calamity. And God almighty had she ever found one.

FIFTEEN

Hewitt had put together the short list of Brandi Kaczmarek's closest friends and was en route to interview one of them, Victoria Semrau, when Spangler's call intercepted her. She listened intently as he conveyed the details, his voice doing its best to sound businesslike but giving way to a lilting incredulity at the finish of sentences. The only details that mattered to Hewitt were the freshly constructed crypt-like structure and the bizarre cat vocalizations, an endless loop of which had been burned to a CD and placed on the stereo unit in Genevieve Bohannon's house to play until such time that the world came to turn it off.

It was one of Hewitt's habits to immerse herself in a particular work of jazz for as many hours, days, weeks as she needed before finally coming up for air. Once a disc was in her car player, it had a tendency to move in and make itself at home. So it was with the Coltrane/Hartman recording. To veer her mind off its linear track, she hit the RANDOM button on the CD player as she exited the Tri-State for the detour to Barrington. She felt her mind hunch up, waiting for the first selection.

Of course. "Lush Life."

The velvet-throated baritone of Johnny Hartman, singing of the sweet, dark loneliness of life inside the bottle. With Coltrane's wild, brooding saxophone interpretation of that place, that special station in life at the end of the bar.

It chilled her enough as it was. But when her mind crossed into speculation of what might have gone on inside the brick crypt in that Barrington residence, her entire spine might as well have been in cryogenic storage.

I'll live a lush life in some small dive . . .

Well, that's what could happen with a roll of the dice. When you set your CD player to RANDOM. Or when a bad brain picked you for his special evening.

Looking through the windshield ten minutes into her future, Hewitt saw the first news chopper, *Eye On Chicago,* already moored in the airspace above the Barrington subdivision. Ten minutes later, she felt the bagged hand of Brandi Kaczmarek squeezing her own hand again, saw her knuckles white on the steering wheel as she parked the car across the street from the Bohannon property. Already she could feel the persona of Victim Two reaching out to her in similar desperation.

There had been a time, a long time, when the first thing that struck a visitor upon entering the Bohannon home was the magnificent stone hearth at the far wall of the great room. Those days were over. She had heard the thing described, but there was no way Hewitt's eyes and brain were ready for the sick shock of the black cinder-block crypt that stood like a waiting room to hell in the far corner.

The smell of acrylic paint hung in the air. Nice touch, Hewitt thought. Not bad enough to seal her up. You had to put a little window dressing on it just for fun.

Hewitt found the primary detective from the Barrington PD. A graying blonde woman, not in terrible shape, with the heavy load of the vocation hanging from her face in all the typical places.

Herself in another ten years.

"We found one of the blocks loose," the detective told Hewitt. "So we pulled it out, got a scope in there. Female victim. Gunshot wound to the head. Dead several hours."

"Did you find anything else inside?"

Hewitt's question took the woman by surprise, caused a shift in the facial baggage. "Well, the firearm."

"I was thinking in terms of an animal."

"There was the recording. The sounds."

"No, inside it. Inside the structure."

The detective shrugged. "We can put the scope in again. When we saw the victim in that condition, we decided to work the exterior before we opened it up . . ."

Her voice was trailing Hewitt now as the special agent moved toward the crypt. She found the opening. At head height.

A young male tech who smelled like peppers and patchouli inserted the camera and jib through the opening and pointed Hewitt to the monitor screen. Her eyes followed the camera and its band of illumination to the victim. A pathetic, god-awful mess. Face-up. Hair all over the place. A big clump of it detached from the rest of the arrangement. Skull spillings, like some kind of bizarre floor art.

"Check the corners," Hewitt said.

The instructions were followed. First in the left corner, at the head of the body. Projected brain tissue, but no animal. The light of the scope painted its way to the right corner. Again, some aerated gore, but nothing else. The light began to run the length of the body. Nothing from the blast had made its way there. Nor had any cat. And for the first time, Hewitt thought maybe she'd miscalculated. Maybe the hellacious sounds of the animal had been enough for the freak. The lower right corner revealed nothing either. Just more of the same light-swallowing nothingness.

"Too literal," Hewitt heard her voice say just before the same voice let out a gasp.

In the darkness that enveloped it, the nether-world visage of the thing was enough to have elicited that response. But the fact that only one eye lit up against the light when the mind expected two was what had pushed the air from Hewitt's lungs. And in the next breath, her brain wrested from its literary archives the long-dormant image of the cat's older, more famous one-eyed twin.

SIXTEEN

The feline Cyclops from Poe was only one of the revelations that danced with Hewitt's thought process during the three hours she spent inside the Bohannon home and, once it was cut open, the cinder-block sitting room.

Foremost was the fact that Genevieve Bohannon's fatal gunshot wound gave every indication of having been self-inflicted. And why the hell not—given the option of being entombed alive or drawing the curtain on the nightmare with one squeeze? Re-creating the victim's endgame decision-making made Hewitt shiver inside the red cashmere sweater she'd changed into for what she hoped would be her final meeting of the day. Why, and at what point, had the inquisitor chosen to give his doomed prisoner the option?

Hewitt was logging much of this in her sketchbook between sips of hot chocolate at a corner table at John & Lila's, the midpoint restaurant she'd chosen for the dinner meeting. It was a classic old supper club that had survived because of its proximity to O'Hare, and its reputation as the place where the girls from the strip club down the road would congregate during off hours. From her acquaintances in Vice, Hewitt knew it was a special point of interest for prostitution as well— an interest that cut both ways. The same male cops who would periodically chase the chickens out of the henhouse were just as likely to visit the restaurant to hire one of them to do the Chicken Dance at a buddy's bachelor party.

Based on the looks she'd gotten from a few of the well-scotched out-of-town businessmen at the bar, it probably wasn't the best place to hang out alone in red cashmere and a black skirt.

Hewitt stopped drawing, took a moment to consider her preliminary sketch of the Bohannon kitchen. The table. The two place settings.

From the photo she'd procured from the residence, she'd sketched the still-alive Genevieve Bohannon at the head of the table. The pink lip gloss on the wineglass at that setting had been an ostensible match to what Hewitt had found on Genevieve Bohannon's otherwise blue lips.

At the place setting opposite the hostess, Hewitt now sketched in the image of the perpetrator, leaving the space for the head blank and adding a Poe-style cloak to the body for effect. They hadn't found a wine glass at this place setting. But Hewitt was sure there had been one. The spillage from an errant pour had been her first hint. The spill could be analyzed. But her nose had successfully matched the faded bouquet of the almost-empty bottle of chardonnay with the spill spot on the glass table.

The crime scene team would continue searching the residence inside and out. But her gut told her the wine glass in question had already been bagged by the headless man in her sketch book—as a souvenir. Which meant that somewhere out there in the big crazy world, a Baccarat wine goblet was hidden away in some closet corner or drawer, as potentially incriminating as a butcher knife or a Saturday Night Special. Then again, and just as likely, it may have already been lying at the bottom of some northern Illinois river.

She took a sip of the hot chocolate, looked up, saw a middle-aged guy in a suit, all rosy-cheeked and alcohol-lubed and smiling at her with a leer that said he was ready to spend some good money. Hell, he hadn't worked his ass off all his life just to put his kids through college and his wife through Weight Watchers. Hewitt declined the commerce with a shake of her head, figured that was as close as the joker wanted to get to soliciting a state special agent. His wife and kids could thank her later.

Hewitt ran her eyes to the hostess station for a sign of her dinner interview. Coming up empty, she returned her attention to the sketch of the Bohannon kitchen scene. How the hell exactly had it come to that? The divorced Lady Bohannon sitting down to table with a headless fiend who would take her life? And on that account, how had it gone from game hen, wine, and conversation to Genevieve Bohannon blowing her brains out in a freshly constructed cinder-block tomb?

She was on a fresh page now, sketching the living room crypt, adding a headless, cloak-enshrouded man standing at the crypt façade, at the open space that had apparently served as Genevieve Bohannon's last view of the world.

"I always said you had a future in comic books," a voice said from less than ten feet away, and a decade and a half if you were counting years.

Seeing Scott Gregory in human form for the first time in all those years gave Hewitt a full menu of potential reactions. But the first, by a country mile, was relief. Relief that he hadn't gone completely to hell like so many men did in the twenty-plus years since graduating high school.

His face hadn't puffed. He'd kept most of his hair. There were a few creases in the face. But they were lines of a stubborn intelligence, not lines of defeat. And his shoulders and chest hadn't done the typical surrender to gravity thing. In fact, they looked solid. His frame in general looked strong. Hell, he must have actually been working at keeping it together. This she fully assessed before she even registered the clothes he was wearing—brown leather bomber, blue oxford shirt, the ubiquitous Levi's.

"Sometimes I think I'm living in one," she said.

"Wouldn't be the worst place to end up. A character in your own comic book."

He gave her the smile then. Christ, even his teeth looked like they'd been working out.

"Better yours than someone else's," she offered .

He smiled again—his *I'll grant you that one, but just this once.*

Hewitt pushed back from the table, stood up, hesitated slightly before extending her hand. From the way he took it, she knew he had expected a hug.

"You look wonderful," he said as their hands separated.

"You beat me to the line," she told him, seating herself.

He sat down across from her. "So we're both wonderful. Seems like an auspicious place to begin."

"You look like you've been putting some serious work into it," Hewitt offered.

"Well, part of my deal at Northwestern is full access to the athletic department facilities and trainers. So I figure what the hell. And you? I suppose that's part of the Spartan-like regimen of being a protector of the people."

"For me, I think it's the stress that keeps the weight off more than anything else," Hewitt responded, not being entirely glib.

He ordered coffee, and they both ordered food. He, a steak sandwich, medium. She, a turkey club. They decided to split a plate of buffalo wings to get things started. Their initial conversation was pleasant, guarded, insulated with cordial humor. Each was able to tap the pulse of the other, without much effort, as people who've enjoyed every intimacy but a kiss at the altar are able to do. But as Scott Gregory neared the halfway point of his coffee, he drew a bead on Hewitt, eyes grabbing eyes.

"What has it been—four thousand years between appetizers for us?"

"I believe Nefertiti was queen at the time," Hewitt offered.

She could see he liked this from her. But not enough to keep the Egytptology theme going.

"I have to say I was a little surprised to hear your voice on my office voicemail," he said as he picked up a buffalo wing, dipped it and set it on his plate. "I mean in the usual sea of students and administrators there's this SOS from Special Agent Hewitt."

"I have two Poe-related murders," Hewitt said. "The first, an emulation of elements from "The Gold Bug." The second, an emulation of "The Black Cat." If I had just the one maybe I wouldn't have called. But now I have a series. And my fear is we may just be getting started. You're a recognized scholar on the author in question. Regardless of the circumstances, I have an obligation as an investigator . . ."

"You've got it wrong twice," he said with a disarming smile. "I was quite happy to hear from you—under any circumstances. I just figured after four millennia, what were the odds? Not that I'd ever sealed the lid on it. Actually, I have to tell you I took small pleasures over the years in keeping up with you through our wonderful American media.

The only problem is someone usually had to die for me to catch a glimpse of you."

Hewitt had taken a bite of a wing. Scott Gregory's pause caught her in mid-chew.

"If there was one thing about my job I could change," she managed, "that would be it."

He looked down at his coffee cup, didn't like what he saw. "I guess that's how it all started, isn't it? Or—for us—set the end in motion. That someone had to die."

Hewitt swiped the side of her mouth with her napkin. "See, that's just it. I never felt she had to die. I never feel that any of them have to die. Sarah Lee. Or anyone else. And I guess that refusal to give in to it is what keeps me going."

"I didn't mean to imply there was anything fortuitous in any of it, ever," he said. "It's just that even in the darkest of circumstances I try to find my own little human victories. I'm a writer. I'm afraid you're just going to have to grant me that."

Hewitt picked up her cup, sipped the last of the room temperature cocoa, cutting it off at the final teaspoon's-worth.

"What's the other way I got it wrong?" she posed.

"Excuse me."

"You said I got it wrong twice. One was my concern over the way you would react to hearing from me. What's the other way?"

"Yes, that. It was just the way you described these murders as *emulations*."

"Well please, professor, correct me," Hewitt said, wanted it to sound cute but coming out bristly.

"My sense is that this would fall into the realm of *the paying of homage*," he said.

It was part of his vocation, of course, to split hairs, to delineate shades of meaning. It was a big part of her vocation as well. She appreciated the delineation, knew he was probably right. Point made, he took a satisfied sip of coffee. As he did, Hewitt caught herself looking at his left hand. He caught her, too, smiled a smile that clearly pained him.

"Yes, there used to be a ring there," he said.

"I wasn't . . . I wasn't aware either way," she said, caught in the flashlight beam, not liking it.

"I was," he said, his eyes clouding, his face darkening. "Married. Quite married."

He took a deep breath that seemed to suck in all the air above their table.

"My wife passed away last year. Died is the more honest but less socially pleasant way of saying it. So, yes, my wife died last year. After, again as they say, a courageous battle against a long illness."

Hewitt felt a dry ache of empathy in her throat. "God, I'm sorry."

She could feel him fighting off his emotions. It was another thing in which he was a world-class expert.

"Why do I suddenly wish we could just make this a social call?" he said.

"I wish life could just be a social call," Hewitt responded. "But given my profession, that would only be possible if everyone agreed to behave like decent human beings. Not saints. Not even being especially nice to each other . . ."

"Just maybe not hanging their heads in trees or walling them up alive," he offered.

"Something like that," she said. "Is that too much to ask from humanity?"

"Seems reasonable to me. But what you're dealing with here doesn't have a whole lot of interest in living in your world of reason."

He took a slow sip of coffee, looked at her, his eyes brighter—as if he had left a shade of their darkness inside the cup.

"You're still doing the hot cocoa thing," he said, nudging the air with his nose in the direction of her cup.

"It's like an old friend. There when I need it, not when I don't."

He nudged the air with his eyes now, detecting something in the margins of her comment. Hotly self-conscious, Hewitt made the leap. Was her hot chocolate old friend statement a metaphor for what she now expected of him? *There when I need you, not when I don't.*

"Don't mind me," he said. "It's just an invasive interest in people's habits."

The way he looked at her then, with the little rounding of his shoulders, made her feel the implication that she was a co-conspirator on that front.

"Do you feel this meeting is invasive on my part?" she asked.

He smiled innocuously. "You've got a job to do. And because of the rule of chaos and ridiculous circumstance over our lives, I might have some insight that could help you. Surgery is always invasive. But sometimes it's the only way to get at the problem."

"Well, I'll try to keep this somewhat less painful than surgery," she said, attempting to be cute, but coming out a little bitchy.

And with that tone in the air, with the smells of their sandwiches grilling in the kitchen, and with the image of a one-eyed cat scratching behind her retinas, Hewitt began the official phase of the interview.

SEVENTEEN

In her dream, Elizabeth sees the one-eyed cat. It paws tentatively at the upstairs window, outside the bedroom where she slept as a girl. It is from her childhood bed that she watches the black cat. Putting its paw to the glass—as if it knows that tapping on the window is the best way to gain entry into little Elizabeth's world.

It is a sad cat, Elizabeth decides. It must be very sad for a cat to be missing an eye. She's heard that people can get an eye made of glass if they ever lose their real one. But a cat. There are no glass eyes for cats.

Her dad would never let her have a cat anyway. First, because her mom was allergic to cats. And now that her mom was in heaven, getting a cat would remind her daddy too much of how things were when she still lived with them in the house. She had once asked her dad how long it would be until her mom was done visiting heaven so she could come back home. But all he had done was look at her real, real sad.

Kind of like the cat with one eye is looking at her now.

Mee-oow. Can I come in?

If she lets it come inside, she could make it happy. She could wrap it in a blanket. She could give it a bowl of milk. She could tickle it behind the ears like she'd seen her Aunt Grace do with the Siamese cat.

But these are just dreams, and she knows it. If she lets the cat in, it will want to stay, she will want it to stay. Forever. And her dad will not allow it. Her dad can't see her dreams the way she sees them. Not even with his two good eyes.

So, little Elizabeth closes her own eyes, knowing it is best for her to get back to sleep. To find another dream. One that might have a better chance of coming true. But like always, with her eyes closed, her ears hear better. And she can hear the sound of the cat hitting the window with its paw. One, two, three times. Then stopping. Then again. One, two, three. The sound of a cat's paw against her window glass. So soft. Like giant raindrops hitting the window. One by one by one . . .

With her eyes still closed, Elizabeth makes a wish, a wish that the one-eyed cat's dream will come true. But when she opens her eyes, the cat has gone away.

IN HER BIG-GIRL bed, Hewitt snapped awake. She looked to her bedroom window. The blinds, cracked open enough to reveal a look outside. No cat. She looked around the room, palely lit by the filtered moonlight. No little girl furniture. No dolls on the dresser. She could feel the fullness of her body in the bed. No little girl there either.

She had been completely out. In a dead sleep. Well, not totally dead. Her mind's eye had kept its periscope poked into that world, wherever it was, where the cat dream had been playing.

Reality tumbling back to her now, like bright shirts in a laundromat dryer. One of them a light blue oxford. With a head, a face that was spinning, too. Scott Gregory. She felt him in her mind. But also, strangely, on her body. As if she'd been with him. Her memory reminded her that when they parted company at the restaurant, there hadn't been so much as an embrace. They were mature now. They'd proven that to each other. She, with her intelligent, analytical approach to the interview. He, with his insightful answers, his resistance to injecting humor into his responses where once he would have jabbed and parried and lampooned the process to death.

Hewitt got out of bed, went about the morning routine, with thoughts of her personal West Nile buddy winging through her intense recollection of her meeting with Professor Gregory. In the shower, she waited for the water to warm, her body abloom with gooseflesh and still with the feeling that their skins had been together. She stepped into the warm, soothing spray, hoping the phantom feeling of him wouldn't completely wash away.

Still in her robe, she went to the computer, checked her departmental e-mail, clicked the message from Kristal Drury at the state lab, read the conclusion that the gold bug was a handmade, one-of-a-kind piece. Checking the department's website for any related tips, she found several. All red-flagged, cockeyed. Nothing credible. All of which confirmed what her gut had told her at the beginning. The bug, as evidence, had been dead on arrival.

She got up from the desk, made breakfast. Swiss Miss, peanut butter and jelly toast, orange juice. The big vitamin. All of it over a generous serving from her sketchbook. Notes from the previous night. A couple of drawings. Both of Scott. One with the tight face of reason he presented as his usual way of being. The other, with the idealized face he'd manifested a handful of times when the euphoria of his fully engorged intellect had overwhelmed all physical obstacles.

When she had asked him what would possess someone to recreate the atrocities in Poe's work, the professor had redirected the question.

"First you have to ask yourself what would have possessed Poe not only to conjure up but to commit to the literary record such terrible things in the first place."

Seated across the table from him in the decades-old light of the supper club, she had waited patiently for his next words. Now, as she began her morning walk, she replayed the rhapsodic facial expression he'd displayed, the one that always came over him when he knew he absolutely had the goods, not only on the person to whom he was proving his point, but on the devil's advocate inside him with whom he was engaged in almost constant battle.

"Poe composed such things," he informed her, *"because it made him happy."*

Despite his cocksure rendering of the opinion, Hewitt had been instantly averse to its plausibility. Doing it for gratification, yes. Whether the gratification was intellectual, fetishistic, psycho-sexual, whatever. Gratification she could buy. But happiness. It was more than a semantic matter. It was a commentary on the moral core of the human species—of which she happened to be a fully committed member. To equate such depraved musings to the pursuit of happiness, to say that the creative fantasy of burying someone alive was somehow equivalent to flying a kite in a park on a breezy June day was something that not only repulsed but scared the hell out of her.

What a freaky Goddamn thing—Scott Gregory's theory that happiness wasn't necessarily a property to be claimed by those on the bright side of the rainbow. But rather, it and its pursuit were equally viable motivators in the shadowy regions where the bad brains lived, loved, and bred.

Christ, that was just wrong.

That had been her initial reading. But as with all ideas she suspected of having a distant plausibility, she'd turned it, rolled it, batted it around. Like a cat playing with a bird.

Shit, there it was again. Just ahead. The crow from hell. More like some black paintball accident with feathers now.

She was walking hard, fast—aggressively putting the damn bird out of her mind. She'd always assumed that some kinds of happiness were superior to others. *Hers,* for instance. The Swiss Miss thing. The lunch dates and movies with her dad. A new leather jacket she couldn't afford but she bought anyway. Getting laid on those rare occasions by someone who was smarter than she was.

Not exactly a bushel basket of universal truths. And what if Scott was right? Maybe happiness was a universal commodity without denomination. Hell, you could fill a room with psychiatrists, and not one of them could talk a schizophrenic out of laughing ecstatically while he methodically pulled out his eyelashes.

Did the Poe-freak revel with unrestrained elation in the final living hours of Brandi Kaczmarek and Genevieve Bohannon? What games had he played with them? What liberties had he taken in pursuit of his bliss?

She had completed the loop, was a little out of breath, having pounded the two and a half miles in what felt like record time. She did not, however, check her watch for any kind of verification. Because by then she had already extracted the newspaper from the plastic sleeve beneath her metal mailbox. And from the front page, she quickly learned that the crime editor at the *Sun* had been the one to christen the killer with the moniker she suspected was coming.

From now on, for as long as human memory held valuable such hideous scandal, he would be "The Raven."

EIGHTEEN

He sits at the writing desk of the hovel, which at this moment is serving the dual function of a breakfast table. He has paused in his composing, paused in the detailing of the events which transpired during his evening with Genevieve Bohannon.

On the plate before him, two poached eggs, toast, a sprig of green grapes, fifteen or twenty. And, of course, his coffee, dark French Roast, with seven drops of anisette. He sips the coffee, drawing up the scent of the anisette during the wonderful interval when the center of his face is inside the cup.

He sets the cup down on the saucer which rests on the two-hundred-year-old desk. Taking his fork, he raises it to his mouth to allow the tip of his tongue to press down on each of the four silver tines, one by one. He stabs the first egg. It is exactly that. A stabbing. Not an incursion into the egg. Not a penetration. The gesture is quicker, more precise, more willful. And he enjoys the feeling of the violation, of destroying the sanctity of the one tiny universe and spilling its contents into the universe in which he dwells.

He hears his voice reacting to this, his laughter filling each of the three rooms of the hovel. There was a time when he hated his laugh, hated its haughty way of announcing his mood. And, for a period, he attempted to control it. Over time, however, the laughter and its capricious power over his greater sensibility became an unexpected comfort to him—like a loathsome in-law with whom, through sheer repetition, one becomes accepting and even familiar—such that now, the laughter is not just a tolerable acquaintance but a welcome confidant.

He and it, they, had worked well together on the Eve of Genevieve. For the amount of time it had taken—he always lost track of the hour during such things—the laughter had served as a pleasant counterpoint to the aural protestations of Mrs. Bohannon.

It was not unlike the two hands on a piano. The left, his laughter, driving and inspiring the right, the full range of her vocal responses. All of it, both hands, fueled by the same heart, the same mind, the same pure well of inspiration.

He pierces the second egg and hears it again—his throaty accomplice parading about the space of the hovel. It no longer surprises him, the laughter. Yet, oh how it had startled the simple mind of Mrs. Bohannon. And the more she had struggled against it, the greater the degree of her protest, the more aggressive his accomplice had become. As if the will of the one ascended to match the will of the other, until each had broken free of its own tiny universe and spilled its contents into the greater realm where only one of them had the conscience to continue.

Grapes are fascinating. The rivers of fluid inside. The succulent flesh, the soft thin skin that envelops the inner workings. Is it any wonder men saw fit to squeeze them into a fluid many equated with hallowed blood?

He considers a grape in his long fingers, pinches it, squeezes it until the soft thin skin ruptures and the fruit plasma ejaculates, some of it onto the writing desk, some onto his hand, some spattering against the side of his face. He ingests the grape, delighting in his crushing and swallowing. He performs the same sequence of actions in ingesting each of the remaining grapes. When this is completed, he draws the last of the coffee from the cup and pushes away from the table.

The sound of his feet crossing the floorboards of the hovel. His breathing. Satisfied breathing. Well-fed breathing. All of it becoming more excited as he approaches the north wall of the hovel. This is the wall that holds the photographs. The dimly lit, smoky, granular images of the subjects of his prevailing interest. The Bohannon woman on the right. The Kaczmarek woman on the left. Both photographed in a similar pose, standing upright, arms to the sides, hands gesturing.

And on their faces, that curious expression. Trepidation mixed with merriment. Eyes wide. Mouths, of course, agape.

He regards them this way until he has worked the series of notions through his mind. Finished, he leaves them and crosses the room to his antique chest of drawers. In the top drawer, there is a single object—a small cedar box. Small, yet just large enough to hold other photographs like the two on the north wall. He slides the top drawer open carefully, mindful of the troubling squeal it makes if opened too forcefully. As if dipping his hands into a font of sanctified water, he takes the little box, crosses the hovel and returns to the writing desk.

He withdraws the photographs and sets them on the desk, one by one until he is left with one final image at the bottom of the box. The woman in this photograph is the same relative age as the women on the desktop and the two already on the wall. But whereas the other photographic images have been captured recently, this last one shows the weathering, the denaturing, the distance of decades. The subject's pose, however, is strikingly similar to that of the others.

He takes his napkin and wipes his mouth before lifting his mother's picture to his lips and kissing it dearly.

NINETEEN

"I sent an MP3 to the Zoology department at Depaul. It's the sound of a female cat in coitus."

Of all the evidence analysis Hewitt had been presented in her career, this was the first time she had interfaced with kitty sex. Art Mitchell, the division's A-V guru-geek, tried to hold back his impish grin, but failed. "So obviously someone was there when a boy cat was proving his true love for a girl cat. And they used a microphone and a recorder to capture the special moment."

Now the resident imp flexed itself fully into the dough of Art Mitchell's face. Hewitt heard Elizabeth Taylor's vestigial voice in her head. *I feel like a cat on a hot tin roof.*

It wasn't until her mother died that her dad revealed he was the one who had pushed to have his only child named after the star of *National Velvet*. Right now Elizabeth Taylor Hewitt felt more like a reclining Cleopatra, the way the faded, middle-aged Mitchell was regarding her with his candy-store eyes.

"The type of disc and the manufacture, et cetera, will narrow your suspect range to something in the hundreds of thousands," Mitchell told her. "And that's just among American citizens. I understand no usable prints were produced."

"No," Hewitt demurred. "It was clean."

"Clean as a cat after a tongue bath," Mitchell added.

She could see his own mother-of-pearl coated tongue twitch a couple of times in the sagging mouth.

"That's a lovely image," she said. "I think I'll let you keep it."

Hewitt left it there, left the crime lab facility, left Art Mitchell to his own twisted inner dialogue, left the body of Genevieve Bohannon in the hands of the people who were resigned to the fact that sometimes life just smelled bad.

The cat theme, however, that she couldn't leave behind. She had a 3x5 note card scribbled with her prioritized list of interviewees and their phone numbers. But upon exiting the underground ramp in the Mazda, the first number she called was the state police evidence bank. Her query was answered quickly. The one-eyed cat—by now they had a name for it, Shorty, as in short one eye—had been taken to an animal shelter pending further instructions.

By noon, Hewitt had paid a personal visit to the shelter. And before the lunch crowds across the city had begun to thin, Elizabeth Hewitt was the proud owner of the first real live kitty of her life. Or at least she was the proud temporary owner.

Her visit to the animal shelter had affected her the way most such visits affect people with a reasonably functioning heart. And seeing Shorty in the cage, surrounded by all the other caged cats on death row had not just tugged at Hewitt's heartstrings but had penetrated her chest and locked both hands onto the big red pump.

Somewhere inside, in the little-girl cortex of Hewitt's brain, there had been an impulse to liberate all the kitties, to take them all home, to make them all happy. But the grown-up cortex slammed the cage door on that. One brief memory montage of a double murder in a cat house, a north-side bungalow where an elderly couple kept more than two dozen of the creatures, had been enough.

So Hewitt had kept her focus on Shorty, the one-eyed wonder cat. The last of God's creatures to have seen Genevieve Bohannon alive. The only witness who had seen the face, the eyes, the moving form of The Raven. And because of that, Shorty would be the only cat in the animal shelter invited to the ISP news conference scheduled for three o'clock that afternoon.

TWENTY

He remembered her back, knew its mapping, its topography, its history. He'd always had such intelligent hands. Each of the fingers seemed to have a mind, a personality of its own. As if, embedded in the flesh of each fingertip, there was a tiny individual brain that knew exactly what to do. No other man had ever been able to work her back like Scott Gregory. And the amazing thing was that after all this time, he remembered the spots, the places to look for the knots of tension, the drumlins of stress, the entrance to the cave of deepest secrets.

"Better?" he asked.

"Only you would know how much," she told him.

"Then mission accomplished."

Which would have been the God's honest truth if she had called this second meeting for the sole purpose of relieving a little muscle tension, and perhaps a small fraction of the outer tension that pressed against her skull like an iron helmet resurrected from a world war.

The truth, as far as her imperfect mortal soul could tell, was that her reason for requesting the meeting had been two-fold. One, with no plausible hits on Poe-related antecedents on VICAP, she was now in the mode of contacting field-related professionals whose paths, by some Goddamn miracle, might have crossed with the bad brain they were seeking.

Of course, there was always the possibility that something would come spinning out of the latest news conference and its call for information on the Bohannon murder and the identity of the one-eyed cat. But it would take time for the flotsam to separate out. And most of the flotsam, she knew, would turn out to be nothing more than that anyway. So she had returned to the personal interview mode. Because Professor Scott Fitzgerald Gregory was an esteemed professional with a

Poe connection and an ancillary connection to hundreds of colleagues, thousands of students, and the occasional letter-writing or e-mailing freak who might have contacted him after dwelling on one of his articles or university press publications.

That was her rational reason anyway—the PR machine of her psyche spinning out the one-page release for the rational criminologist that resided inside her. The other reason, of course, was the handwritten, perfumed note from the horny, starstruck undergrad who just wanted to be in the same room with him.

Professor Scott Fitzgerald Gregory. He was the one who had deigned to permanently place that sparkling A on her University of Illinois-Chicago transcript in an English course called "An Inquiry Into The Mind Of Poe." She had probably deserved something closer to a high B. But her extra-credit work with the young associate professor hadn't gone unappreciated.

The first time she'd gone to see him during office hours, it hadn't been with the notion of raising her grade. She had rationalized it, justified it. But the fact that she spent significantly more time in front of the mirror for that meeting than any other meeting she ever had with a teacher was her first clue. They screwed on his desk that first time. He had cleared off all his books and papers and laid his leather jacket on the desktop to cushion the hardness for her. At the time it seemed like the most chivalrous act a man would ever do for her. And she had wanted to feel that feeling forever.

But eighteen months to an undergrad can feel like a lifetime. And a wild year and a half of turning on to sex, mind trips, and his other passion, jazz, was not the kind of foundation upon which a long-term relationship was going to be built. Hewitt had known that, even before her half of the story took its own horrible turn in the middle of a Halloween night on the roof of a campus apartment known as "The Springs" at the time, and "The Splat" ever since. And once that had gone down, UIC, its students, its faculty members were too haunted for her to continue there.

Sitting alone with him in the present, with his hand playing puppeteer to her central nervous system, she was feeling haunted in a different way. For this there was the obvious, unfortunate explanation. They weren't really alone. And what privacy she had initially perceived had been a mirage much less palpable than the ghost of Mrs. Scott Fitzgerald Gregory who continued to inhabit the three thousand square feet of the L-shaped ranch.

For the truncated Q&A part of the meeting, Scott had moved from the suede camel sofa and settled into the fan-shaped rattan chair directly facing her. For the record, Scott had come up dry when asked if he recalled any students, colleagues, associates, or pen pals who might have transmogrified into the thing the media was now calling The Raven. Although Scott, to his credit, hadn't come up dry without a splash of humor.

"I did know an associate professor—lovely woman—who surprised one of my colleagues when she took him home to her private little dungeon after dinner and drinks. And on their next date, he surprised her by appearing at the door dressed like a big black bird."

The bird reference made Hewitt feel compelled to share her neighborhood crow story.

"You were actually going to shoot the thing?" the professor posed at story's end.

"It was one of those impulses," Hewitt explained. "The desire to put the thing out of its misery. I would think you'd approve. Aren't you the writer who was fond of saying poets like to play God?"

"Actually, I've amended that woefully self-aggrandizing statement."

"To?"

He traced a smile with his lips without fully executing it. "Poets play God only half the time. They other half, they try to fool God."

Hewitt was quick to delineate the critical difference in the two statements. Sitting on the suede sofa, with her stockinged feet snug to the polished oak floor, she paused to take a really good look at him. The professor, the scholar, sitting back in his big rattan chair like some jungle-republic governor, with his bare feet, his Northwestern football T-shirt, and the signature jeans.

"Playing God is one thing," Hewitt proffered. "Playing God doesn't assume the existence of a model upon which to base the behavior."

He sketched another smile, as if he already knew where she was going.

"Fooling God," Hewitt continued, "is quite a different enterprise. Fooling God presupposes there's a God to fool."

This time when he traced the smile, it held and affixed itself to the invisible wall between them.

"So you're suggesting I may be one of the legion of lovers and hallucinators who've traversed the belief system from pretending to accepting the existence of The Big Man."

"Assuming it's a male."

"I'm a male. I have no other choice but to hope God is, too."

Hewitt felt a smile tracing itself on her own face. Without arousing suspicion, she projected it onto the opposite side of the invisible wall where Scott's smile was already on display.

As it turned out, it was the only form of a kiss they would share.

"Outliving a very close loved one has a way of messing with a person's belief system," he volunteered.

And with that, the smooch-art came down from the wall and the ghost of Rose Gregory danced its way into the room. She was not a quiet dancer.

Scott began by apologizing for the conspicuous absence of her photograph from the rooms Hewitt had seen to that point. "I'm not sure if it's a customary thing. But after the one-year anniversary I decided to have some of the things put away."

Hewitt considered her similar process in the chronology of her father's afterlife. The gradual thinning of some of the more poignant, painful reminders. The anniversaries, birthdays, Christmas.

Under the heaviness of his admission, Scott buckled noticeably. Hewitt straightened up from the sofa and, mindful not to bump into the whirling dervish of Rose Gregory, went to his side. She put a palm to his face and then to the back of his neck as he tilted to the front edge of the rattan chair and released some of the memory with a series of harsh, deep breaths that in a woman would have been sobbing.

With the rudder of her hand, Hewitt helped him steady things, to the point that after a few minutes, he went to the kitchen to prepare a bourbon on the rocks for himself and an ice water for her. The traipsing shade of Rose Gregory seemed to follow him out of the room.

Hewitt returned to the camel sofa, happy under the circumstances to be alone with her thoughts. She had never seen Scott this way before. And one dynamic aspect of the altered Scott was clear to her. If she was ever going to end up cheek to cheek with him, she would first have to do a little dancing with Rose Gregory.

Hewitt resumed her seated position on the sofa as Scott returned to the room, a detectable effervescence preceding him that couldn't be attributed solely to his cocktail. He crossed the room, delivered her tumbler of ice water, and sat down next to her on the sofa. After a sip of his drink, he set his own tumbler on the glass table in front of them and slipped his right hand inside the back of her sweater one more time.

A few minutes and several degrees of reduced tension later, he picked up a remote control from the table with his left hand and clicked on the music track that had been cued on his personal stereo for a decade and a half.

Coleman Hawkins. "Body and Soul."

Of all the songs in the jazz universe, this was the one she thought she would never listen to again. It had been his personal favorite—the one he'd cued to repeat during their lovemaking on occasion after occasion. It was the track they'd fallen asleep to the night Sarah Lee fell from the roof. It was the song she was compelled to hate or fear—and certainly to avoid—the rest of her life. Despite its beauty, its sensuality, its place at the altar of the Temple of Jazz.

She knew Scott Gregory could sense all of this in her back, knew he was using the intelligence of all those brainy fingers to control it, to calm it, to tell her enough time had passed, to convince her it was time for the ghosts to leave them alone.

It would be as far as they would go that night. The intelligent entities in his fingers had been able to feel that, too. And for Hewitt's part, she wasn't even as aware as he was that she wasn't ready to go all the way home with him just yet.

They had waited four thousand years to reunite. One more night wouldn't alter the course of human history.

TWENTY-ONE

Hewitt paused at the top of the steps, let her fingers linger on the switch for the basement lights. She was down there. Sarah Lee Hooker was in the basement. And even though Sarah Lee was in the basement in memorabilia only, there was a palpable sense of her radiating up the steps. And it unnerved Hewitt, the idea of stirring up those bones.

She flipped the switch. Right away that helped. Ghosts were always more manageable with the lights on. She descended the steps, went to the box, retrieved the white envelope. And it was odd, once she had the envelope in her hands, how the sense of Sarah Lee, the suggestion of a local apparition, disappeared. As if the contents of the envelope were communicating the unsubtle message: *Really honey, this is all that's left.*

Hewitt sat down on the floor beside the box. In the sagging incandescence, it struck her that she was presently about as subterranean as Sarah Lee—though they were in different states. Literally. She was in Illinois; Sarah Lee in Wisconsin. And figuratively. She had a living, breathing body; Sarah Lee was dust.

Opening the envelope, Hewitt inhaled the emission of time and must from the deteriorating newsprint. The first thing she pulled to the surface was the newspaper clippings. The stories of the tragedy. The Halloween suicide of a University of Illinois-Chicago coed. A UIC coed dressed as a witch.

It wasn't the yearbook photo of Sarah Lee in the body of the article that stunned Hewitt then. It was the face of the young woman in the larger photo. A shocked and desperate face. Shocked by the tragedy. Desperate for some kind of answer that would have a chance of making some kind of sense.

It was a picture of herself. With a decade and a half less age on her face. But the face itself, that look hadn't changed. She knew, sitting on the cold basement floor, that if she held up a mirror right then, that look was exactly what she would see.

She sifted through the other articles. The follow-up. The suicide ruling from the M.E. The interview with Sarah Lee's parents. The numb bewilderment that still emanated from their quoted words, and definitely, from their look in the accompanying photo.

At the time of her Halloween death, Hewitt had only known Sarah Lee Hooker since that same August. It began when they had showed up simultaneously at a housing complex, both looking to lease an efficiency. But when the manager had informed them he only had one-bedroom doubles available, they had eyed each other up, asked the manager to hold one of the units for thirty minutes, and proceeded to the nearest coffee shop for a two-way interview and a couple of hot chocolates.

Sarah Lee's ordering of the hot chocolate had been all Hewitt needed in terms of character testament. A half-hour later, they were filling out the application together. For Hewitt, there had been no inkling, no dark sense, no flutter of the psyche that ten weeks later one of them would be dead. And dead in such an unfinished way that all these years later the other of them would be sitting alone in a cold basement with tears in her eyes, still wondering why.

Picking through the rubble of memory now, Hewitt reencountered the one element that had always bothered her about her meeting with Sarah Lee's parents in the wake of the tragedy. It was the way they had accepted the county's ruling on their daughter's death. They had down-shifted so quietly from the question *How could this possibly be?* to the much more self-contained question *Why?*

It had always made Hewitt feel a little arrogant that in the two-plus months she had known her, she might have drawn a tighter bead on Sarah Lee than her parents had managed in twenty-plus years.

She was fingering the white business-size envelope that held the photographs now. These were the pictures of Sarah Lee, the ones she had taken with the old Olympus her father had given her. These were the pictures she had always considered to be the best evidence of her premise. In a court of law they wouldn't have added up to squat. About all a veteran judge could've said after carefully examining them would've been something along the lines of *nice girl*. Yet that was exactly it, the basis of Hewitt's case. The pictures depicted a nice girl doing nice things in a nice world.

Shit, it was all right there. The pictures of Sarah Lee hanging around the apartment. The one of her sitting on the edge of her bed with her wet hair wrapped in a towel. What could be more normal than that? Or the shot from their camping weekend in Wisconsin. Posing with a handful of fallen red maple leaves. Christ, she'd pressed them in one of the textbooks she'd taken with her. That was Sarah Lee Hooker. She did things like wash her hair and press leaves, for God's sake. Hardly the antecedents for jumping off an apartment building.

With her feet pressed to the fire of her own investigative thinking, however, Hewitt had to admit that Sarah Lee Hooker's perfect sky wasn't without its turbulence. There had been the sense of a boyfriend problem. Someone Hewitt had never met. Someone she presumed to be from back home in Black Earth. Sarah Lee didn't talk about it—whoever it was. And for her part, Hewitt was still in her drooling gaga stage with the associate professor she had so impressively bagged. So maybe she had missed some of the telling signals Sarah Lee might have been flashing to the world.

The old doubt skittered across Hewitt's mind, like a millipede on the basement floor. She brought her focus back to the photographs. As far as she could gather, looking at a close-up of Sarah Lee and her harmless eyes and too-big-for-her-mouth smile, she still failed to see the face of a suicide planner.

She returned the photos to the business envelope, tucked it back inside the big white one. She dug past the newspaper clippings to the bottom of the envelope, found the one real artifact she'd kept, the one Sarah Lee's parents had missed when they came to pick up her things. Hewitt had discovered it a few days later. While sitting at the foot of

Sarah Lee's abandoned apartment bed. She'd seen it underneath the built-in dresser Sarah Lee used.

Hewitt pulled the object from the envelope, held it in her cupped hand in the halo of the basement light.

Sarah Lee Hooker's rosary.

TWENTY-TWO

There was something funky about the floor. At the end of the living room, where the Persian rug gave way to the polished oak, something looked funky. Jasmine Rudella set her black suede jacket down on the candy-striped love seat and proceeded to assess that section of the floor, like a surveyor, from a number of calculatedly stepped-off angles.

It was the light.

What else could it have been? One of the track lights overhead must have shifted in its bracket. Ever-so-slightly. But enough to have caught her eyes when she'd entered the room and flicked on the switch.

Jasmine Rudella felt a little smile break on her lips. Then again, maybe it was just the four champagne cocktails talking. Those and the half-dozen hits of pot she'd enjoyed in the ladies room at the Petrified Rock.

Still grinning, she studied the polished wood, the vanilla pools of light wet against the polyurethane skin that protected the wood against the outside world. Even though the outside world, in this case, was the inside of a house.

That was definitely pot-thinking. When in was out and out was in. And the walls changed directions. And the edges of things evaporated. And the measurements of normal things got stretched. And all the things you always believed in, you weren't quite so totally sure about.

Like the floor. The way the wood slats fit so snugly together in a pattern that screamed solidarity. Yet if a person took the time to look really closely—maybe after four champagne cocktails and several lung-fulls of THC—you could see each little seam, each potential little weakness in the otherwise solid floor. Again, pot-thinking. She was damn good at it.

Having removed her heels at the back door to protect her floors, she now removed her stockings. To allow herself to stand barefoot on the warm wet wood beneath her, in those little pools and eddies that were springing up from the cracks.

She liked the feeling—of her feet imagining they were standing in liquid. Did her feet have their own imaginations? She looked at them, let her eyes think they saw the little ripples of vanilla light washing over her toes. There was something funky about the floor. And rather than fight the funk, she was letting herself immerse in it, be one with it. Goin' with the frickin' flow—in keeping with what she'd done to the music on the dance floor at the Petrified Rock in the hours before her little foot bath in the wood.

It had been a dancing night. No singing for laughs and vanity on this evening. She and Caroline. The two of them. The weird pattern of their lives, continuing. The dancing for the boys in high school. The double dating in college. The almost double wedding. The double dating with husbands. And now, weirdest of all, that they'd both gotten divorced in the same year. On nights likes this, their lives seeming to have peeled back and away from themselves, returning to some essence, revealing some hidden layer of succulence. On nights like this, they were dancing for the boys all over again.

Jasmine Rudella watched as the muscles of her lower legs pulled her bare feet from the tide pool of the solid oak floor. The same sweet feet—how many men had seen fit to suck her sweet little toes?—transported her to the master bedroom of the split-level ranch.

In the left back corner of the bottom drawer of the birch veneer vanity, she kept a snack-size plastic bag with about two joints-worth of pot she'd been saving. She watched from that special perspective behind the invisible mirror that only pot provided as her fingers—sweet fingers, too—picked their way through the strata of long-sleeved T-shirts and turtlenecks until they located the plastic bag.

She had always sucked at rolling. For years she had relied on her pothead lawyer husband to do the honors. But in a pinch she could manage to get enough of the green leaf into the paper and seal it with a big wet kiss to create something she could smoke without setting herself on fire.

On the third attempt, sitting on her bed, she managed to create just such a joint. Having enjoyed so much the feeling of her suckable toes in the healing waters of her funky living room floor, she waited until she had returned to that same spot before lighting it. The first hit she sucked down hard and held it—the space between inhalation and exhalation like a decadent little visit with her evil twin. When she finally exhaled, she blew out not just the burnt leaf and the sickly sweet pungency but the last layer of caring about who she was and what she would do next.

Another hit. This one sucked and held with less intensity. And when she let her breath go, it was with a chesty resignation that, while not exactly articulated, made the clear enough sound of *Fuck It.*

Jasmine Rudella crossed the funky floor to the stereo cabinet and set the joint down, knowing it would burn out before it burned far enough to damage the wood. An illegal but harmless stick of incense for her dancing pleasure. She reached inside the CD rack, selected a CD the color of drying blood. The Doors. *L.A. Woman.* She punched in the title track.

Crossing the room, she caught sight of herself in the reflection of the bay window that faced her backyard. Stoned Sally. In her red hooded sweater and tight black jeans. She still had the body, even on the other side of thirty. The dancing and the pilates helped with that.

The song was up and running. The beat too fast for a sedentary body to keep up with for very long, but just right for a dancing body. In a sudden impulse, she pulled the hooded sweater up and jerked it free of her head. A bra-wearing cavewoman with wild hair stared back at her from the bay window, both of them moving snakelike to the John Densmore beat. And both, in the next blood-pump of beats reaching back and freeing themselves of their bras.

Tits ablaze in the lamplight of the bay window.

She didn't watch herself remove the black jeans. Nor did she pause to observe the quick slide and kick-away of the panties. So it was in her birthday suit that she finally saw herself, deep set in the bay window, her body hustling now to the music as Morrison's voice began to preach and seduce from the bookshelf speakers.

If she could have stayed there inside the flattering glass of the window, free to move, to dance wherever the breezes of her brain blew her, she would have traded that for any future reality. If she could have stayed the naked dancer in the window, for all eternity, her mind and body never changing from the way they felt right now. Nirvana. Jasmine Rudella style.

In the incandescent light, the V of her pussy danced its own inner dance, inside the movement of her limbs. As she watched herself, this window image made Jasmine Rudella revise her assessment of her naked dance Nirvana. For the dance to be enough to keep her happy for eternity, she would need to add one thing, one dimension, one psychic-gymnastic possibility. The ability to transport herself from one windowpane to another. Not just within a single house. Or even a single subdivision. Or a single town. But to be able to move freely, soundlessly, to any window in any place she chose.

The possibilities. To show up unannounced in her ex-husband's bedroom window as he returned from one of his pot and drinks and titty bar nights. To come home to the image of her, dancing nude and untouchable in the light of his window.

The Doors were into the big "L.A. Woman" instrumental thing now. Robby Krieger's guitar wailing like a sex voice. Ray Manzarek's keyboard pumping blood to all the special veins.

Jasmine Rudella began to twirl. It was an inevitability. Whether she was on a public dance floor or in the privacy of her own in-home fantasies. The twirling was always something that had to happen.

Moving faster now—so that each glimpse in the window was increasingly fleeting. So fast now that even the V of her pussy was just barely catchable if the lamplight hit just right. Yet inside, from the core of her, she was disseminating her essence to the outer realm, beyond the window, through the window. And she wondered if maybe somehow, somewhere, Jim Morrison could see her dancing in the window of his penthouse on either the lowest floor of heaven or the top floor of hell.

She could see the Lizard King lying on his netherworld bed, shirt off, in the leather pants, his feet bare, his eyes fixed on the window between realms, watching this naked Aphrodite twirl and twirl and twirl for his pleasure. She could see his hard eyes, his hard smile as his hand rubbed his belly, as the hand made its way to the top of the leather pants and began to work its way inside.

Shit!

She saw him. In mid-twirl. The Lizard King. His face in the window. His mouth at the V of her pussy.

But in the next tight, screaming, breathless twirl, he was gone. And she fell out of the twirling, the dizziness hitting as her pilates-and-dance legs fought their way to the window. Her dizzy face and her tits blooming back at her in the light of the reflection. She hurried to turn off the lights. So it was a dark window she was looking out for a sign of someone—The Lizard King, she hoped—to be there in the darkness, in the patch of grass that rolled into the opaqueness of the woods. But there was no one, man, reptile, or otherwise.

On the stereo, "L.A. Woman" had ended. Jasmine Rudella hurried over to the cabinet, the fluid in her ears still rolling, rollicking like Lake Michigan in a storm. She turned off the CD before the next song could start.

The dance was over. She was a naked Stoned Sally in her dark living room. And somewhere beyond her dark bay window she knew Jim Morrison was back asleep, the covers pulled up over his body so that now she would never know how far her dancing had taken him.

TWENTY-THREE

She awoke at first dawn to the face of her houseguest beside her on the bed, its single eye regarding her with caution, its front paws testing the softness of the bedding as if kneading a delicate pastry dough. She wondered how long it had been in the bedroom, how long it had taken her new pet to make its way from the corner of the dining room where it had chosen to hole up under one of the extra chairs she kept in the unlikely event a dinner party broke out, and she actually had to add the leaf to the table and increase the chair count from four to six.

"I hope you're ready for your first full day as a celebrity," Hewitt said, her lips plastic with sleep.

By the time she had gone to bed the night before—after returning the earthly remains of Sarah Lee Hooker to the cardboard reliquary—Hewitt had learned that the calls to the tip line and the website messages generated from the news conference numbered more than a hundred. Many of them were inquiries about the cat and whether it was available for adoption. The one piece of information Hewitt had regretted withholding at the conference was the fact that Shorty was already spoken for.

The rest of the tips fell into three categories. The first consisted of those who claimed to have had a past relationship with Shorty—the vast majority of which Hewitt knew would be from crazy cat people. The second grouping was connected with the second Poe homicide, namely sightings of Genevieve Bohannon in the days before and, particularly, on the night her strange novella of a life came to its sad ending. The third category was comprised of tips concerning the possible identity of the Poe killer himself. Again, the lion's share of these would be messages from the reality-challenged. A handful would be nothing less than full and, of course, fully bogus confessions to the crimes themselves. Hewitt had assigned two detectives from the unit, Pete Megna and Val Patterson, to pan through the silt.

She ate her peanut butter and jelly toast at the kitchen table while Shorty took a meal of Meow Mix and a saucer of milk in the corner next to the fridge. Hewitt had the morning paper lying flat and unfolded in front of her. There'd been no need to go any further. The photo was on the front page, upper half, the photo that showed the lone witness to the latest atrocity snuggled in Hewitt's arms.

As media manipulation went, this was a beauty. As inverted strategy went, it was capricious, risky, maybe even borderline crazy. It was a strategy for which she hadn't needed the help of Minerva Vann to explain her position. Nor had she needed the approval of Captain Spangler—though she was fairly certain he had an inkling she was persistently stroking the cat at the conference for something more than personal comfort.

Hewitt knew only too well that she was in the age range of the victims. Whether or not she hit any of the other hot buttons, she didn't know. Not yet anyway. And beginning with the day's slate of lead rundowns and interviews, she hoped to put a little meat on those bones. Not unlike what Shorty was doing by way of his little bowl of pressed tuna, the vapors of which had already overpowered Hewitt's peanut butter and jelly.

Hewitt left Shorty to finish his breakfast in peace. She went to her breezeway and put on a windbreaker and her crow-walking shoes. It was time to face that bad music again. As she walked past the kitchen window on the stone path outside, she looked up to see that Shorty had jumped onto the counter to give her a proper feline sendoff. Cool, diffident, a little dismissive.

Yet even in the coolness of it, there was an affinity communicated. It was about all you were going to get from a cat. No howling, slobbering *I'm gonna miss you so much I might have to hurt myself* goodbye you'd get from a dog. At best, this was an *I wouldn't mind too terribly much if at some point we saw each other again*. In other words, it was a perfect complement to the good-bye she had experienced with

Scott Gregory the night before. Not in so many words, but in the look on his face, in his academic eyes.

I'll massage your back. I'll absorb your tension. I'll put my fingers into your nervous system and right up into your brain. But for now, that's as far as we'll go.

As Hewitt's shoes hit the asphalt road, her pace quickened. Not just her walking, but the rate at which her mind moved along the innumerable neural pathways that connected her to Brandi Kaczmarek, Genevieve Bohannon, and, in a bottomless shaft of memory, the reanimated spirit of Sarah Lee Hooker.

TWENTY-FOUR

She awoke from a deep, black velvet sleep with the sense she'd been dreaming intensely, but with no sense at all of what her dreams had been about. That the dreaming had been vigorous she had no doubt. Because the first thing she encountered upon opening her eyes was the feeling of her heart pounding.

Reacting to the bunching of the bedding around her, taking in the smells of the room—the smell of marijuana dreaming—the sheer intensity of her beating heart at first surprised and then, as her brain locked onto its cadence, frightened her.

Jasmine Rudella had never felt her heart beat this way, had never heard it beat this way. She felt a cold shrinking sensation in the small of her back. She tried to sit up, but her hips were wrapped in the bedding. As she kicked her way out and managed to untangle herself, her mind began to unwrap itself from the sound of her heart. In a moment she understood, THC in her system or not, that the sound of the heartbeat wasn't coming solely from inside her own chest. And as the heartbeat moved from her body, it instantly took up residence in not only the atmosphere of the house, but in the wood, metal, and plaster. Which left Jasmine Rudella with the only perception her through-the-looking-glass mind could conjure.

It was not her heart, but the heart of the house that was beating.

She was still nude, the fact of it sweeping over her as she extricated herself entirely from the bed and stood up, her feet pressing into the wood floor and instantly connecting with the pulse that pounded from within. There was no doubt about it now. The house was the thing that was making this impossible vibration, drumming this outrageous sound.

She made no concession to the needs of her body as she put forth from the bedroom. No clothing, no slippers. It was a sound the house was making—or a sound her mind was making the house make. Either way, sound was like water. No jagged edges to it. In water you needed no clothing. Being naked in water was a birthright.

Down the hallway now, her feet padding against the floor, she flashed the thought of her feet awash in the liquid wood the night before. In the funky floor.

Bursting upon the living room now. Her body entering the room, becoming it. Like a chick outside the egg, filling the world. The world filling her ears. Her own heart beating as fast as the hatchling—much faster than the rate of the house heart. The double hit of the thing, the rise and fall, like a musical instrument. Not quite a drum. Not quite a woodwind. But low in pitch. Low like the voice of a man.

The embryonic chick followed the vibration. Connecting with, homing in on the sound with her unborn ears. Instinctively ignoring the relentless waves of idiotic clucking. Knowing, recognizing the perfect quality of the pulse that ran this world.

Her hatchling feet clawing their way across the living room floor. Her ears, her mind, her bloodroot drawn to the source of the sound. To the thin membrane between worlds. Where the laws of the universe suddenly and shockingly changed. Where liquid became air. Where wood became water.

It was coming from the floor. From that same place in the floor where the bounce of the light had seemed out of place the night before. The sound wasn't coming from the floor itself, but from beneath it. And in her mind, Jasmine Rudella configured the history and the design of the split-level ranch. This section of the floor wasn't part of the original home. It was an addition. An addition without a foundation. A raised floor with a crawl space.

Someone had been in that space. Someone had pulled up the strips of oak flooring to install a heartbeat.

In the echo of the next palpitation, she caught a scent she identified as a man, and she knew the thing that had been in the crawl space was now inside the room.

TWENTY-FIVE

She could only hope Shorty was okay in the house. The thought was never far from her mind as she threaded her way through the first interview of the day. The lead had come in from the tip line. Pete Megna had followed up a call from a bartender at a Rush Street club called Outrage. Hewitt had arranged to meet the man at the club at 9:00. By 9:05 she was sitting on a barstool across from the dark-eyed, nice-looking but bony, twenty-something bartender, Mitch Martino, who, out of habit, had assumed his usual place behind the bar.

Three stools down from Hewitt was the spot where Genevieve Bohannon had spent much of her time in the club two nights earlier. The nightclub stank with the morning-after smells of smoke, spilled beer, piney cleanser, and now, the air of psychotic calamity.

"Did it appear she was with anyone?" Hewitt inquired, a cube from her ice water interfering with her tongue.

"From what I could tell, it didn't look like she came in with anyone—if that's what you mean," the bartender answered. "But there was one guy who was talking to her for quite a while."

"Anyone you recognized?"

"Yeah, he's in here pretty often. His name's Ricky. They call him Ricky Ricardo. On Karaoke Night he sometimes gets up there with a conga drum and plays along."

Hewitt stopped fiddling with the ice cube in her mouth. It was still too big to swallow, so she redeposited it in the glass as gracefully as she could.

"Did Genevieve Bohannon ever attend any of these Karaoke Nights, ever participate?"

Mitch Martino drew himself a glass of Coke as he answered. "Well, yeah, that's the thing. I guess maybe I should've started there. As much as anyone who comes in here, she was a regular."

"A regular at karaoke?"

The bartender took a quick sip of his soft drink, wrinkled his nose at the fizz. "Well, I'd see her in here other times. But Thursday nights, she was definitely in the house."

Hewitt felt an icy wind against the back of her neck. If she had wings, she would have felt the cold wind beneath them, too.

"She could sing," Hewitt said.

"It's pretty rare when someone gets up there who can. And this girl could. And you could see guys were attracted to it. Hell, I was attracted to it. That's why when I heard . . ."

He might've finished the thought, but Hewitt was already running away with one of her own. It was the appalling but edifying possibility that The Raven preferred the company of women who could raise their voices in song.

VICKY SEMRAU WAS Brandi Kaczmarek's best friend. They'd know each since elementary school. But it was in high school that the friendship had become the lifelong kind. They'd done everything together, including two years as bench players on the basketball team. Upon learning this, Hewitt had no problem creating her own little home movie of the two girls shooting at the backyard hoop while Vic Kaczmarek and his wife sat at the kitchen table sipping their coffee, the beat of the ball against the concrete comforting, like an all-night rain against the roof.

As nice as it was for Hewitt to have her answer on the question of Brandi Kaczmarek's basketball history, her history as a singer was much more provocative. Brandi and Vicky had honed their vocal skills in the high school chorus and later at various points of interest in Chicago and its suburbs.

Sitting at the kitchen table of the Irving Park loft, Hewitt had just received an affirmative nod from the interviewee on the first critical question.

"And *how often* did you go out for karaoke together?" Hewitt followed up.

"At least once a week," Vicky Semrau answered, her face drawn, her body too thin in its black leggings and T-shirt. Eating-disorder thin. "Sometimes more often. I mean I liked it okay. But Brandi was the one who pushed it."

"What clubs did you go to?"

This follow-up made Vicky Semrau visibly uncomfortable. She directed her unease to the tin of Altoids on the table, situated between the black-and-white cow-pattern salt and pepper shakers. She opened the tin, fumbled with the thin white paper that covered the mints. She finally took one, nervously popped it into her mouth—like some kind of breath-mint addict.

She offered the open tin to Hewitt.

"Thank you," Hewitt said, taking one of the mints, at the same time wondering if that single white mint was going to be Vicky Semrau's lunch.

"The question, Vicky," Hewitt said in her cop voice. "The places you went for karaoke."

Vicky Semrau blew a sigh of resignation. "Okay. There were four places. Chameleon Club. O'Donahue's. Petrified Rock. And . . ."

This next club would be the sticky one. And Hewitt already had a pretty good idea.

"Muffy's," she said, rolling her eyes at herself at the naming of Chicago's most popular lesbian club. "We went there for the dancing."

"And the karaoke, I assume," Hewitt said flatly, making it clear she had as much interest in any sapphic mysteries as she did in uncorking the bovine pepper shaker and ingesting its contents. So she moved the focus to questions about any men the teammates had encountered on their karaoke nights who, in retrospect, might arouse suspicion.

With the questioning falling into the category of men only, Vicky Semrau not only seemed relieved but gave herself to the task, providing as many descriptions as her memory could manage. She even produced a jewelry box with a little pirouetting dancer in which she kept the business cards, torn-off matchbook covers, and scribbled cocktail napkins with the phone numbers she had collected. A handful of these were of interest to Hewitt. Though deep down another corridor of her mind, she knew it was highly unlikely The Raven would have been so untidy.

He was a carrion crow. And any useful scraps would have been picked cleanly from the body of evidence.

Yet despite his best efforts, The Raven had managed to leave traces. For now they were invisible, existing only at the ends of the beguiling questions Hewitt was beginning to ask herself regarding his specific ways of acting. His decisions. His choices. Why in the hell, for instance, had he chosen Brandi Kaczmarek over Vicky Semrau? With the two of them such evenly matched teammates, why had he chosen Vic Kaczmarek's daughter to be the one to join his horrible glee club?

TWENTY-SIX

It is quiet now. The hovel is filled with the last red tones of the October sunset. The Raven sits at the writing desk, erect and attentive. He enjoys this moment as much as any other, this time when the activity has been completed, the fuss has been made, and the tribute has been received. That the sun has graced him with its blood-tinged dissolution is only an added dividend.

The silence, of course, is never truly silent. There is always the background echo that is only exposed when the quiet becomes quiet enough. The greater the perceived silence, the deeper the throat of echoes reaches for its memories.

He opens the journal on the writing desk, turns to the next blank page, and prepares for composition. Against the impending dusk, he lights the candle. He prefers to write when the memory of the events are fresh in his mind. And so he writes, relating the story of his encounter with the late Miss J. Rudella.

He is several paragraphs into the exercise when he pauses, distracted by the sudden flickering of the candle which until that point has been perfectly still. Drafts are not uncommon in the hovel, and it interests him each time when such a disturbance occurs. These interloping house winds mimic so well the air current associated with the passage of a living body through the room. Of the three rooms in the hovel, this, the composition room, is the second smallest. In a room its size, any movement, even spectral, would be all the more discernible. In the large room, by contrast, the passage of an ethereal body would be more easily swallowed by the volume of space.

The door to the large room remains locked, of course. There is a small measure of joy in this, a heartening, such that even now, considering it, the thought brings an upward curl to his lips. Such small pleasures he measures appreciably, knowing they are meted out by the fates in precious increments, like the seven drops of anisette that graced his coffee moments ago. Knowing the large room is available to him, to host the eventual unfolding of his most ambitious work, is a promise from the future he has no intention but to honor.

There are four, perhaps five sips of the anisette coffee remaining. He allows himself the first of these before returning his attention to the journal and the lines and swirls of ink that vibrate into a hundred dancing snakes before his eyes.

He reads the last line he had composed before the candle intercession.

She remained frantic, even in death.

In his mind's eye, he sees his latex-covered hands working at the deconstructing of Miss J. Rudella. He recalls, vividly, the spastic twitching, the vigorous trembling of the limbs as each was summarily disjoined. Certainly by the time of the first severance, Miss Rudella was already flying among the angels. Yet even in death, her body had retained the nerve-driven capacity for disbelieving gesture.

Yes frantic, even in death!

He imagines her there, in that brighter sphere, that Elysian sky, flying with her new wings. He hears the sonorous tone of a man beginning to laugh, and he senses the entity is none less than God himself taking pleasure in the maiden flight of his newest angel. Presently the composer then realizes—he must admit this—that the laughter is not from heaven but from the composition room.

He emits another hovel-filling laugh at the notion of it—of plucking that angel from the Elysian sky and bringing it down to earth, to the home of Miss J. Rudella, and detaching those heavenly wings in the same, twitching, shivering manner and commending them to the same temporary resting space as the other parts of the body.

With this picture of the wingless angel fallen from God's sky, he turns his attention away from the pictures and embraces the thought-world of sounds. For next he will add to his journal's nest of snakes his interpretations of the outpouring of music from Miss J. Rudella's shocked and shimmering throat.

He will hear them again, as they resound in his ears, as they articulate incessantly in the bell tower of his memory. He will hear the sacred music. He will hear the perfect voice of God's only daughter.

TWENTY-SEVEN

Among the jazz CDs in Hewitt's Mazda was another disc that, while not exactly jazz, possessed more than enough fire of the body and mystery of the soul to be included in her car collection. Hewitt was scheduled to circle back to headquarters for a briefing with Spangler, Pete Megna, and Val Patterson. To accompany her on the ride, she'd gone with the anomalous musical selection. *The Essential Janis Joplin.*

Hewitt's head was swimming in karaoke, and Janis Joplin, more than anything she could think of, was the anti-karaoke. The back of the jewel case featured a psychedelic purple image of the legendary singer at a microphone, her hair wild to the point of feral, her hands open in a pleading gesture, her face contorted in a manner that conveyed one thing. Anguish. And why not? You couldn't put anguish into the blues the way this girl did unless anguish attended your daily life like a sadistic valet.

In the live version of "Ball and Chain"—track five/disc one—that anguish was offered up like entrails on a Civil War battlefield. Spilled guts wasn't something you could fake.

About eight minutes out from headquarters, Hewitt switched over to the second disc and forwarded to the song that, for reasons she knew only too well, had gotten inside her head the most. Track four. "Little Girl Blue." It was a bluesified version of the Rogers and Hart number. But the lyrics—the way Ms. Joplin sang them—always managed to mess her mind at every possible level.

Sit there counting your fingers. What else is there to do?

When she had lost her dad, in the long sad days that followed, she would catch herself staring at her hands. Until eventually it dawned on her why. Her dad had always been a hand holder. And for little Elizabeth, there had been no safer place to be than walking at her daddy's side, her little hand in his massive but impossibly gentle one. She remembered the time when she was eleven, when one of the girls from her school had seen her walking that way with her dad at the mall. The hell she'd had to pay to the little teasing bitch clique the next day. She remembered how that had put an end to it. And she couldn't forget the look on her father's face the first time he had reached for her hand and she had pulled it away.

Jesus Christ, she was going to have to do her eyes now before the briefing. Catching the look of herself in the mirror, while Ms. Joplin wailed in anguish inside the car, inside her head, Hewitt saw the usual collateral damage done to the eyes whenever she thought too long and too hard about her father.

She took a tissue from the travel pack in the glove box and dabbed at her eyes. She checked the mirror again.

Sit there counting your fingers. What else is there to do?

The finger count of The Raven's victims was two. As Hewitt continued to speed toward headquarters, she wondered how many more digits would be added before she could make the counting stop.

TWENTY-EIGHT

"Ricky Ricardo doesn't wear two-tone jackets or act anything else like a Cuban bandleader."

Pete Megna didn't look up from his notes for Hewitt's reaction as he continued to weigh in. He was sitting across from Hewitt, flanked by Captain Spangler and Val Patterson, at the conference table in Spangler's office.

"He's a drywaller who likes to bang the conga drums and any women he can persuade to spend a few hours in his life. But he's not The Raven."

"I assume he had a story," Hewitt said.

"Oh, yeah. Damn good one." Megna responded, his busy face pushing away from his thick neck like something in the hamster family. "He ended up with another honey from Outrage that night. Took her home. Introduced her to his sensitive side."

"Did you talk to this other woman?" Spangler asked.

"Yeah, but I really didn't need to. I saw plenty of her in the opening scenes of the video Ricky Ricardo made of her and, sad to say, him."

Val Patterson popped a laugh. "He showed you his love movie?"

"Right down to the date and time and close-ups. Seemed pretty damn proud of himself. Again, not the kind of thing the real Ricky Ricardo would have done."

Hewitt almost made a comment about the twin beds Lucy and Ricky slept in to keep 1950s America safe from carnal reality. But she tossed it off, looked at Val Patterson. "Anything from your end of the pool, Patterson?"

Val Patterson was young, intuitive, smart, but definitely young. Her dark-skinned face was still brimming with her amusement over the sex tape. But under Hewitt's watch, she pulled things in.

"I talked to the manager of the other club where the victim was known to hang out. The Petrified Rock. Like Outrage, they don't have security cameras. But the guy, the manager, Trey Walsh, he says they sometimes videotape the functions, the shows, you know."

Hewitt felt herself perk up at the notion. In a brain-flash she compared it to the way Shorty perked up at the first whiff of tuna.

"Do we have access to the tapes?" Spangler said.

Val Patterson had done some theater in college and wasn't shy about turning on the floodlights when there was an opening. She reached back behind her chair for her leather satchel, lifted it onto the table, unzipped it, and proceeded to pull out a mini-library of eight-millimeter tapes.

"You all are welcome to join me," she said. "You bring the popcorn. I'll bring the Mountain Dew."

"Beats the piss out of my afternoon," Spangler offered. "Division heads with Spivak. I'm sure he plans to probe my ass on this. It's always been my bad karma to be one name ahead of his in the directory. So anything else—Hewitt, I believe you had your hand raised—would be welcome."

Hewitt stared into the tabletop. "I've got a book over a thousand pages long with everything Poe wrote, in the order he composed it. But based on these two scenarios I'm not sure there's any rhyme, reason, or pattern to the stories he's selecting. Any more than Poe had a logical order in the chronology of the stories. Whenever something creepy and crazy enough came into his brain, he picked up the pen and wrote until the pressure to get it out was gone. I mean it's possible—I don't like to use it, but it's apparently here to stay—it's possible The Raven might have some personal kind of preference for the stories. Some ranking system. Either way, it doesn't give us much in terms of predictability. Which means the best thing we have right now is the singing connection."

"The karaoke thing, right?" Spangler injected.

"Yeah," Hewitt answered, refusing to avert her eyes from his. "The karaoke thing. I've got two victims, both of whom were active participants in the local karaoke scene. Karaoke is an entertainment offered up for public consumption. I believe The Raven is one of those consumers."

"What are you saying—he's going around and picking his victims based on the songs they sing in some nightclub?"

Spangler wasn't buying. But Hewitt wasn't done selling, either.

"I'm saying he may be looking for something. Some common element in the singing. In the way they sing."

"And you base this conjecture on two victims," Spangler posed. He waved a glance at everyone present. "Anybody here not sung karaoke at some point in their lives?"

Val Patterson's answer was a given. Pete Megna shrugged with resignation. They looked to Spangler who shrugged as well.

" 'My Way.' The Elvis version. At a friend's birthday party. Hewitt?"

"Yeah. A few times," she said. "But this isn't some half-assed once-in-a-while thing. These women were regulars. And more important, both of them could actually sing."

"So what do you want me to do—pull a Chief Brody and close down the beaches?" Spangler said. "Until further notice, there will be no more karaoke singing in the state of Illinois."

"You start there, and next you'll be banning singing in the shower," Megna added. " 'Course then my wife might move back in. So let's not tempt fate."

The phone rang. Spangler took it. Whatever it was that he downloaded made him fix his pupils on Hewitt. He scribbled a few lines on his legal pad, signed off.

"In Wilmette, they found a woman's body buried under her floor. With sound effects this time, too."

" 'The Telltale Heart,' " Hewitt said as Spangler tore the page from his pad and handed her the prescription for another mind-altering afternoon.

TWENTY-NINE

It was a prototypical 1950s suburban neighborhood. Nice, solid ranch homes with giant willows that stood like doting parents over the lindens that had replaced the great elms long gone to the disease known as Dutch Elm.

Other than the absence of the elms and the presence of the news helicopters in the sky, it might have been just another nice fall day during the Eisenhower administration. That, of course, and the parking lot of emergency and information-gathering vehicles around the home of the victim whom Hewitt now knew to be one Jasmine Rudella. One poor, sad, dismembered-under-the-living-room-floor Jasmine Rudella.

Inside, Hewitt made the acquaintance of Brady Richter, a Wilmette PD detective who looked to be several years her junior and a puppy on the seniority scale. The way he approached her in the front room, big-eyed and a little out of breath, made Hewitt wonder if he was going to put his paws on her and start sniffing. She also half-figured his voice would sound like Scooby Doo. But it was actually a rather nice voice, reminding her of another one, a movie voice she couldn't place.

"Who found her?" Hewitt asked as they crossed the polished wood floor to the section where the boards had been pulled up.

"Cleaning lady," the mystery male lead answered. "She arrived about one o'clock. Heard the recording of the heartbeat coming up through the floor. She went to check the basement. But there's just a crawl space down under that part."

Hewitt surveyed the room, saw the cleaning woman standing well back into the dining area, talking to another local detective.

"Was the door left open?" Hewitt asked.

"Yeah, but that wouldn't have been unusual. According to the woman, the victim would leave the door open on the day she came to clean. This is Wilmette."

An actor who'd been in a huge hit and then hadn't been heard from much.

They were at the opening in the floor now. The techs paused for a moment to let the big girl from state have her look-see.

"I'll want to talk to the cleaning woman," Hewitt heard herself tell the puppy detective, her voice sounding metallic to her as she made visual contact with the body in the hole. As she had expected, but hoped she wouldn't actually have to see, the body had been portioned as in the original Poe. Head removed. Limbs separated.

"Where did he do the surgery?" Hewitt asked Richter.

"The bathtub. Down the hall. Did a pretty good job of cleaning up. But luminol revealed a few spots on the porcelain and the tile."

Hewitt's eyes had been commandeered by the screaming flesh and bone of the dismemberment sites on the body. So it was only then, as her focus moved to the face of the victim, that she noticed the left eye, half-closed like the right one, but different.

"You're looking at the eye," Richter said. He was pretty sharp for a puppy. She was starting to like him.

"You've been looking at it, too."

"We didn't know what the hell to make of it. But I get the feeling you do."

She knew. And it made her shudder that with all the brutality that had been visited upon the body, the killer had taken his time to do such a delicate thing with the eye.

"In 'The Telltale Heart'—the Poe story that's been re-created here— the storyteller kills the victim, the old man, because of his weird eye. Which, like our victim here, had a pale blue film over it. A vulture's eye. That's how Poe described it."

"Do you think he put the thing on her eye before or after he killed her?" the detective inquired.

"I hope after," Hewitt said. "I hope to hell everything happened after."

*   *   *

THE CONVERSATION WITH the cleaning woman yielded a couple of insights for Hewitt. The first was that despite the fact that one of the woman's clients had been decapitated and quartered and buried under the floor, she was clearly responding to all the attention.

It was a strange phenomenon Hewitt had seen before. In the extreme, it could be very unsettling. Especially when the attention crossed the footbridge from law enforcement to media. She had seen them on the news so many pathetic times. Wide-eyed family members of homicide victims, just hours after the tragedy, affecting a pleasant face for the cameras, with the occasional self-conscious grin. As if the lens of the camera was some kind of eye of a higher power, imbuing the griever with a greater strength and understanding—so long as the cameras were running.

Hewitt's other insight was more directly related to the atrocity at hand. Hewitt had learned that the cleaning woman had a standing appointment with Jasmine Rudella on Wednesdays like this, at one o'clock. Which gave Hewitt something textural to chew on. An inference could be drawn that the Poe-freak had timed out the murder and the display for a timely discovery by someone he knew would be coming to the house. It definitely fit the pattern. The Gold Bug skull had been left on a well-traveled hiking trail in a way that a five-year-old had been able to find. The Black Cat crypt had been presented with such a booming attention-getter that an old man a half-mile away had been able to track it.

These were the last material thoughts Hewitt had as she approached the bathroom door to see the female tech continuing to work the darkened room with luminol. It was in the corner, between the toilet and the bathtub that a blood-traced shoeprint materialized in all its glowing green-blue eeriness.

Hewitt moved gingerly into the room for a closer look at the print.

"We can definitely rule out Chuck Taylor's," she said to the tech.

"Looks like a hard sole, something really old," the tech offered.

The words were only partially out of her mouth when Hewitt heard a burst of piercing cries coming from the other side of the house. Jasmine Rudella's first family member had arrived. From the sound of it, a sister.

Crossing the house, Hewitt saw the distraught woman being handled by Brady Richter who, despite his efforts, had been unable to keep the next of kin back from the hole to hell. While Hewitt took a moment to sketch out the floor plan and the principle players of Poe #3 in her notebook, Brady Richter did what she had to assume was a hell of a job with the woman, the sister, Maggie Corbett. Waiting for the proper opening, Hewitt slipped a 3x5 to Detective Richter with the one question that was burning a hole in her brain.

When the question drew a fresh round of tears from the sister, Hewitt had her answer. And having that little part of the picture resolved had the ancillary effect of relaxing the part of her brain where the names of forgotten movie stars were catalogued.

"Mark Hamill," she said, mostly to herself, but loud enough that Brady Richter heard it and reacted with a couple of deep blue question marks in his eyes.

Hewitt nodded professionally, appreciatively to her colleague. Then she turned away and wrote the name Luke Skywalker next to the figure of the young detective she had already sketched in her book.

THIRTY

Well, a girl had to eat. And they were colleagues working a case. So after an afternoon of evidence gathering and a brief stop to feed the cat, Hewitt met the puppy for dinner. It had actually been his idea—all very businesslike, very professional. An opportunity for a couple of detectives to work a case over a couple of charred pieces of steer. Of course, Hewitt knew full well he wouldn't have messed with her, wouldn't have taken one step in her personal direction if she hadn't left the door cracked.

In a way, an almost resentful way, she felt she'd earned an hour and a half outside the shadow of the big black wings that had come to dominate her life. She and Detective Richter had done everything professionally possible at the crime scene. The five pieces of Jasmine Rudella were now in the best of hands at the state crime lab morgue. The shoe print was being forwarded to the FBI's best shoe guy, Ira Tarnoff. The third in a series of depressing news conferences wasn't scheduled until nine o'clock the next morning. And, well, a girl had to eat.

"How would you like that done?"

The ruddy waitress from Ty's Steakhouse was smiling patiently enough, but her eyes were darting like a gazelle's at a hyena family reunion.

"Medium-well with a little horseradish on the side. Baked potato. Salad with the house."

The waitress turned to Brady Richter.

"I'll have the same," he said with a smile at Hewitt. Nothing smarmy about it. For all she could tell, real.

"Ditto for the dude," the waitress chimed as she took the menus and moved on.

"Is the devil playing hardball tonight?"

Brady Richter's question made no immediate sense, was not particularly welcome, and Hewitt knew her face was reflecting it.

"While we were waiting to order," Richter reloaded. "You looked
like you might've been doing a little internal negotiating."

Hewitt figured if he was going to go direct, she would, too. "I was
just trying to rationalize my being here. As opposed to sitting at a desk
and digesting my own organs for dinner."

He gave her a harmless smile. "Hey, we're just two public employees commiserating over a couple of steaks."

She knew he could tell she was having a little buyer's remorse over
the he/she thing. Especially the younger he and older she.

"Hey, you know what always works?" he said, a little too loud,
even for Ty's.

"A craniosacral massage?"

"Onion rings."

It caught Hewitt by surprise, pleasantly so. She knew her face was
showing him this, too.

"Onion rings are life's great equalizer," he said.

He was a puppy, but he was a smart puppy. No golden retriever
here.

"Okay, you've sold me," Hewitt told him.

They did the jumbo basket. And the little joke of it, the mind game
détente, had the desired effect—at least from where Hewitt sat. She loos-
ened up. And he stopped trying so hard to make a positive impression.

They split a carafe of red wine and washed it down with tenderloin.
They talked about the case. Initially she was going to explain the nature of her 3x5 question and lay out the whole singing connection. She
decided not to. But ultimately that didn't matter when, over dessert, he
forced the issue.

"That question for the sister. Whether the victim liked to sing
karaoke. What was that about?"

Hewitt finished a bite of banana crème pie. "Well, the whole world
will know at nine o'clock tomorrow morning. So I suppose telling you
isn't going to melt the polar ice caps."

Detective Richter took his fork and continued scraping the last of the frosting from the top of his piece of marble cake. It was something only a guy that young would do.

"There's a connection between the first two victims. And now this one."

"A karaoke connection."

"Yes. But also the fact they were singers with legitimate talent."

Richter set his fork down. "The only way he could know that, could put that together, is by going out and looking for the kind of thing he liked."

"That's my take exactly," Hewitt said. "That he's been conducting auditions at area clubs."

"Have you traced it down to specific clubs, checked security tapes?"

"The clubs we've looked at didn't have systems. But one of them had some home video of the events. Contests. That sort of thing."

"But what the hell would karaoke singing have to do with Poe stories?"

"Tell you what," Hewitt said. "You figure that out, and you can have my job."

"Will you throw in a company car?"

"You got it."

"Well, if you could find something in the writings of Poe where there was some kind of musical thing. Singing. I don't know. Maybe that's too linear."

"Too linear," Hewitt echoed. "The murders themselves, the stagings, those are fairly linear in terms of re-creations. But that's just the flower of his brain popping through. It's what's beneath the surface. All the mixed up stuff down there in the dark. That's the shit that made this asshole come to life."

Brady Richter didn't counter right away. He took a long sip of his coffee. "But as a man who's been affected, touched, messed up, by the siren's song—I'm talking me now—it seems that somewhere along the line there must've been a voice that set him off."

Now it was Hewitt's moment to reflect. She didn't know if it was her half-carafe of the wine that was talking, but her mind was actually batting around the notion of offering him a job under her at State. As soon as she thought it, though, she realized such a hiring would also come with the hidden clause that he would probably end up working on top of her at some point.

"You're good," she said. "The world needs more good detectives."

She raised what was left in her wine glass and held it until he joined in her half-assed toast.

"Here's to good detectives. And good guys."

THIRTY-ONE

Samantha Griggs is a curious name. Samantha Griggs is a name one would expect to find in colorful feminine script on the cellophane-wrapped box of a little girl's birthday present.

Samantha Griggs is a doll's name.

He has been watching Samantha Griggs for some time. He has both his eyes on her now. If only his adoring press could see him. How exquisitely it would feed their active little imaginations. How beautifully it would fill their news-gathering faces with some badly needed color.

Raven stalks next victim from tree perch.

Or something of its nature. His mission, of course, is not to amuse the humorless members of the press. His mission is not even to amuse himself—although life, in this current manifestation, is rife with observable humor if one only opens one's eyes.

His eyes are wide open now. This is his mission. For the next amusement-strewn hour of his life. To observe the movements, the reflections, the passions of Samantha Griggs.

Not Samantha Griggs, the doll. Samantha Griggs, the real live girl. On this evening, she is in her upstairs bedroom. And the best place, the only place from which to adequately observe her is the arthritic oak tree outside the bedroom window.

He hears the voice laughing in the tree and for a moment entertains the notion that the laughter is emanating from the tree itself. Does a tree have a mouth? Could a tree laugh without such an opening?

Samantha Griggs has a mouth. On this there is no equivocation. It is not some porcelain doll's mouth. Samantha Griggs has a very active mouth. An industrious mouth. Even now as he observes, the mouth is enterprisingly engaged in fellatio on the young man for whom she had prepared a fine supper earlier in the evening. After a dessert of what ap-

peared to be Black Forest Tort, Samantha Griggs and her guest had
moved to the living room for an after-meal brandy. The brandy, in twin
snifters, had remained downstairs, only partly consumed. The more immediately desired form of consumption was now being practiced on the
big bed upstairs.

Such a busy mouth. A mouth built for such animalistic activity, yet
equally well designed for the articulation of far more cerebral, if not ce-
lestial, expression. Left to her own devices, this was the kind of activity to which Samantha Griggs would dedicate her mouth. Clearly, she
was in need of an infusion of greater purpose.

Soon enough, she would receive it. Of course, he preferred to engage her alone, with an acceptable buffer of privacy around the encounter. Yet here she was, giving this young man every reason to make
a return appearance, perhaps even settle into a running engagement.

Again, the old oak groans with laughter. Inside the upstairs bedroom, Samantha Griggs looks up from her quarry to peer out the window, almost as if she has heard it. But there is nothing to be seen. And
the maker of the sound will not utter another for her until she is able
to feel the gust of his breath upon her skin.

THIRTY-TWO

Hewitt didn't sleep with Brady Richter that night. But she did take a man to bed with her. All 1,178 pages of him.

With a mug of Swiss Miss on the nightstand and her table lamp on high, Hewitt crawled beneath the blankets with the unabridged Poe, the massive volume of everything he had ever published—the poems, the essays, and, especially, the tales.

There'd been three murders. Three re-creations from three of the stories. She knew if there were plans for a fourth victim, the blueprint was already somewhere in the heavy pages in her hands.

It was an unnerving enterprise. So unnerving that not even this, her second serving of hot chocolate and marshmallows, could melt the cold feeling of dread against her neck, her shoulders, her face, and any other skin not covered by the down comforter.

So she thought of Brady Richter. She could have slept with him. It would have been one of the easiest things she'd ever done in her adult life. Brady Richter had apparently figured it would have been just as easy for him. Outside the restaurant, when she'd made it clear with her body language and her sign-off that they were going their separate ways, he had done his best to buck up like a good soldier. But his eyes had given him up. Eyes always gave a guy up. The only time you ran into trouble with a guy was when you let him get away with not looking you in the eyes.

She let down the comforter a little. Thinking about Brady had warmed her some. At best a mixed blessing. While neither had known it at the time, the sex fate of the evening had been determined by a line from the young detective with the Star Wars voice which, in the moment, had seemed nothing more than incidental to Hewitt. It was his premise that a song must have gotten inside the sick fuck's head and continued to bounce around the walls of his skull until the only way to quiet it was to act out.

She played Brady's words back in her head. *As a man who's been affected, touched, messed up, by the siren's song—I'm talking me now—it seems that somewhere along the line there must've been a voice that set him off.*

As they had proceeded through the end of dessert, the paying of the check, the exit through the smoky bar, Hewitt had rationalized the horny puppy away. Because she'd be damned if the next siren song that fucked up Brady Richter's mind was the one she would sing loud and strong with him all over her. For the next weeks, months, who knew?—years—she sure as hell didn't want to have to worry about tying him to the mast whenever his wooden ship wandered into her waters.

That was one way to rationalize it. Over another several sips of Swiss Miss, she put a little heat on herself and admitted the real reason she'd sent Brady Richter home with his tail between his legs. She was saving herself for Scott Gregory. Jesus, that was good. And it got even better when she finally had the balls to admit to herself the possibility that Scott Fitzgerald Gregory was the love of her freaking life.

It had been a long time. But if she hooked herself up to a polygraph, she would have been forced to admit that Scott was still her lifetime high score in the pinball game of love.

Christ, if Sarah Lee hadn't died, who knew? Right, and if Lincoln hadn't gone to the theater that night. If the asteroid that killed off the dinosaurs had been a few degrees toward the moon.

The mug of chocolate was back on the nightstand. The phone was in her hand. The number to Professor Gregory's cell phone—the one he told her he was mostly likely to pick up—had already been dialed. He answered on the second ring. By the time they had exchanged greetings, she detected the wide humming ambience coming from his end.

"Sounds like you're outside," she said. "Not that it's any of my business."

"But since you've so softly and sweetly made it your business, you might as well know that I'm on my patio at the table smoking a cigarette and looking at the North Star. Oh, and one more thing. I'm wearing a dark blue bathrobe."

"Aren't you a little cold?"

"Now that you mention it, maybe a little."

She visualized him sitting there. It was a picture of cool: understated and utterly confident in a way of being. It was a picture in which she couldn't imagine Brady Richter. Not tonight. Not next week. Maybe never.

"And you took your phone with you," Hewitt said.

"I saw the news. I figured it wouldn't be totally unreasonable to think that I'd hear from you. Although I had supposed if I was going hear from you, it would've been earlier."

It would have been. But Brady Richter's pheromones had created a detour.

"I was taking care of a puppy."

"I won't ask."

"Some new information has come to light," Hewitt said, clicking on the business switch. "And it leads me to think there might be some kind of musical element, some female-singing trigger with the person we're seeking. So here's the trillion dollar question. Is there anything in the Poe record of that nature that comes to mind?"

She could hear him smiling through the phone. "And how long do I have to come up with an answer for you?"

"As long as you need," Hewitt said. "Or immediately would be even better."

There was a weighty pause from him during which Hewitt took a hopeful swallow of Swiss Miss.

"Well, I have to tell you right off the bat there isn't some musical smoking gun that pops to mind," he told her, more resigned than disappointed.

Another heavy pause. Hewitt drummed her fingernails against the handle of the cup.

"There is one thing, of course," he offered, a little tentative. "I'm not sure you needed to call a Poe scholar for this. But you might want to have a look at his poem—arguably his second most famous—"The Bells." Or . . ."

Whatever the "Or" was that he'd dangled out there, she wanted it. "Or?"

"I could just recite it for you."

She was paging as quietly as possible through the table of contents of the Poe book.

"Well, I have to admit I'm pretty well in chrysalis form in my bed," she said. "And my book is downstairs. So if it wouldn't be too much of a pain . . ."

She had located the poem. The last title in the table of contents. Which meant, given the chronology, it was the last published piece Poe had written.

"Reciting Poe is always painful," she heard him say. "But it's a necessary and ultimately rewarding and edifying pain."

It would take Professor Gregory more than four minutes to recite Edgar Allan Poe's "The Bells." He would deliver the poem in the low passionate voice he always used when reciting, quoting, or discussing one of the great works. In the time it would take him to complete the poem, Hewitt would sketch in her notebook her image of Scott Gregory in his robe, reciting "The Bells" at his patio table in the dark, the North Star ablaze in the sky above. She would sketch him, but her focus would be affixed to the unfolding recitation and the dark, pathetic, brilliant beauty of the words that flowed from Scott's voice by way of Poe's mind:

> *Hear the whisper of the bells—*
> *Silver Bells!*
> *What a world of merriment their melody foretells!*
> *How they tinkle, tinkle, tinkle*
> *In the icy air of night!*
> *While the stars that oversprinkle*
> *All the heavens, seem to twinkle*
> *With a crystalline delight;*

Keeping time, time, time,
In a sort of Runic rhyme,
To the tintinnabulation that so musically wells
From the bells, bells, bells, bells,
Bells, bells, bells—
From the jingling and the tinkling of the bells.

Hear the mellow wedding bells—
Golden bells!
What a world of happiness their harmony foretells!
Through the balmy air of night
How they ring out their delight!—
From the molten golden notes
And all in tune,
What a liquid ditty floats
To the turtledove that listens while she gloats
On the moon!
Oh, from out the sounding cells
What a gush of euphony voluminously wells!
How it swells!
How it dwells
On the future!—how it tells
Of the rapture that impels
To the swinging and the ringing
Of the bells, bells, bells, bells,
Bells, bells, bells—
To the rhyming and the chiming of the bells!

Hear the loud alarum bells—
Brazen bells!
What a tale of terror, now, their turbulency tells!
In the startled ear of Night
How they scream out their affright!
Too much horrified to speak,

They can only shriek, shriek,
Out of tune,
In a clamorous appealing to the mercy of the fire—
In a mad expostulation with the deaf and frantic fire,
Leaping higher, higher, higher,
With a desperate desire
And a resolute endeavor
Now-now to sit, or never,
By the side of the pale-faced moon.
Oh, the bells, bells, bells!
What a tale their terror tells
Of despair!
How they clang and clash and roar!
What a horror they outpour
On the bosom of the palpitating air!
Yet the ear, it fully knows,
By the twanging
And the clanging,
How the danger ebbs and flows:
Yes, the ear distinctly tells,
In the jangling
And the wrangling,
How the danger sinks and swells,
By the sinking of the swelling in the anger of the bells—
Of the bells—
Of the bells, bells, bells, bells,
Bells, bells, bells—
In the clamor and the clangor of the bells.

Hear the tolling of the bells—
Iron bells!
What a world of solemn thought their monody compels!
In the silence of the night
How we shiver with affright

At the melancholy menace of the tone!
For every sound that floats
From the rust within their throats
Is a groan.
And the people—ah, the people
They that dwell up in the steeple
All alone,
And who tolling, tolling, tolling,
In that muffled monotone,
Feel a glory in so rolling
On the heart a human stone—
They are neither man nor woman—
They are neither brute nor human,
They are ghouls:—
And their king it is who tolls:
And he rolls, rolls, rolls,
Rolls
A Paean from the bells!
And his merry bosom swells
With the Paean of the bells!
And he dances and he yells;
Keeping time, time, time,
In a sort of Runic rhyme,
To the Paean of the bells—
Of the bells:
Keeping time, time, time,
In a sort of Runic rhyme,
To the throbbing of the bells—
Of the bells, bells, bells—
To the sobbing of the bells:
Keeping time, time, time,
As he knells, knells, knells,
In a happy Runic rhyme,
To the rolling of the bells—

Of the bells, bells, bells:
To the tolling of the bells—
Of the bells, bells, bells, bells,
Bells, bells, bells—
To the moaning and the groaning of the bells.

The recitation complete, he took several seconds and a couple of deep breaths. "Anyway, that's 'The Bells.' "

"That's a hell of a lot to remember," Hewitt said.

"At this point," he responded, "it would be a hell of a lot more to forget."

She waited for some sort of elaboration, but none came.

"So in other words," she offered, "the bells may not always be what they seem."

"Oh, the bells are what they are," he countered—not contentious, merely academic. "It's how the bells are heard, how the bells are interpreted. I suggest you dedicate a large flotilla of brain cells to thinking about that."

Hewitt wasn't sure if the last of this amused her or made its way under her skin.

"Is that an assignment?"

"That's up to you."

"Correct me if I'm wrong. But something tells me you already know what I'll find on the other side of all those brain cells."

In the silence that followed, she saw him grinning into the phone again.

"You're not going to charge me with obstructing an investigation are you?"

"No, but I might have to cite you for being a dick."

She knew the grin had widened now.

"Elizabeth, you're the brilliant criminologist. I'm just a tweed-wearing English teacher."

"So you won't tell me."

"There's no reason I should. My interpretation could be completely wrong. But yours . . . yours could be the one that sets the church bells ringing."

Minutes later they were done. By then he had convinced her that he wasn't trying to be difficult. He was just trying to avoid steering her in a potentially wrong direction. To his mind, "The Bells" was the quintessential look into the mind of Poe. And since the ghoul they sought was a psychological child of Poe, the insight she was after might well be resonating somewhere inside the brilliantly articulated tones of the poem.

Before she fell asleep, Hewitt reviewed the entire text of "The Bells." And it was with a distant, disturbing tolling in her ears that she finally gave herself to the sanctuary of sleep.

THIRTY-THREE

The bells awoke Hewitt at 3:27 A.M. according to her clock-radio. But it could have been any early morning in her childhood for all she knew. The sleep into which she'd fallen had been that timeless.

In the two additional rings she allowed before picking up, her brain fired off a short list of potential callers. First, Professor Gregory was calling to admit he actually was a dick and to tell her what she needed to know. Second, Luke Skywalker was reporting in from whatever lonely planet he had returned to after his evening of steak and wine and rejection. Third, Captain Spangler was calling with news of yet another sortie flown by the bird from hell.

The East Coast crackle of the phone voice informed her it was *None of the Above.*

"Agent Hewitt, Ira Tarnoff. In your e-mail you told me to call anytime night or day with anything conclusive."

"I absolutely did. And although I may not sound like it, I'm happy as hell to hear from you."

"Now it's not totally conclusive," Tarnoff barked. "But I can give you some pretty Goddamn intriguing parameters."

"I love intriguing parameters," Hewitt said, shaking off the torpor.

"First of all, it's an old boot. But not just your garden-variety old boot. This is an old friggin' boot."

"How old is old?"

In the short pause, while Ira Tarnoff cleared his middle-of-the-night throat, Hewitt anticipated the math.

"It's a special kind of gentleman's boot that became popular in America in the eighteen-thirties. It's called a Congress Gaiter or Boston Gaiter. In this case, we'll say Boston. Because the Flynn Brothers of Boston, Massachusetts had the marketing foresight of burning their company imprint into the heel of their boots. It was pretty well worn, but with enhancing we picked it off."

"Any idea where an enterprising psychopath could get his hands on something like that?" Hewitt asked, wide awake now.

She could virtually hear the wrinkles bunching on Ira Tarnoff's forehead. "Really not a hell of a lot of options. A museum. Some kind of theatrical wardrobe place. A private collection."

Hewitt shifted her hips, sat up a little higher in the bed, bumped the back of her head a little too hard on the headboard. "Do you have a visual reference for this style of boot?"

"Yes. And so do you. It should be in your in-box right now."

They wrapped up, Hewitt thanking him profusely, and Ira Tarnoff claiming just as profusely it was all in a day's—or a night's—work. Hewitt thought about getting all the way up and going downstairs to have a look at the thing on the computer—with, no doubt, a stop at the pantry and the microwave. But it was just short of four o'clock in the morning, and not even the earliest birds were stirring. She figured if the boot in question had waited more than a hundred and fifty years to walk into her life, it could wait another couple of hours.

THE REFERENCE PHOTO of a pair of Boston Gaiter ankle boots was disseminated to the media at the nine o'clock news conference. It was such an unusual find that it seemed like the kind of thing that might shake something loose. Whether a lead would come from a vintage footwear collector, some nutball with an old boot fetish, or from an heir to the Dr. Scholl estate remained to be seen.

The news conference wasn't being held just for the displaying of a pair of antique boots. Its main purpose was to put a name and a face and a life on the latest victim. And so between them, Hewitt and Spangler put the dismembered pieces of Jasmine Rudella back together and petitioned the moral outrage of the public for whatever help it could provide.

At the end, as the Q&A was winding down, Hewitt spotted Val Patterson entering the back of the media room in her long leather coat, with the same leather satchel on her shoulder that she had carried the karaoke club tapes in the previous day. It was pretty clear she was straggling in after a late night of scanning and logging the tapes at home. She made eye contact with Hewitt, gave her a nod and a tightening of her jaw and mouth that said she'd found something.

Fifteen minutes later they were in the screening room, Val Patterson cueing up the find.

"Now who knows if it's anything more than coincidence," she said. "But both of the first two victims were in the house when this tape was shot. Each one got up and did their thing. As to whether or not our creepy crawler was in the house that night, well that could stand the help of some fresh eyes. Mine started to bleed about three o'clock last night."

"You didn't notice any close-ups of a pair of really old boots on a mysterious male dancer did you?" Hewitt tossed out.

"No, but there's a couple of honeys that would look real nice across the table picking up the check on a lobster and champagne dinner," Val Patterson tossed back. She started the tape, took a quick sip of her official State of Illinois coffee. "They're out of order. I mean the second victim sang first that night. The first victim came later."

And there she was, in all her sweet, doomed, karaoke glory, Victim Two, Genevieve Bohannon. Trouble was the camera appeared to have been set on a tripod at an angle of no more than thirty degrees from the right of the stage. Too close and too tight an angle to yield much of the dance floor or the club's interior.

The song was Whitney Houston's "I Will Always Love You." And Genevieve Bohannon was using everything in her arsenal to do justice to the demanding peaks and valleys of the track. Hewitt could see that Genevieve had put away a few drinks to that point. But that only added to the endearing fearlessness with which she approached the song. As she sang on, there was something about her, the way she sang, the way she sounded that gave Hewitt the dizzying chill of déjà vu. A number of human bodies and faces passed in and out of the shot as she sang on, but none that gave her pause enough to ask Val Patterson to freeze it.

As Genevieve Bohannon belted out the closing lines, Hewitt noticed Val Patterson mouthing the lyrics, syllable by overblown syllable. The song ended, the audience applauded enthusiastically. Val Patterson hit FAST FORWARD.

"Okay, so that's Ms. Bohannon," she said. "The first victim . . ."

"Brandi Kaczmarek," Hewitt helped.

"Ms. Kaczmarek sang the same song. They all did. That was the deal. A contest where the audience voted for who sang it best."

With the tape winding forward and Val Patterson nuzzling her Land of Lincoln coffee mug, Hewitt slipped into her own thoughts, to the Poe poem that had now become a featured wall-hanging in the lobby of her mind.

Of the bells, bells, bells, bells, bells, bells, bells.
To the moaning and the groaning of the bells.

The VCR clicked to a hard stop. Val Patterson scrolled ahead on the tape until Brandi Kaczmarek, in a tight black skirt and gold top, did a self-conscious walk across the stage before taking her place at the microphone.

"Okay, let's see if you and I end up with the same takeaway here," Val Patterson said.

The ghost of Brandi Kaczmarek was already into the first verse of "I Will Always Love You." Hewitt flashed back to the home video she'd viewed in Vic Kaczmarek's living room. This was the same person singing. But the difference was this was more of the *woman* singing. Gone were those trace elements of daddy's little girl. And the stripping away of that vestigial vocal nuance brought the updated big-girl voice into perspective for Hewitt.

Although Val Patterson was once again mouthing the lyrics, this time her eyes were focused on Hewitt with game-show-host expectancy.

"Well, in addition to the fact that each of them wore clothes that were a little small for their bodies," Hewitt said, "there's only one other observation I can make."

Val Patterson had stopped her lip synching but hadn't entirely closed her mouth as she waited for Hewitt's answer.

"If you put a gun to my head, I don't think I could tell their voices apart."

THIRTY-FOUR

It was the right answer, of course. And Hewitt's prize was a fun-filled getaway to the inner recesses of her consciousness to figure out what the hell it could mean.

With a third victim mirroring the profile, Captain Spangler concurred it was time to put the karaoke/singing connection into the public's consciousness as well. His disclosure, in a prepared statement to the media, had definitely fallen under the *Hey, there's something else we think you should know* heading. In Hewitt's book, that was one step above the FYI category. Unlike Chief Brody closing the beaches of Amity, the Illinois State Police didn't have the power to shut down karaoke nights in greater Chicago. But they could sure as hell put a crimp in attendance. Whether or not that was a credible tactic or a misguided missive under the *Too Little, Too Late* heading would be borne out in the days to come. Hewitt knew it was quite possible The Raven had selected his talent well in advance of taking action.

Hewitt had no doubt that the latest victim, Jasmine Rudella, had possessed a vocal quality similar to that of the first two victims. But a corroboration would only help build the case and give her even more just cause for staring at the bedroom ceiling at night while the bells banged in her head.

She was sitting in her office, running down the hard-copy list of calls and Web hits Pete Megna had seined from the volume that had come in, contacts that had at least some potential beyond wishful thinking. And she was just about ready to set it aside when the phone rang.

"Agent Hewitt, my name is Victor Sweeney," the caller announced. "I'm curator of the Poe Museum in Baltimore."

The voice had such a theatrical lilt that it seemed too affected to be legitimate. Hewitt was sure someone was screwing with her.

"Mr. Sweeney," she said, "if this is a membership drive, I'm already a card-carrying member of the Ernest Hemingway Museum and Distillery."

It was then that she glanced at her caller ID screen, saw a number with an area code she didn't recognize.

"No, Agent Hewitt," the voice bit back. "I'm not looking for new members. What I'm looking for are my boots."

Hewitt got an instant adrenaline rush that, mixed with the cold froth of embarrassment, gave her a wave of nausea that wouldn't dissipate fully until several minutes after she'd hung up the phone.

"A colleague of mine contacted me," Victor Sweeney continued. "He'd seen your press conference. I called the number you gave out. And whoever answered, transferred me to you."

"Mr. Sweeney, I'm the special agent leading the investigation into the Poe-related homicides in the Chicago area. I assume you're referring to the boots we identified from the most recent crime scene."

"I'm looking at the reference you have on your website as we speak. The boots are the same style as a pair that have been missing from our museum for several months."

"And what boots or whose boots were they?"

There was a hesitation from Victor Sweeney, the kind of hesitation where the incredulity of the hesitating party fills the hole in the conversation like the bang of a gong.

"Well, Mr. Poe," he sniffed. "They were Mr. Poe's boots."

"Mr. Poe's boots."

"They were part of a diorama of Mr. Poe's personal effects. A desk. Some books. Other personal items, including some items of clothing."

"Are you saying the boots were stolen?"

"Well, unless Mr. Poe summoned the items to join him in Valhalla, yes, Agent Hewitt, they were stolen."

Hewitt let his sarcasm roll off. After her opening statement, she figured she had at least that coming. "Mr. Sweeney, was anything else noted as missing from the display or from other areas of the museum?"

"Yes," the curator said. "A cloak and a scarf."

Hewitt flashed the sketch of the headless, cloak-wearing man from her notebook. She would have to remind herself to add the scarf and the pair of boots.

"When the items went missing, did you report it to the Baltimore police?"

"Yes, but after a modicum of initial poking around, they quickly lost interest. The case remains open, but I'm not sure they're terribly keen on the idea of ever resolving it."

"If this is connected to our investigation," Hewitt said, "you may notice a sudden increase in their interest level."

This seemed to brighten and even warm the curator's tone. "You do understand why it's important for us to get these items back. I know this isn't exactly the theft of the Hope Diamond. But these are actual items that belonged to Mr. Poe. Needless to say, there's a certain price-lessness attached to such artifacts."

"I do understand," Hewitt said, which was only partially true. Of course they wanted the items back. In a perfect world—a perfect museum of a world—all items would always be accounted for, catalogued, and loved. And, hell yes, Mr. Poe's stolen items would be terribly missed in the world were such things were treasured. But in the bigger world, the bigger and far less orderly world, there were things that would be missed even more terribly. Like the sound of a basketball bouncing in Vic Kaczmarek's driveway. Or the special sound of a daughter's voice on birthdays.

Victor Sweeney was no slouch at telephone-pause interpretations. Into Hewitt's interlude he neatly inserted, "Now, obviously you have much bigger fish to fry. My only hope is that in the long run, if these items should reappear in the investigation of your case, it would be a wonderful outcome for everyone."

S'wonderful. S'marvelous. If you could return Poe's boots to me . . .

"Mr. Sweeney, it's possible your theft is *not* related to our situation. But if it turns out that it is, we'll keep an eye out for the items."

An eye out. She wondered if she'd left enough Meow Mix in the kitchen corner to get Shorty through what was shaping up to be a long day.

Hewitt proceeded to take Mr. Victor Sweeney through the investigative process. She inquired about security cameras. For budgetary reasons there were none. She asked about a visitor registry. This they had. Hewitt requested a list of all employees who had keys or access to the displays and any behind-the-scenes activity. As the questions continued, Hewitt doodled in her notebook and noodled with the notion of going to Baltimore herself. When the questioning and scribbling were over, Hewitt had left herself with a nice sketch of what she imagined the Poe museum façade to be, with a headless figure fleeing the premises in the missing boots, cloak, and scarf.

By then Hewitt had also decided that, given the curator's tendency toward theatricality himself, she would send Val Patterson to Baltimore. She informed Victor Sweeney of this and pledged to do everything she could to keep the curator and his little museum beneath the media radar until they had determined if there was a connection between the Baltimore and Chicago crimes. If there was, he would be on his own to deal with it, a possibility that didn't exactly alarm the curator.

"Truth be told, we could use the attention," he told her.

And then as they were signing off, he offered one final elucidation that would echo in Hewitt's head for the rest of the day. "Please understand that my interest in reacquiring the missing items isn't for me. It's for Mr. Poe."

THIRTY-FIVE

It had been a long day at work for Samantha Griggs, and a hot shower is the perfect therapy for that. She washes and conditions her hair first—to get that out of the way. The soaping and sponging come next. Quickly. Perfunctorily. Again, to get it done.

The rest of the time in the shower will be hers. To let the water work its magic. To paint the skin back to a respectable shade of pink. To give her muscles the feeling that they're eighteen again. To reach down to the bones and tap them awake.

This is her time. The water is her love slave. And she, its thankful master. It wasn't unusual for her to stand in the flow of love for twenty or thirty minutes. On this occasion she takes a good twenty-five. Not that she is counting. But the seashell clock on the bathroom counter informs her as she steps from the shower and takes the pink towel, now only a half-shade rosier than the skin of her thighs.

She towels off, again taking her sweet time. The seashell clock ticks off the seconds. They are, each of them, like a single drop of water, rolling off her skin, her life.

Reasonably dry, she leaves the bathroom, leaves the seashell clock to count the seconds in solitude. It is on the way to her bedroom vanity that she notices the flower lying midpoint on her pillow.

Quickly, she draws the picture in her head. Since Kevin had spent the night, and since she had needed to be at work earlier than he did, she had given him a spare key so he could lock the deadbolt as he let himself out. At some point Kevin had doubled back, white rose in hand, to thank her for a wonderful night. And to thank her most appropriately, he had placed the rose on the pillow. Which made it the sweetest gift he could have given her.

And she hadn't gotten him anything.

Given his imminent arrival, she doesn't have time to run out and reciprocate. But a reciprocal gift didn't really have to come from a store did it? Not if it came from the heart. He would have his reciprocation. He would have all he wanted. This, she is only too well reminded of when, after she has dressed, she pours herself a glass of wine and moves to the front room to await his arrival. It is when she opens the drawer of the bureau, to get a couple of coasters, that her eyes hold the photo she keeps there as both an ugly reminder and a lovely motivator.

It is a picture of the three of them snapped during his company picnic, already two summers removed. The three of them, in petty picnic conversation. Herself. Her husband Richard. And his twenty-one-year-old employee, fresh from her two-year associates degree, with whom he was already sleeping at the time the photo was snapped. She had, of course, noticed the attention the woman was showing her husband. But she had seen that sort of thing before. He owned a business, and there would always be women interested in a piece of that business. But this one, this twenty-one-year-old with her two-year degree—and Brittany yet, it had to be fucking Brittany—she had already positioned her mouth firmly around the one piece of business that mattered most.

Sitting on the sofa now, she takes a sip of wine, closes her eyes, continues to see the photo. The three of them smiling cheesily for the camera in front of a picnic table topped with chips and beer. She, the willing wife. He the successful businessman. And Brittany, the husband-stealing blonde cunt.

The wife is always the last to know.

As it turns out, hard to argue with. And as she sits now on the sofa, squeezing the stem of the wine glass, her eyes still closed, her thoughts turn to the bigger picture. It is a question she has asked herself again and again. At the moment the photo was snapped, how many other company picnickers had also known?

The doorbell rings. Samantha Griggs opens her eyes. The sounds, smells, and especially the sights of the picnic begin a slow fade. She relaxes her grip on the wineglass.

Her first eye contact with Kevin comes through the front-door window. And the look in his eyes surprises her. After leaving a rose on her pillow, she would have expected the look of a boy coming forward for his pat on the head. Or an extra piece of dessert. But his eyes, his face show no such anticipation.

She lets him in. The bottle of Veuve Cliquot in his hand and the tight T-shirt under his jacket catch her eyes. But still no glint of mischief in his.

"That was a nice touch upstairs," she says.

His head cocks slightly, oddly, at the words.

"The rose."

"Okay," he says, smiling at her as if it is something he has just remembered.

"I've never had someone leave a rose on my pillow before."

He smiles again. "Well, who deserves it more?"

She loves him for it, rushes in, pushes her abdomen, her pelvis hard against his. She feels her breasts spreading against the hardness of his chest. In seconds her hand is inside his pants. In minutes they are upstairs in the bed. She is fucking him. She is fucking all of them.

The wife is always the last to know.

Kevin is good. When she first saw him on the dance floor she knew he would be. He had strong arms and legs, active and flexible hips. He could grind with the best of them. He is grinding her now. On top. All the way into it. But as much as he is focused on rocking her world, he is sneaking little looks at the solitary white rose in the clear glass vase on the nightstand.

Kevin is good. Who cares where his eyes go? Everything else is exactly where it needs to be. He has a thing, a technique—he is doing it now—where he holds himself up by one arm and reaches back behind the bumping zone with his free hand and works her that way, too, while he continues to grind. Not many men can do that. Not many men would think of doing that.

The wife . . . is always the last to . . . know-oh-oh-oh-oh-ohhhh . . .

Kevin is great.

She closes her eyes, feels him shift positions slightly, the grinding never missing a beat. Something new from him now. His hand, his fingers, pinching her perineum, that G-spot in the no-man's land between her vagina and butthole. Pinching it hard. Too hard.

Her eyes are squeezed shut. She makes herself go with it.

Kevin is fantastic!

Grinding. One hand working her pussy. The other pinching like crazy just below.

Kevin is a god!

Her eyes pop wide. All the way wide. She sees Kevin is still using his arm to hold himself up.

But he can't. Because Kevin doesn't have three arms.

As the scream begins to form in her throat, she hears a loud, bony smack. The grinding stops.

THIRTY-SIX

Shorty had dinner late that night. And it wasn't exactly an elegant affair. Chicken pot pie from the freezer. The kind with a few pieces of broccoli thrown in to make human diners feel it wasn't a total caloric and nutritional wasteland.

Shorty liked the chicken part. Which was fine with Hewitt. She only ate a bit of the chicken anyway. The crust, what passed for vegetables, and the yellow-green creamy stuff—whatever the hell that was—she polished off herself.

"I know it's not Spago. But it's been thoroughly heated. If there's one thing I know, it's how to thoroughly heat a frozen entrée."

As had become the case over the time she'd had him, Shorty gave her his one-eyed attention while she spoke to him and, when she'd finished, gave a little nod of his head. As if he agreed with what she was saying. And for Hewitt, being agreed with at the end of the day—even if it was only by a Humane Society refugee—was something that had its value.

"You're the only one who's seen him. The only one who lived to tell," Hewitt said from her seat at the kitchen table. On the chair beside her, the black cat did the head nod again, and Hewitt dished it some more chicken.

"Did he whistle while he was walling her up? Did he sing? You heard it all, didn't you? You saw everything."

Shorty made short work of the chicken. His eye was focused on Hewitt again. And in the next span of minutes, while Hewitt stopped thinking out loud and kept her conjecturing inside, Shorty seemed to stay with her train of thought, nod by nod, blink by solitary blink.

If The Raven didn't hear the bells when the bells were ringing, she asked herself, what did he hear? If he didn't hear the singing while the voices sang, what was he listening for?

Of the bells, bells, bells, bells, bells, bells, bells.
To the moaning and the groaning of the bells.

As the black cat stared at her, Hewitt's mind spliced something entirely unanticipated into the track of the poem.

Janis Joplin. *The Essential Janis Joplin.*

The revelation came to Hewitt in four distinct images. The first was the Janis Joplin photo from the CD, her mouth wide open in agonized song. The next three images followed in rapid succession as the Joplin wail grew louder. The imaginary pictures took their places alongside the wailing singer, in identical poses. Brandi Kaczmarek. Genevieve Bohannon. Jasmine Rudella.

But the legato wailing of Janis Joplin that accompanied them all was no longer music. Because the singing wasn't singing. The singing was screaming.

THIRTY-SEVEN

Christiane Mons hears the screams. On this night it is the scream of her own inner conscience superceding the imagined sounds of the women who have already been taken and the women who were almost certain to follow. All her life she has kept the secret, and for so many of those years the secret actually seemed something she could keep. But the screams have begun to penetrate even the deepest rooms where the truth has been sequestered.

She sits in the dark, cross-legged on the quilted pads of the big bay window, facing outward to a front lawn bathed by a mixture of street-lamp and moonlight.

Hers is not a big house. Her life is a modest life. Were she some business leader or civic trustee or congresswoman, then the shroud with which she has covered that part of her life would make eminently more sense to the reader of her story. But she is none of these. And what she is, she is barely that.

She is a custodian of the human mind. In the official directory, she is listed as a librarian. But to her way of thinking, it is not the physical items, the books, which she tends. It is the minds that generated them.

It is one thing to have a secret. It is quite another to keep it. And now she held in her possession not just one, the old, but this new one as well. Inevitably the one would expose the other. It is time for this to happen. It is beyond time.

Christiane Mons knows that in time the pale empty lawn will be colored with visitors. They will come. There is no question they will come.

Rubbing the toughened bottoms of her bare feet, she reviews the catalogue of information she has assembled in her mind. For a moment, a tatter of clouds catches on the moon, taking away some of its illumination, allowing the lamplight a more prominent role in lighting the lawn.

By the time the clouds pull free of the moon once more, Christiane Mons is sure of her conclusion.

It has to be him. It is something her intuition knew immediately with the news of the first woman. *The Gold Bug.* Her intellect had played its brilliant game of second-guessing. But then another victim had come. *The Black Cat.* Which had stunned her into a nearly catatonic torpor. Only to be shaken out of it by the news of yet a third victim. *The Telltale Heart.*

It is difficult for her to imagine what the reporters will look like on her lawn. By day perhaps it will be easier. Soon enough she will be able to abandon imagining. In the morning she will call. She will sleep with the secret for one more night. Then she will call. And with that one pull of the thread, the entire shroud will unravel. The truth is that she is sick to death of wearing the shroud. It will be good to walk free of its weight, even if it means walking into the arms of a new nightmare.

She is kneading the bottoms of her feet again. No amount of pumice stone or moisturizing cream will ever bring back their softness. All those years of wearing hard shoes eight hours a day on the unforgiving tile floors.

She remembers rubbing her sister's feet in the hospital. With the rest of her body securely strapped to the bed, at least her feet could be liberated. They were always soft, her sister's feet. In her world, there were no hard shoes to be worn. She can feel her sister's feet now, in the form of her own. On this night, on the quilted pads of the bay window, this is her connection to her. These vestiges of skin at the bottom of the world.

THIRTY-EIGHT

Scott Gregory was not an early riser. But on this day he would have to be, at least temporarily. On the third ring, he picked up her call.

"Paradise Hotel," he managed groggily.

"It's screaming isn't it?" Hewitt said. "The music of the bells. The singing he hears. He isn't auditioning singers. He's auditioning screamers."

"Is that the official finding?"

She could hear he'd gotten out of bed and was making his way through the house, phone in one hand and she figured she knew what in the other.

"There's nothing official about anything yet," she said. "It's my interpretation."

"Sounds pretty reasonable to me," he said. Now she could hear he was in the bathroom, pissing like there was no tomorrow.

"Why the hell didn't you just tell me?"

"Because I wasn't sure," he said. "That was my interpretation, too. But I've been known to get a thing or two wrong in my life. God knows."

"There's still a problem," Hewitt said. "The screaming alone doesn't get me there. This guy's a serial psycho. Serial psychos always base their actions, at some level, on the taking of pleasure. Like a Poe character who derives pleasure from tormenting his victim. From, in some cases, making them scream."

"It wasn't just the characters who derived pleasure," the professor interjected. Hewitt could hear that he was moving through the house again. "I would contend the writer of the tales derived pleasure as well. For that matter, no one is immune from the taking of such pleasure. I'm afraid it's a basic instinct."

"You make it sound like food or sex."

"Because it is," he said matter-of-factly. He was in the kitchen now, clanking the carafe as he got some coffee going. "Maybe not as directly cerebral cortex as those two. But definitely in the same family."

Taking pleasure in the suffering of others, on the same human-desire menu as food and sex. And not only that, but the opinion so casually served up at 7:30 in the morning. It was an observation He-witt voiced to him and for which he had an immediate and well-shaped argument.

As he proceeded with the illustration of his point, Hewitt couldn't stop herself from imagining him at a chalkboard, but still in the just-out-of-bed attire—whether that consisted of an old bathrobe or, as she suspected, his preferred sleeping outfit, nothing. It wasn't the most flat-tering way for a scholar to be visualized. A man-toy, yes. But not a tenured professor.

"Think about it," she heard him say. "In human coitus, but cer-tainly in other sex acts, is there or is there not a certain degree of dis-comfort—if not pain—in the actions, gestures, sounds of . . . let's just call it *the receiving party*."

He was sounding way too much like a scholar and nothing like a man-toy. In her mental sketchbook, Hewitt quickly tied a tweed jacket around him.

"I believe Dr. John Cougar Mellencamp referred to it as 'The Hurts So Good Principle'," Hewitt said. "So what?"

She could hear the water from his coffeemaker bubbling, hissing. "So I will tell you that when a man tenders the hurts so good to a woman, those looks, those sounds, those signals turn him on."

Hewitt could hear the coffeemaker at full boil now.

"You're making a blanket statement that during sex, men get off on the idea that they're hurting women."

"The blanket is even bigger and fluffier than that," he said. "It ex-tends to the other side of the bed as well. Such that the painful-pleasure inflicting of Dr. Mellecamp's principle runs both ways."

"Women take pleasure in hurting men."

"Yes."

"All women."

"With the possible exception of a handful of saints and perfected beings. And even that I'm not totally sold on."

Hewitt didn't want to let him have the pleasure of hearing her get emotional, but damn it if that wasn't exactly what she heard in her voice. "So what the hell are you saying?"

Over the phone, she heard the sound of the carafe hitting a cup, knew he was catching a sneak pour.

"Only this. That the sounds, the moans, the shrieks can push a man to the edge of his pain-inflicting, animalistic nature. Now most of the time, it's like a temporary seizure, a controllable seizure that gets shut down the moment the act is over. But for some, the OFF button gets stuck. And that brutal craving—well, there may not be a way to shut it down."

Another sip of coffee.

"Anyway," he yawned, "that's my story, and I'm sticking to it. So what are you doing for dinner tonight?"

In the next few minutes, he came down from the dais, and she came down from her high horse. He had been about as bellicose as possible in making his point, but it was a point to be considered, and she knew it. For his part, the professor agreed to comb through his mental archives for any specific Poe parallels to the screaming pleasures of his theory. And she, without a whole lot if hesitation, agreed to meet him for dinner. At her place. Schedule permitting.

Within seconds of clicking off, the hardness of her chair registered against her nervous system. A moment after that, her hot chocolate registered cold against her lips.

At exactly 0:38 of her microwave beverage reheat, the telephone called her back to the kitchen table. It was Pete Megna reporting in with information about a predawn call to the tip line from a woman in Downer's Grove. A woman named Christiane Mons.

THIRTY-NINE

It only made a certain twisted sense that she would visit a library to pursue what had the promise of being the most significant lead in the case to that point.

The library meeting hadn't been her idea. It had been the librarian's. Over the phone, Christiane Mons had explained to Hewitt that it was a workday for her. And she was very nervous about all of it and thought the library would have a quieting effect. Hewitt had no choice but to agree. It was a library. The only thing quieter would have been a mausoleum.

The Downer's Grove Public Library had an orange-tan brick façade from the 1950s, recently sandblasted, and what had to be one of the largest American flags in the state of Illinois ruffling in the autumn breeze.

Inside, Hewitt found Christiane Mons at the front desk. Although she had given Hewitt a well-detailed description of where she would be and what she would look like, she could just as easily have told her, "Look for me at the front desk. I'll be the one who looks like a head librarian."

When Hewitt approached and introduced herself, Christiane Mons' periwinkle eyes seemed to freeze solid for a moment—as if, despite the fact that she had made the call to the authorities, she was still surprised that someone had actually showed up. With her eyes fixed, her jaw began to tremble.

Hewitt was an only child, and it was in interviews like this that she had to dig deep to get in touch with her latent big sister.

"Christiane, I know how hard it is, how frightening it can be to come forward like this. But I want you to know that you're doing the right thing. For that you have my respect and gratitude. And I'm here to help in any way I can."

This seemed to thaw the woman's eyes somewhat. But the jaw still had some work to do.

"I appreciate that," she said.

She looked across the sparsely populated landscape of the library, made eye contact with a younger female employee—a younger version of herself—and gave the woman a nod.

"There's a room," she told Hewitt. "A study room where I thought we could talk."

Hewitt followed Christiane Mons across the library, through the biography section, to a series of small personal study rooms, originally labeled A, B, C, and D on plastic placards. Someone with a bibliophilistic sense of humor had neatly added the names Alcott, Byron, Cicero, and Dostoyevsky on the placards, respectively. It didn't surprise Hewitt when they walked past the first three rooms and Christiane Mons inserted her institutional key into Dostoyevsky.

It was a tiny room. And when the lights were switched on, it was a tiny room with too much fluorescent light. It was the kind of light that highlighted every imperfection on a person's face. Hewitt could see the results of the lighting on the librarian's face. She knew Christiane Mons was seeing the same effect on hers. In that strange, unflattering way, it had the effect of breaking down any pretense between them, made them fully exposed equals, like strangers in a public shower.

There was a built-in desk and a single wooden chair and a sign that read: NO FOOD OR DRINK IN STUDY ROOMS.

"Please, have a seat," the librarian said uneasily, with an equally uneasy *have a seat* gesture.

"Thank you, I'm fine standing," Hewitt replied, implying with a look that Christiane Mons was the one who deserved the chair. When the librarian declined, the lines were drawn. They would stand facing one another in the unforgiving light, close enough for noncontact dancing, or guarding each other in basketball.

"I'm sorry I wasn't as forthcoming as I might have been on the phone." Christiane Mons offered. "I just felt I could only really explain this to someone in person."

"You were forthcoming enough to convince me you might have some valuable information. If it helps us find the person responsible for these homicides, I would've been happy to meet you in a bathysphere at the bottom of Lake Michigan."

It was only a modest exaggeration of the conditions they were actually in.

"I have it. I have the documentation," the librarian said. "The letters, the poems. They're here. In my car. You can have access to all of it. But first I want to tell you how, where, and when it all began. And especially why"—her voice cracked—"why I waited to come forward."

The big sister in Hewitt wanted to put an arm around this faltering wisp of a woman, to give her a few good pats between the shoulder blades. But the space of the room was too tight to maneuver to such an angle. And a straight-on hug would have been too much too soon, might in fact have been as *verboten* in that setting as the food and drink.

"Take your time," Hewitt reassured. "Sometimes a nice deep breath . . ."

The breath Christiane Mons took was anything but nice or deep. It was a sudden, violent intake followed immediately by a tearful outburst.

"I lost my sister last year."

And with that, her lungs pushed out a series of sobs that drenched Hewitt in their grief. With no place to hide, no room to even step back, Hewitt had no other option but to absorb it.

"She spent most of her life, her adult life, at Mount Prospect State Hospital," the librarian continued, struggling with each new phrase. "That's where she lived. If you could call it living."

"Mount Prospect is a psychiatric facility," Hewitt said.

"She was schizophrenic. It came on in her teens. But well before that—even as a child—it was clear things weren't the way they should be."

Hewitt maneuvered to reach the chair, pulled it out, turned it so Christiane Mons could sit. "Please . . ."

This time her gesture was accepted. Hewitt carved out the only other available space in the room and sat herself down on the floor. "Just take whatever time you need. I'm not going anywhere until you tell me to."

Between the chair and Hewitt's reassurance, the librarian seemed to gather herself. Hewitt's guess was that it had been a long time between cries for the woman. Once she got it under control again, it would probably be a long time before the next one.

Christiane Mons reached into the front pocket of her tea-green house dress and produced two wrapped pieces of butterscotch candy. She extended her hand. Hewitt reached out, took one of the pieces.

Once the candy was safely inside her mouth, Christiane Mons began. "Her name was Anna. Anna Magdalena Mons. I know—named after one of Bach's wives. That probably didn't help."

Her voice sounded a little steadier now, her jaw relaxing too under the influence of the butterscotch.

"The way I see it, it isn't quite food, and it's not a drink," she continued, dipping her face in the direction of the sign that warned against both.

"I won't tell if you won't," Hewitt said as she began to unwrap her own candy.

"His name is Gabriel Rafferty," the librarian offered, her eyes softening, glazing over with the relief of the confession. "He was a patient at Mount Prospect. On the same ward. Down the hall from Anna. Not long after Anna's death, I began to receive the letters."

"Letters from Gabriel Rafferty?"

"Yes. With each letter there would be a poem included. Written in the style—at least it was apparent to me—of Edgar Allan Poe. Sick things. Sick love poems to my sister. And eventually to me."

Hewitt felt the butterscotch beginning to coat the lining of her mouth. "If it's okay to ask," she said, "how did your sister die?"

Even in the harsh brightness of the Dostoyevsky study room, a darkness rippled across the librarian's face. "She tore some pieces of a hospital gown and made a rope. And she managed . . . She hung herself from a closet door."

"God, I'm so sorry," Hewitt said—what you always said, but meaning it, really meaning it this time.

"My sister went through hell on this earth," Christiane Mons said bitterly. "And once she was gone, I hoped the hell was gone, too. But it's not. It's worse. It's worse than hell."

FORTY

As far as Hewitt knew, she had never actually been all the way to hell.
She didn't know if Christiane Mons had ever been there, either. So she
had to take her word that what was going on now was, in fact, worse.
But after an initial perusal, the documentation supported her claim.

Before turning over the collected works of Gabriel Rafferty, Christiane Mons had elucidated her own private vision of earthly hell for
Hewitt. Her sister's mental illness had been one of those fiercely held
family secrets the rest of the world knows about but never speaks of in
anything but a whisper. Now, however, with this monstrous possibility,
the whispers would escape their containment and a full blown cacophony would ensue. As Christiane Mons had explained in her neat, polished, librarian diction, it would be awful enough when the rest of the
world attached her sister's story with the story of Gabriel Rafferty. But
what was even more punishing was that her own private thoughts of
her sister would always be draped in the shadow of a ghoul.

Throughout this disclosure, in the brazen light of the little room,
the librarian's composure had held—at least outwardly. This Hewitt attributed to the years of facial pinching and pursing that attended her
vocation. A less sternly muscular face would have broken under the
strain.

Hewitt took the accordion folder of writings quietly, appreciatively,
and did not read any of them in front of Christiane Mons. It wasn't
until she had returned to the parking lot, to the relative safety of the
Mazda, that she ventured the first look. It was a few chilling moments
later, when she was forced to look away from the pages, to stare into
an unspeakable void, that she found instead the face of Christiane
Mons peering out from a library window with a pitiable look that said,
simply: *See?*

Hewitt saw. And she knew, after spending those first minutes inside the monster's mind, that these words, these images, these visitations from Worse Than Hell, were things that would take up residence in the recesses of her own mind for as long as she lived. Still, there was nothing empirical in the accordion file that could prove the writer was The Raven. The psychological underpinnings were there. The three Fs were definitely there. Fantasy. Fetish. And the straw that stirred the drink, Fury. But that alone couldn't put a gavel down on Gabriel Rafferty or anyone else.

Before leaving with the folder, Hewitt had asked the librarian if she knew if Rafferty was still at the Mount Prospect facility.

"Of course not," had been the terse reply. "Obviously, he's out."

"If you believe that, why didn't you contact Mount Prospect?" Hewitt questioned. "Weren't you afraid that if he was out he might come looking for you?"

For this she had an answer just as terse.

"The last thing a poet is going to do is kill his only reader."

Solid. About as solid as it could be in a tiny room with a librarian freshly liberated from a lifetime secret. With the accordion file on the seat beside her, Hewitt was speeding north on the Tri-State for what she hoped would be an edifying encounter at the Mount Prospect state psychiatric hospital. With her music off, she was waiting for whomever was going to pick up the ringing phone at the mental health facility. As it turned out, a cheery-voiced older woman named Julia.

"Mount Prospect State Hospital. This is Julia. How may I direct your call?"

"Well, maybe you can help me figure that out," Hewitt said. "I'm looking for either the administrator or the physician who has overseen the treatment of a patient named Gabriel Rafferty."

Cheery-voiced Julia became momentarily mute. When she reclaimed her voice, it was at the expense of the cheeriness.

"Yes, I'll connect you with Dr. Willis," she intoned. "May I ask who's calling please?"

"Special Agent Hewitt with the state police," Hewitt intoned back.

Hewitt was put on hold long enough to wonder why. She took the delay to mean one of two things. Either formerly cheery-voiced Julia had lost her call. Or concerned citizen Julia was making a concerted effort to bring the proper party to the phone.

It was scenario two.

"This is Dr. Willis," a calm, reedy voice said into the phone.

Hewitt introduced herself.

"I know who you are," the psychiatrist said. "And I have a pretty good idea why you're calling. But if you're looking for Gabriel Rafferty, that would make two of us."

Twenty minutes later, Hewitt was inside Willis' office at Mount Prospect. Not huge, but a decent-size office. After the Dostoyevsky study room, anything would have been spacious. It was a good thing the office was roomy. Because Dr. Burton Willis had a certain bigness about him. He was from the large-boned end of the gene pool. To Hewitt, he looked more like a guy who should have been supervising a meat locker. The way mental health cases were processed and packaged, maybe it made sense.

One thing was certain. There was a large cut of Grade-A Bad Brain missing from the warehouse.

"Weren't you a little concerned that a patient had walked away from your facility?" Hewitt heard herself ask in an aggressive, accusatory tone. At that moment, she was glad Willis was holding a pen in his big fingers and not a meat cleaver.

"The first thing you need to understand, Agent Hewitt, is that this is a treatment facility," Willis lectured back. "This is not a lockup for the criminally insane. And if you're here today, as I assume, to tell me Gabriel Rafferty is, as you say, a person of interest in this Raven case, I have to tell you I think it's a reach."

Hewitt was in her book, sketching a side of beef hanging from a hook. Without looking up she said, "I have some evidence that suggests something to the contrary, Dr. Willis. Some writings from Mr. Rafferty that were sent over the last several months to the sister of another of your *missing patients,* Anna Magdalena Mons."

"That's a rather insensitive way of referring to Anna Mons," Willis said. "Anna Mons was a suicide victim."

Hewitt looked up from her beef sketch, smiled curtly. "I'm aware of that opinion. But I'm not ready to assume anything until I have a chance to take a good look at everything there is to see."

Willis set his pen down, rolled it on the desk blotter from one hand to the other. "Agent Hewitt, there's a dartboard on the wall behind you."

Hewitt turned, saw it.

"I keep it there," Willis continued, "as a daily, hourly, sometimes moment-to-moment reminder that, despite our best intentions, psychiatry is still not an exact science. Anymore than what you do is. So if you want to come here and throw a dart at this institution in the hope that you'll hit something, I can't stop you. All I ask is that you try not to put it in my ass."

Hewitt smiled, the way a she-wolf smiles at an unexpected guest in her nursery.

"The best way for you to avoid that," she said, "is for you to remain seated right where you are and start telling me the Gabriel Rafferty story."

Willis smiled back, a smile of pure conciliatory politics—the kind that would serve you well if you were a player at a state-funded psychiatric facility. "Please understand, Ms. Hewitt, I'll be happy to help. Just don't expect the smile to stay on my face indefinitely."

FORTY-ONE

The way the two o'clock sun breaks through the window of the hovel, through its perimeter of raised glass, creates a wash of prismatic color on the writing desk that spills onto the next blank page of the journal. It is time to write. But he cannot write. Not with this spillage of light upon his desk. Not with the resultant spillage of memory that inundates his mind.

The Raven sees his mother's hair. For a moment he sees her hair in its performance shade of blonde. And then he sees it in the familiar shifting shades of light. A cheap rainbow sent by the gods of the profession. Lighting her hair. Imbuing her hair. Coloring her hair. Changing her hair. Possessing her hair. Hurting her hair.

With his eyes closed, he does not like what he sees. He does not like to see her this way. He does not like to see his mother change colors.

He does not like to see what it does to her hair. Her face. Her mouth. Her voice.

When it changes like this, she is not his mother. She is the mother of them all. She does not sing to him. She sings to them. And they do not, cannot possibly love her voice the way he does. The way he always has. The way he always will.

He sees the changing colors on the faces of the men who watch his mother. He hears their voices. Their laughter. Their calls. He sees with perfect clarity the way the men attach themselves to the changing colors of his mother's hair.

He opens his eyes once more to the desktop, to the journal. Outside, the sun has shifted, enough that the pattern of light on the blank page has faded to all but the shallowest tones of the spectrum. He watches as the color proceeds to pale completely. It is the same disheartening moment as the final dissolution of a rainbow. That moment when the promise of a more interesting world, a more beautiful world, a better world is rescinded. And all that remains is the cold howling blue of the perfect sky.

The Raven picks up the pen and begins to write about the lost rainbows.

FORTY-TWO

Dr. Burton Willis told her about Gabriel Rafferty. He started with the clinical aspects, but Hewitt quickly steered him into the personal. What did Willis *know* about Gabriel Philip Rafferty? The takeaway from all of that didn't surprise Hewitt. Getting to know Gabriel Rafferty was kind of like being in the cell next to Charles Manson, hearing him rant and rave and whisper sweet nothings in the middle of the night.

How much would a mind like that ever let you get to know it? To get to know a human being, there had to be a human being there.

Yet there was a history. The tenets of an abusive childhood—again separating fact from fiction was something upon which Willis could only speculate. But there were a few hard pieces of information. His father had died during his adolescence, the mother in his early adulthood. His mental illness had been recognized in late high school. With the help of medication he had been able to enroll at Illinois State University for a semester and a half. It was in the half of his only college year that his mother passed away. And that event had apparently led to a precipitous downward spiral for the son she left behind. In his brief college experience, Gabriel Rafferty had apparently demonstrated an affinity for the English language, its study, its history, its creative use. That helped Hewitt a little. But troublesome was the fact that there was nothing in Rafferty's intellectual history to suggest he had ever dipped his wings toward Edgar Allan Poe anymore than he would have focused on Hawthorne, Whitman, or Longfellow.

Student Rafferty left Illinois State and lived off the small inheritance he received as the only child of his deceased mother. He had no known relatives in the area. And no one had ever come forward to claim him from the mental-health slag heap which he proceeded to orbit as a diagnosed paranoid schizophrenic, in and out of treatment, on and off medication. Of course, it was always the off times that would send him crawling and muttering back to the heap. Until such time that the bees in his brain got too far out of control, stinging more aggressively, more frequently, with increasing amounts of venom.

In the course of their conversation, Willis would eventually share his insights on the apparent absence of Poe-related antecedents in Rafferty's past. But not before Hewitt would share with the psychiatrist what now appeared to be the manifesto Gabriel Philip Rafferty had penned prior to beginning his assault on the sane world.

As they would with anyone who would see them for the first time, the works of Gabriel Rafferty, as collected by Christiane Mons, had the power to fully unnerve Dr. Burton Willis. Which was saying something for a shrink who had spent his share of time swimming with patients in the deep end of insanity. His visceral reaction to the writings led to his rational decision to take Hewitt's interest in Gabriel Rafferty more seriously. About one hundred percent more seriously.

At Hewitt's request, and with the help of an administrative assistant, he was able to locate a sample of Rafferty's handwriting. The writing sample ended up being an extensive note Rafferty had written on the inside of a Christmas card he had given to one of the psychiatric nurses involved in his care. The unscientific handwriting analysis that followed—basically Hewitt eyeballing the samples side by side—drew the conclusion that if the two examples of sweeping grandiloquent script weren't a match, a handwriting expert would have to make a pretty Goddamn compelling case against it.

In the wake of Gabriel's Rafferty's sudden flight to freedom, the Mount Prospect psychiatric hospital had also been left with two office storage boxes of the patient's personal effects. Under Willis' direction, these were brought to his office. As Hewitt looked on, the psychiatrist removed the covers of each box and beckoned her to come forward for as much sniffing as she cared to do.

Hewitt pushed in for a look, half-expecting to see a large decomposed crow interred in each box. Her first reaction was one of disappointment. The items in the box appeared far too ordinary for someone who had wreaked such hateful havoc on the world. There were no doubt plenty of viable prints on the items. But with The Raven's immaculate approach to his crimes, it was of little consequence. Hewitt snapped on a pair of latex gloves for her rummaging.

"It's entirely possible he took other things with him," Willis advised. "This is the stuff that was left behind."

Hewitt's gut told her there wouldn't be much there. If Gabriel Rafferty was The Raven, a brain as calculating as his wouldn't have left behind anything incriminating for the likes of her to find, unless it was intentional.

Her rummaging confirmed her gut feeling.

"I'll take these with me," Hewitt said. "But I don't expect a calling card. The thing I find surprising is that in the course of your treating Gabriel Rafferty, there were no particular antecedents to suggest an affinity for Poe. It's as if these writings, this Poe fling, just came in out of left field."

"From my experience that wouldn't be terribly unusual," Willis said. "I once had a patient who took twelve years to reveal to me that the reason he decapitated the family poodle was because he thought it was the reincarnation of Marie Antoinette. He wasn't exactly your everyday schizophrenic. But neither is Gabriel Rafferty. If there is an obsession, it wouldn't necessarily have to be a lifelong interest. It could've been something that simply tripped his trigger one day."

"Like one day he got out on a day pass and went to Blockbuster, rented a hotel room, and spent the next week eating malted milk balls and watching Vincent Price in *The Pit and the Pendulum*?"

"Right now I can't prove he didn't," Willis said. "Hell, it might've been something even more ridiculous. Here's the thing, Agent Hewitt— the bottom line, if that's what you're looking for. We all have secrets. We all invest a great deal of time and energy into keeping those secrets. Especially the bad ones."

He paused then, let the comment breathe, as if he'd just opened a special bottle of wine for the occasion of secret-keeping. A new side of Dr. Willis. When he looked at Hewitt over the dispersing vapors, it was with an expectancy that fell just short of solicitation. She knew what it meant, or what it was intended to mean. *We all have a secret or two, don't we, Special Agent?*

With that on the table, Hewitt also knew she didn't want to know any of *his* secrets. And she certainly wasn't going to share any of hers. In other words, the big shrink would be sipping his secret wine alone.

Sensing the ice crystals forming in the air, Willis opened the thick patient file and produced a Polaroid that he handed to Hewitt. "I believe you might be interested in this."

Hewitt took the photo, took in the visage of Gabriel Rafferty. A pleasant, line-less face, with eyes that focused either too hard or too soft, depending on how you looked at them. And then there was the characteristic that jumped out at Hewitt and pressed its forehead hard against hers. In the Poe anthology there was a picture of the great author, the classic photograph of Poe—the dyspeptic mouth, the sunken eyes, the high collar and loosely tied cravat—and the feature Hewitt was seeing right before her own intermittently focusing eyes, the signature hairline. She was seeing that hairline in the Rafferty photo now. They were damn near identical, raised to reveal the high façade of forehead, as if to announce there was one very large and extremely active brain inside the casing.

"Do you have anything on tape of this guy?" she asked. "Video? Audio? What I'm looking for is anything with his voice on it."

"Well, we don't exactly make a practice of recording our patients in their natural habitat," Willis responded.

"If there was something, you'd tell me, right?" Hewitt said, squeezing his eyes with hers.

"There's no one I'd rather tell," Willis said.

It was time to get the hell out of the psychiatrist's cage. Before leaving, however, Hewitt did procure the name of the local Mount Prospect detective who had been looking into Rafferty's whereabouts—to the extent that such a case would remain much of a priority beyond the first couple of weeks. She was in her car, on the phone with Detective John Huberty when headquarters cut into her call with news that The Raven had made yet another creative statement. And this time it sounded like his magnum opus.

FORTY-THREE

At the time of the first call, Hewitt was less than five minutes from the Palatine residence where the latest atrocity had been discovered. So in addition to the two local uniforms and a plainclothes who had responded, Hewitt was the first detective on the scene. It was a hell of a scene to walk into, both in its shocking twists and its even more shocking barbarism.

First, the victim was male. Second, he was found naked outside. And third, his throat had been slashed more deeply, brutally, soullessly than anything Hewitt had ever seen, heard of, or imagined possible. As she observed the victim splayed face-up on the backyard patio, one of the local guys was speculating on the type of blade and the force it would have required to inflict such damage. What wasn't debatable was that the decapitation could have been finished off with a butter knife.

Against the smooth cement surface, the blood had pooled into a shape that seemed familiar to Hewitt in a vague geographic sense. Was it Antarctica? It was at the bottom of the bottommost continent that a fourth element of note was there for all the world to see.

In the victim's blood, the words "For Edgar."

Had it not been for this chilling sign-off, given the anomalous nature of the rest of the crime scene, Hewitt might have struggled to connect this slaying with the others. America's third-largest city was certainly capable of producing more than one active homicidal maniac at any given time. According to the Bad Brains Charter, the page for rules governing its members was as blank as the eyes of the victim on the patio.

"Any ID on this guy?" Hewitt asked.

"His name is Kevin Kell," the plainclothes said. "Wallet was with his clothes upstairs."

Again, a plink of dissonance in the MO for Hewitt. "Who's the homeowner?"

The plainclothes checked his notes. "John and Samantha Griggs."

"Any sign of them?"

"The woman's the one who lives here. The master bedroom upstairs is a total shambles. The rest of the house is intact. We've been through the premises. Closets. Basement. Garage. Something else you'll want to know. The husband and wife are legally separated."

"How'd you get that so fast?"

"Fresh papers on a desk downstairs."

At least that part of it fit. The divorced, separated, or otherwise estranged wife. Yet that dynamic laid additional credence at the feet of the other possibility. That this wasn't the work of The Raven. That some enraged, opportunistic bastard had seized upon the situation, killing the boyfriend and trying to pass it off as the work of a serial killer. If that was the case, then the news chopper that was just rising over the eastern horizon—and the others to follow—were about to crash the party under false pretense. A big, juicy, hideous story, yes. But not the one they craved.

That evaluation took a hit, however, when Hewitt went into the house. It wasn't anything she saw right away as much as what she felt. Death was never invisible. Death always left a shadow. Sometimes the shadow was obvious as hell, especially if some time had passed and the sense of smell got involved. This time it wasn't smell for Hewitt. It was taste. Something in the environment on that first floor. An acrid, almost burnt sense of something that hit Hewitt's tongue within moments of entering the house. And the sense of it, the taste, only grew stronger when she entered the living room.

She scanned the room for whatever might be the source of such a taste. She didn't have to scan long. It was right there. Surrounded in fieldstone, with a dark gaping mouth.

The fireplace.

And then it hit her. She could practically hear the smack of it.

"The Rue Morgue," she heard a voice say—hers, and yet not

wholly hers. Her voice with a hand of revulsion tightening around her throat.

On one of her late-night encounters with the Poe book, she had gone through a number of the tales, looking for references to torture, mayhem, execution. They hadn't been hard to find. The words had a way of jumping out at you, as if they had already been highlighted in a sickly shade of red.

"The Murders In The Rue Morgue" had not been cheated of such highlights by its author. And now, standing there in the living room of the Palatine saltbox, Hewitt replayed the highlights of the section of the story that had caught her attention. In 1840s Paris, according to the tale, a series of bizarre, ghastly murders had been committed with an element of the nearly superhuman in their degree of violence. Hewitt knew that now, more than a century and a half removed from that fictional nightmare, she was standing in the midst of its reproduction.

As the story dictated, the one body had already been found outside, with the victim's throat slashed to within inches of severance. The second body would be found inside. By now Hewitt had made her way across the living room and was standing at the cold face of the fireplace. Like some wandering pilgrim at a long abandoned altar. She recalled the headline from the Parisian newspaper in the story, the way it communicated the essence of the fictional crime in two words.

Extraordinary Murders.

With one murder already in the book, Hewitt would have bet her entire jazz collection that the results of the second were right there in front of her.

One of the uniforms was back in the house, and Hewitt asked to borrow his flashlight. The other investigative tool she needed she found in a downstairs bathroom—a hand mirror.

Returning to the living room, and with the uniforms and the plain-clothes observing, Hewitt moved the screen and knelt down at the fireplace opening. She turned on the flashlight and extended her right arm into the hearth to shine the beam upward. Tottering on her knees and in a compromised position she knew was at some unspoken level entertaining to the Palatine cops, Hewitt slowly pushed the hand mirror into position to reflect back whatever the illumination and "The Rue Morgue" had to offer.

For a moment, she struggled to hold the flashlight still enough and straight enough to force the light upward. Instead, she saw in the mirror's reflection the shiny buildup of carbon on the lower parts of the flue. Cold, black, demoralizing. The reverberations from Hewitt's nervous system didn't help the steadying of the flashlight.

"Fuck it, fuck it, fuck it," she said under her breath, but loud enough in the big empty room to be heard by her colleagues. Yet the profane mantra helped. The flashlight steadied. And the upturned mirror followed the rising plume of light.

Incredibly, disarmingly, the first thing the light encountered was a little ball hanging from a string. Like a Ping-Pong ball on a fleshy tether. But Ping-Pong balls didn't exude moisture from within. Ping-Pong balls didn't have retinas.

FORTY-FOUR

The rest of Hewitt's day was swimming laps underwater. Exertion. Tension. Burning lungs. Exploding heart. Wanting to quit. Rallying the mind.

And that was just the action beneath the surface. While you were down there gutting it out, there was still the rumbling muted pressure of the world above water, the expectations, the anxieties, the harsh reality of results.

The feeling had started with the shockingly harsh reality of Samantha Griggs stuffed upside-down in the chimney, her eyeballs pulled from their sockets. At that, it was debatable if those were the worst injuries to her face. The victim was not just brutally beaten. She was annihilated. Then jammed up the Goddamn chimney. Feet first. Already dead—the hope. Or still somewhat alive—the worst case.

For that, they had forensics. For all of it, they had forensics. And yet at the end of the day, all it would tell them was that they were dealing with an unprecedented monster.

So that was the afternoon. Hewitt's evening began with a briefing in Spangler's office, with the usual attendees. To Hewitt, Captain Spangler and Minerva Vann had become like teammates above the surface as she continued her underwater marathon. She knew they were there for her. She knew they wanted her to win. But she was struggling to understand anything they were calling to her.

From the briefing to the news conference, it didn't get any better. Again, all the usual attendees. Faces she was used to seeing from her couch at night, while curled up in the corner, waiting for the latest cup of her beloved blend to cool enough so it wouldn't burn her tongue. Here, too, she heard the compressed, distorted voices, even responded to their questions. But all of it seemed to have been swallowed alive.

She had already assigned Pete Megna to interview the estranged husband of Samantha Griggs once he returned that evening from a business trip to St. Louis. But Hewitt knew full well that no matter how estranged he was from his wife, it wouldn't have been enough to pull out her eyes and stuff up her up the chimney.

It was a little before 8:30 when Hewitt finally got around to the ride home. For much of the trip, she tried to listen to Coltrane soloing on the tenor sax. But the Samantha Griggs eyeball thing was playing its own solo on a much higher pitched instrument in her head. Why the eyes? There was nothing in "The Rue Morgue" about the eyes. If you were going to do the extra work, wouldn't it have made more sense to act out a particular from the story? If, in fact, this was being done *For Edgar*.

Shit, there she was again. Trying to make sense of a brain that had absolutely no interest in making sense for anyone other than itself. Sure, maybe at some level he had convinced himself he was paying some kind of overdue tribute to Poe. But the bottom freaking line was that he was doing this *For Gabriel*. And he was doing it because . . . A white bullet flashed in her brain, and in the echo of its report she heard Scott Gregory's voice.

Because it makes him happy.

Pulling out her eyes had made Gabriel Rafferty happy. But why the eyes? What exactly had they seen? The eyes . . .

Eyes. Shorty had been alone in her house all day. Having a pet, with the kind of hours she kept. What the hell was she thinking? Another of her history of relationships that was doomed from the start.

Hewitt parked the Mazda in the condo surface lot and rewarded herself for all that underwater swimming with an extra minute of Coltrane/Hartman, the end of "My One And Only Love." With that melody floating just beneath her thoughts, she made her way across the lawn and past the big maple to the stepping stones that led to her front door.

It was within the first few steps on the stones that she looked up to see a man sitting on the top step of the entrance. Her dinner date. Professor Scott Fitzgerald Jesus Christ Gregory.

"Oh, shit," she heard herself mutter in a voice of pure exasperation.

"And a good evening to you, too," he muttered back.

"How long have you been waiting here?"

"Not long," he said. "A few minutes. Or was it hours?"

Nearing the end of the walk, she paused, the length of a chalk outline body between them. Close to him now, she could feel herself losing it a little. "What time did we say—seven? Oh, shit. Sorry. I . . ."

"Somehow in the midst of your very pedestrian day, you forgot about your critical dinner date with me."

He overstated it like such an unmitigated shit that Hewitt couldn't stop the laugh that pushed up from her chest.

"No, that's fine," he continued. "Fuck the academics. They don't contribute anything to the Gross Domestic Product. So the hell with them. Fuck the academics. Fuck me."

He lowered his head, put his hands on his knees, and sat there on the porch step, a picture of defeat. Hewitt was laughing. Within a few seconds, she could see from his shoulders that he was, too.

"So what are we having?" he said as he reached behind his back and produced a bottle of wine. "Besides this."

"I'm surprised it survived the wait," Hewitt said.

"You're surprised? I think the wine is in shock."

"A pinot grigio. Good. It'll be a perfect complement to the Chicken and Stars."

Scott Gregory stood up, quiet, effortless. He spread his arms and just kind of opened his body as if to say that whatever it was she needed, she had come to the right place. And that was pretty wild. Because in all the times she'd come home to her condo after all the shitty days, no one had ever welcomed her home like that.

She climbed the two steps to join him on the porch, and when he reached out his hand to assist her, she took it and then she took the rest of the offer and let herself flow into his arms, her eyes closed, but her face finally above water.

FORTY-FIVE

He is alone in the dark. He has always been alone in the dark. He knows he will be alone in the dark forever. It is a fate he has chosen for himself. This he has come to accept, to believe.

There is no escape now. There are no escapes in the offing. Yet he knows deep in the deepest well of his heart that the words will continue to be his way of finding escape, his way of squeezing some life from the corpulent body of the darkness.

Staring across the black void of this space, this room, he sees the first words of the poem burst into flames, then settle into glowing letters etched in the velvet plasma of the darkness that is now his mind, his world, his immortal concubine.

The shimmering, finger-painted letters now legible against the black page.

From childhood's hour I have not been
As others were

His lips unseal. His lungs expand. With his tongue licking the escaping air, he blows breath across the room, extinguishing the words. The next words burst into flame instantly.

I have not seen as others saw

By now he recognizes the sound of the two voices reciting the words as they appear to his eyes, paced, articulated through the movement of his vigorous exhalations.

I could not bring
My passions from a common spring

For some time, the voices have blended together in a kind of dual command of his throat and tongue. But it is the other voice, the one not originally his own, that has become the louder.

From the same source I have not taken
My sorrow I could not awaken
My heart to joy at the same tone
And all I loved I loved alone

The words burning hotter now, line by line, at the far end of the darkness. Burning hotter, whiter. Requiring greater amounts of breath each time to drive them back to the other side of the darkness.

And with the increased demands on his lungs, the voices having to labor more intensely in order to give the words their articulation.

Then in my childhood, in the dawn
Of a most stormy life was drawn
From every depth of good and ill
The mystery which binds me still

Little gasps now beginning to be heard in the spaces between the phrases. The words continuing to be recited with the advancing presence of the other voice. The voice not originally his. Inversely, the sound of the breath struggling, the intermittent gasps coming in his own oppressed voice.

From the torrent or the fountain
From the red cliff or the mountain
From the sun that round me rolled
In its autumn tint of gold

The scripted flames burning an indolent blue, as if fueled by the breath of the devil himself. Almost impossible to blow them out now. His breath losing its sense of rhythm. Struggling, gasping, heaving. Desperate to keep up, to contain, to manage the searing light of the words, to tend this darkness, this mind, this world, this immortal concubine.

The new voice fighting madly for primacy now. On the cusp of victory. Even against the raging storm of the gasping, the shrieking, the hell-born howling. And still the words keep coming, they keep coming.

From the lighting in the sky
As it passed me flying by
From the thunder and the storm
And the cloud that took the form
When the rest of heaven was blue
Of a demon in my view

The poem is long finished, the burning plasma-configuration of the words is long gone, the darkness is once again all-consuming as the long sustained cries of the vanquished voice continue to fall upon God's deaf ears.

FORTY-SIX

Before she could even consider what to do with Scott Gregory, she had to feed Shorty. The pressure to take care of him reared its little one-eyed head midway through the porch hug. When the hug had seemed to turn the corner past support and into something even more needful, the feed-the-cat reminder had been a convenient out.

The funny thing was that she wasn't convinced she wanted an out. Scott, to his credit, had demonstrated his typical adroitness in sensing, if not anticipating, her need to exit the hug. To an outside observer, it would have been impossible to tell whose idea it was to end the embrace first.

Once inside, with Shorty slinking in from the living room to the edge of the foyer, Scott immediately understood the end-of-hug dynamic. And it was all cool, and it was all nonverbal, and, once again, typical Scott. Not being a cat person, Hewitt wasn't surprised when Shorty took a look at the dinner guest and did his slinky thing back into the shadows of the kitchen. Nor, once he was set up with his own dinner in the kitchen, did the cat deign to make any additional appearances in the time she and Scott were together in the condo.

Which was fine with Hewitt. With the investigation squeezing her like an anaconda, in the little window she was going to grant herself to grab a hint of sanity, she was definitely more interested in petting Scott than Shorty. If she was feeling it, she knew Scott was feeling it, too. Feeling her need. Whether or not that would fit into his current curriculum was another matter.

She returned from the kitchen with her own slinky thing going on and two glasses of red wine in her hands. She handed the fuller one to Scott, who had begun to stand up from the sofa but who had abandoned the formality when Hewitt waved him off.

"A little stingy with yours, no?" Scott said upon taking his glass.

"Technically, I'm still on duty," Hewitt responded as she sat down on the chair across from him.

"Any projection on the next time you'll actually be off duty?"

"Why—do you want to get me drunk?"

"I think you're the one who wants to get you drunk."

"The only way I'd get drunk right now would be if The Raven was getting drunk with me."

"What makes you think you could outdrink him?" Scott said with a smile, a nice smile, as if he knew this was exactly the talk therapy she needed after the day she'd had.

"I'd be willing to take my chances," Hewitt answered. "Just to be able to look into his eyes. To see what kind of horror movie was playing there. And if he started acting up, I'd kick his nuts up into his brain to see if that improved his fucking attitude."

Scott Gregory smiled, a smile of genuine amusement. He raised his glass.

"To Elizabeth Hewitt," he said. "The woman who can use the word *fucking* more eloquently than any woman on earth."

Hewitt found herself raising her glass with him.

"Right now I'll take that," she said as their glasses touched.

They sipped their wine. With the alcohol in play, it got quiet. Quiet enough that they could hear Shorty knocking his bowl around as he ate in the kitchen.

"I assume you heard most of what went on today," she said.

"At this point, a person would have to work really hard to not hear about it."

"It was . . . It was pretty Goddamn . . ." She paused, searching.

"Don't bother," he said. "There aren't any words."

She took another sip of her wine, wished she had been more generous with her pour.

"The Rue Morgue, the Poe version, was hard enough to believe," she said. "That the perpetrator of the atrocities ended up being an escaped orangutan. But then all these years later, to have a copycat crime carried out by, I can only presume a human being. I don't know if even Poe would have hallucinated that one."

She watched him take a nice, easy sip of his wine.

"Would you like to switch glasses?" he asked.

"Why—is that what my face says to you?"

"Your face says a lot of things to me."

"Then I better tell it to shut the hell up before it tells you everything."

He took another draw on the drink, smacked his lips, smiled his all-accepting smile. More silence followed. More cat-and-bowl echoes from the kitchen.

"There's something you should be aware of—maybe you already are," he offered as he set his glass on the table with his usual economy of movement. "There's a sequel. Poe wrote a sequel to 'The Murders In The Rue Morgue.' It's not a sequel in terms of story. It's a reprise of the detective character, Dupin, in the same Parisian setting."

" 'The Mystery of Marie Roget'," Hewitt volunteered.

"See, you do know."

"What I remember is that it was a case of one murder being influenced by the similar—I believe simultaneous—circumstances of another murder. A gang of thugs had been implicated in the first murder. So it was assumed the second murder, under such incredibly similar circumstances, had to have been committed by a second group of thugs. But circumstantial evidence and popular opinion aside, the murder of Marie Roget was eventually pinned, through the brilliance of Dupin, on a single killer."

"Yes, a naval officer with whom the poor Marie was romantically involved. And Dupin, in solving the crime, made a concerted effort to circumnavigate the huge preponderate pile of circumstance and opinion and to seek the minutiae, the fluky little details that would suggest something entirely unpredictable, *unguessable*."

Legs crossed in the masculine style, wineglass in hand once more, he was on his academic high horse now. And Hewitt, sensing a significant turn of information, had no choice but to hop on. The professor

took a drink, then lifted the glass in the identical toast-proposing gesture he had tendered moments earlier. But instead of paying another
tribute, he made a request. "Do you have a pair of dice?"

She did. But the request didn't exactly resonate with the logic she
anticipated.

"You don't remember it do you?" he quizzed. "In 'The Mystery of
Marie Roget,' Poe lays out the calculus of chance, of fluke happen-
stance. The probability exercise. If we had the dice, it would help."

The dice were in the junk drawer in the kitchen. Looking at her reflection in the kitchen window above the sink, she took a moment to
freshen herself. A little cold water around the eyes. Then a wet hand
through her hair to coax it into something resembling a shape. She noticed Shorty looking up from his deliberate eating in the corner, a
quizzical look in his eye.

"It's a girl thing, Shorty," she said. "You don't want to know."

With a pair of dice and the bottle of wine, Hewitt returned to the
living room. She refreshed Scott's glass first, then her own, being a little more generous with herself this time. When she was done, Scott
took the dice and positioned them on the table to show double sixes.

"This was Poe's illustration of the principle," he said with an intellectual excitement in his voice she hadn't heard since their previous incarnation at UIC. "Imagine that I've just rolled these dice. And for the
second time in a row they've come up double sixes. Because I have
rolled consecutive double sixes, does it mean the odds of me rolling
double sixes on the next try are diminished?"

Hewitt waited to see if he was going to answer his own question.
When he didn't, she did. "Of course not. The odds of rolling double
sixes are exactly the same with each new roll."

Scott Gregory seized on her answer with a glee fueled by both his
intellectual zeal and the rising level of alcohol in his blood. "So even if
you, Elizabeth Hewitt, even if you had never before rolled three straight
double sixes in your life, it could very well happen on the next roll."

"Are you trying to draw a parallel with accidental evidence or
chance discovery?" Hewitt posed.

"What I'm saying, simply, so ridiculously simply, is that just because something has never happened before, it doesn't mean it can't happen in the next day, hour, minute, nanosecond."

"And this bears relevance to my case exactly how?"

"Poe himself articulated if perfectly, through the mouthpiece of Chevalier C. Auguste Dupin. If you give me a moment, I think I can give you the exact wording."

He took his moment, let his eyes drift to the glass tabletop. "I have before observed that it is by prominences above the plane of the ordinary that reason feels her way, if at all, in her search for the true, and that the proper question in cases such as this, is not so much 'what has occurred?' as 'what has occurred that has never occurred before?' "

Hewitt took a sip of her wine, felt the warm redness of it lubricating her tongue, her throat.

"In dealing with a brain that's gone as bad as this one has," she said. "I would assume nothing less than outrageous circumstance to be lurking at almost every turn."

He looked at her with the glowing leonine eyes of the great teacher. "That's very well stated. And very well realized. All you have to do now is roll the dice to find out whether or not you actually believe it."

Hewitt reached down to the table, to take the dice. But before she could pick them up, she found the hand of the teacher suddenly cupped over hers.

"No, Elizabeth," he said. "Not tonight. Tonight let's just enjoy the sweet intoxication of wondering."

FORTY-SEVEN

She would have slept with him that night. There was no question of it. Reason One, jazz. Coming from her stereo. Pheromones encoded in musical notation. Jimmy Smith. *Standards.* Beginning with an achingly slow, languidly longing version of "Little Girl Blue." Reason Two, intellectual foreplay and psychological petting, mixed with red wine had heated the beaker to the point where there was nowhere else to go with the energy. And Reason Three, the strongest indicator, was the fact that she had her hand inside his underwear and he had his inside hers when the phone line she absolutely had to pick up began to ring like a warning from the Libido Security Company.

If the news had been anything other than what it was, they would have probably returned to the underwear thing and let nature take its course from there. So appalling was the new information that by the time she put the phone down, Scott Gregory was all over the fact that the night games would have to be postponed, that Jimmy Smith would not be playing them into the oblivion of lust, at least not on this evening.

"I prefer your complexion when it's a little less white," he said as Hewitt put the phone down.

"They found semen in one of the eye sockets," Hewitt informed him.

To that, the only English professor she'd ever slept with offered a one-word reply. "Yuck."

Even if Hewitt hadn't been motivated to jump on the forensic find, the crashing of their little love party by the yuck factor was enough to turn out the lights.

At the front door, she apologized for the evening, her career, her life. The cat had come out from the kitchen to observe the good-bye scene, though it kept its distance, as if it understood the need to give them their space.

"I believe I'm the one who suggested getting together. You were gracious enough to invite me here. Unfortunately, the rest of the world wasn't as gracious to you. There will be other nights."

"I hope so," Hewitt said.

From there, it was clearly her move that initiated the big good-night kiss. And it was a good one. Wet, deep, vinous. With a serious, full-body embrace—flesh commingling, bones bumping. The kind of thing people exchanged when there was some true long-range feeling between them. Scott Gregory gave his own little postscript to it as the bodies and beta waves returned to their rightful owners.

"Let's hold that thought," he said. "Good night, Elizabeth."

With human gore, body fluids, and DNA samples swimming in her head, Hewitt still allowed herself the mind-glow of watching him walk away, his gait strong and measured, not deflated, as if he knew he'd be back soon enough to cash in the rain check. As far as she was concerned, he was right. Although it surprised her a little when he paused at the end of the sidewalk and turned to look back at the door he had just exited. What really surprised her was that her instincts had fired off, and she had instantly ducked down from the window.

Was she afraid of being caught looking? Of being caught *caring*?

She was being foolish, of course. And she felt more foolish still when she repositioned herself as surreptitiously as possible for a look from the corner of the front window to see if Scott was still there.

He was. Which sent her undercover again. This time she moved to the side window to observe him through the gauze of the fringe curtains.

He continued to stand there, facing the house. His face was fully hidden by the dark, and yet she felt she could read it. The thought that rose to the surface of her mind was that he was going to come back to the house, or at least that he wished to.

She felt the startle of something against the back of her leg.

Shorty. Looking for a little loving, too.

"Settle down," Hewitt said—as much to herself as the cat.

With that suggestion relaxing her own back and shoulders just a little, she turned to peek through the window gauze once more. But this time the object of her affection was no longer there.

FORTY-EIGHT

The feeling of not having sex with Scott wasn't entirely supplanted by the merging of the melted marshmallows with the liquid chocolate. But it was as close as she was going to get under the circumstances. Counting down the beverage cycle in the kitchen, Hewitt's mind had projected a short list of the reasons for the shift in The Raven's MO. On the living room couch now, mug in one hand, her sketching pen in the other, she worked through the conjecture again.

There were two lines to her thinking. First—not necessarily in the order of plausibility, but of cognition—was the notion that The Raven had entered the Griggs home to find his next victim already in the arms of another pursuer. If he had encountered the couple in a sexual situation—and there was evidence in the bedroom to suggest this—it might have been more than enough to set him off. It would have angered him. It might have stimulated him. Hewitt's feeling was that it would have done both.

Enough to have added a sexual component to his atrocity protocol? Yes. Hell, yes. The motherfucker was insane, inventive, and totally without conscience. And who was to say what would trip his trigger when the lights were low and the mania high?

Hewitt's second line of thinking wasn't exclusive of the first. And it had its roots in the disturbing but illuminating conversation she'd had with Professor Gregory. Maybe The Raven was just having fun. Getting his ya-yas. Pursuing his happiness on a new ride in the amusement park of his brain. And maybe he wasn't doing it so much for the perverted pleasure of the physical act as the psychological kick of playing a head game with the people he knew were pursuing him. Leaving a sickening little signature, a calling card, an in-your-face taunt.

And Hewitt hoped like hell such an indulgence would be his critical mistake. Because somewhere in the big wide world of test tubes and blood bags and cryogenically stored samples, there had to be a piece of Gabriel Rafferty floating innocently in the forensic stew. The good news was she had established her portal to the medical data earlier in the day. Although neither she nor Dr. Burton Willis had known she would come calling so soon. On the phone now, in the Mazda, she went through the process of tracking down a physician who wasn't on call and who was, as it turned out, on the town for a night of fine arts with his wife. Within three minutes of her emergency page, Willis called Hewitt's cell phone. And he was none too pleased with the *entertainus interuptus*.

"I'm at the Schubert Theater," he huffed. "Enjoying *Swan Lake*. With my wife. I *was* enjoying *Swan Lake* with my wife. And no, I did not have anything close to an aisle seat."

"We found semen in the eye socket of the latest victim," Hewitt told him. "If this isn't your guy, it's a golden opportunity to prove it. If it is Rafferty, it's also a perfect opportunity to prove that. As his attending physician, I'm hoping you can lead us to a stored blood sample, tissue sample, something we can test."

"You know this is going to put us right in the center ring of the circus," Willis groused. "Regardless of the results."

"My gut feeling is your ticket to the circus was punched a long time ago."

A hard pause from his end. In the interlude, Hewitt could hear the muffled strains of the orchestra.

"Okay," he said, resigned. "I'll get on it right away."

"If it helps, I can tell you the ending to *Swan Lake*."

"I think I'll be getting at least that much from my wife," Willis sighed before signing off.

Hewitt put her phone down, returned both hands to the wheel, got the feeling of the car and the freeway back into her arms, her nervous system.

Her next stop was the one she hated most. But she had to be there. As much as she wanted to sit this one out, she couldn't. She had to be there for her. If there was an afterlife, Hewitt had to show Samantha Griggs, from the other side of the looking glass, that someone gave a shit, that someone was there to hold her invisible hand.

ON THE ISLAND of the blind, Cyclops is king. But what if Cyclops is a cat? It was the thought pirouetting through Hewitt's mind as she stood at the metal table with the body of Samantha Griggs on display before her.

Hewitt saw a mental sketch of a crown-wearing Shorty surrounded by a court of smiling, eyeless females. The forensic assistant dropped an instrument on the table, the metal-to-metal sound jerking Hewitt from the bad imaginary place and into the much worse real one.

"This is one of those where it's really a matter of how much to put out for public consumption," the voice of Carlton Zoeller stated, bringing Hewitt all the way back.

He was there in the bad reality, too, across the table from Hewitt, all gowned, gloved, and visored.

"I mean, God almighty, I've seen some things," he continued wearily, but not entirely without theatricality. "But never, shit, never . . ."

"Is it really necessary to swear with the victim lying here?"

Hewitt's ringing question caused both sets of visors to turn her way and hold for several seconds. The assistant returned her focus to the body. Zoeller kept his on the steam curling from the ears of the special agent.

"I didn't realize you were wearing the Clean Language Seal of Approval these days, Hewitt," he said. "But point taken if it makes you happy. Then again, you're the one who crashed the party here. Not that I don't welcome your visits. Of all the Homicide and VC people I know, you definitely wear the most coordinated outfits."

It was what he did. The condescending commentary. Especially around women who threatened him. At another time, his comment would have pissed her off. On this night, she knew her anger would have been misplaced. Right then she had more important things to focus her anger on. Like the eyeless naked girl on the table. Didn't someone have to rage for her, too? It was one thing to care, one thing to be devastatingly sad. But someone had to be royally, mortally out-raged enough to go and get the demon who desecrated her.

"All I know," Hewitt said, "is that when I see something like this, like her, it makes me wonder how it could happen in the same world where I live."

"I'll tell you, Hewitt," Zoeller responded. "When screwy brain chemistry and its partner, libido, get together on the dance floor, *any-thing* can happen. And we have no way of predicting what that any-thing might be."

There it was again. The Poe-Dupin-Gregory connection. *The proper question is not so much "what has occurred?" but "what has occurred that has never occurred before."*

An orangutan as the perpetrator of brutal murders in "The Rue Morgue." Two nearly identical murders committed at the same time in Paris by two completely unrelated killers. And now, more than a cen-tury and a half since those tales were conceived, a twenty-first-century madman hell-bent on some kind of mind-melding mission of homage.

For Edgar.

This eyeless, lifeless body on the steel table. Some sort of sacrificial offering, some grotesquely depraved tribute to a troubled genius dead and buried a decade before the Civil War.

FORTY-NINE

It hadn't been the same as the usual Thursday-girls-night-out. But that was the whole point. Girls night out for karaoke, *bad*. Girls night out for something else, maybe okay. Then there was their example, just ended. Girls night in, *good*. What else were you going to do? With all the buzz. The warnings. The freaking out. The whole crazy thing.

So with all that on the table, the Fab Four of them had decided to leave the Thursday-night fun car in the driveway. And that would be the Thursday-night thing for a while, getting together at one of their places, feeding their faces, lubricating their brains, chatting each other up like they were back in an all-girls dorm.

The other three had been gone for no more than ten minutes. Toward the end, the last half hour or so, she had been ready for them to go. Now after they had, and just ten minutes out, she already missed them. At least she had the cleanup to keep her company.

Surveying the interior of the house, it looked like it had been a pretty successful evening of entertaining. The bowl of guacamole dip, practically licked clean. The chips and cracker remnants. The quartet of smudgy wineglasses—each with a different shade of lip gloss. With no men on the premises, and with full prior awareness of that, it was interesting that, without consulting one another, they had all gone full treatment in doing their faces.

It was the Thursday-night thing. She wondered if the makeup and the dress-up part would start to wane over time. That would depend on how long it would be until it was safe to get up on stage and sing with a machine again.

She picked up the four wine glasses, clanking a couple of them a little too hard. She recognized her shade of lip gloss on one of the clankers. Turning toward the kitchen, she caught sight of someone looking back at her from the wall mirror—someone who looked just like her. Only a little too puffy. A little too tired.

Deborah Deverona. In all her freaking dressed-up, lip-glossed, wine-buzzed, manless splendor. Little Debbie. The shortest of the four. Hell, of any four. Cute, though. Very cute. The guys were always quick to point that out. And the boobs. They couldn't resist the gravitational pull of those babies. But there was and always would be the other part. The short thing. Little Debbie.

So nice for all those middle school and high school years to be nick-named for a snack cake. Well, that was then. Now at least she was Deb. At least the "Little" part was gone.

She took the wineglasses to the kitchen where the rest of the mess was. Food prep dishes and utensils. The extra-large pizza box. As always, nowhere to go with that. Too big for the wastebasket. And if she turned it on its side and stuffed it behind the wastebasket until the next time she went to the garbage cart, a thousand crumbs would fall through the side. Not that she hadn't done that many times before. But she'd been fighting a war with ants since the summer. So there was really only one way to deal with it. Take the damn thing out to the cart. Sooner than later.

First, though, she'd straighten up the living room, starting with the highlight of the evening. The X-rated version of Mystery Date she'd put together for her buds for being nice enough to drop by. The game she'd bought after some spirited bidding on eBay. For the prizes, the dream dates, and the dud, she had visited a couple of Internet porn sites. The dreamy studs in all their erectile glory had been easy enough to find. But the dud, well that had been a little trickier. She hadn't wanted just some goofy-looking naked Gomer. There were plenty of those on ama-teur sites. She wanted something a little more interesting. Somewhere between bizarre and hilarious. With a little controversy thrown in.

And, man, oh man, had she found him. On a fetish site. So she printed the images—the beauties and the beast—and made stand-up cutouts of them to substitute for the original game guys. And it had been a hit. Big time. Really, it had been the perfect antidote, the perfect replacement therapy. In lieu of real live men to play with, game-board cutouts were the next best thing. But as she had anticipated, what put the game over the top was the fact that one of the cutouts was shaped so differently from the others.

Tyrannosaurus Dick. That was his trade name. Deb Deverona had found him under the fetish heading of Abnormally Large Men. And of all the abnormally large men in the subgroup, Mr. T. Dick was the abnormally largest.

He had a thing that came down to his mid-thigh. And it just didn't look right. It was shaped more like something you'd see on a pachyderm than a man. But it was definitely there, in all its freakish reality, with the disclaimer that swore to the unretouched authenticity of it.

Unfortunately, that was easily the most attractive part of Mr. T.D. He had a truck driver's body. Not fat, but nowhere close to toned. And at the top of the sloped shoulders, a face that brought only one thought to mind.

Caveman.

In the first round of the game, Larissa—the tallest of her taller friends—was the lucky winner of the dud and all that came with him. Upon opening the little door and seeing that giant thing on that body, the ladies just lost it. Roaring. Snorting. Spitting pieces of unswallowed hors d'oeuvres. They had never, in fact, been more unladylike. And after a good two or three minutes of hysterics, Larissa had made an intriguing point. Or at least a valiant attempt at spin control.

"I don't know," she'd said. "Seems to me he doesn't fall into the total loser category. From what I can see, he does have his redeeming points. Or should I say *point*?"

Of course, that had set them off on a wine-slickened discussion of the whole *size matters* issue and how much you'd be willing to give up on the rest of a guy for a one-time ride on a nuclear warhead.

She caught herself smiling in the kitchen window as she stood up from loading the final handful of silverware into the dishwasher. She had to take one more private look before she could decide. The game and the makeshift man-prizes were on the dining table where she and her friends had left them. She turned to head that way when her elbow caught the pizza box on the counter and flipped it in the air. At which point she made an amazing crumb-saving catch of the box and decided to take the damn thing out to the garbage cart right then.

The cart was kept along the outside wall of the garage, about thirty feet from the side-door exit of the house. It wasn't the most convenient arrangement, but she just couldn't handle the smell of the thing inside the garage.

After dumping the box, Deb Deverona took a few extra moments to take in the night sky, in its autumn crispness, the stars popping like camera flashes so far away, taking pictures of the small woman on earth with the great big boobs. And it was from there, that general area of her body, that she felt the song well up, and only seconds before her next best physical attribute began to sing the words.

She'd performed better renditions of "You Light Up My Life," and certainly longer ones. And it wasn't like she was exactly singing at full volume. There was no one in the audience anyway. Except her. And the picture takers in the sky were too far away to hear. It was special anyway. Just the one time through. First verse and chorus.

But it was early October and the night air had its chill and it was time to go back in and maybe have that last analytical and anatomical look at Tyrannosaurus Dick. Although the night, the stars, the song had changed the mood.

Dammit. At the side door now. Shit. She'd locked herself out. She couldn't imagine how she'd done it. Even if the doorknob lock had been set, she didn't remember closing the door all the way. She replayed the door and the pizza box removal sequence in her head as she walked around the garage and went to the backyard to get the hide-a-key from under the loose piece of flagstone where she kept it.

Ah fuck, what did it matter? At least she had the sense to hide a damn key. Back inside the house, she made a beeline to the dining table, to the X-rated Mystery Date game. One of her friends had apparently stacked the pictures of the guys—although she didn't exactly recall when. Wine. It always made her goofy, she thought, as she picked up the pictures. The dream guys were on top and . . . *what was this? Who the hell did this?*

After all her hard work, which of her three buds had the sick sense of humor and the horrid taste to desecrate the body of Tyrannosaurus Dick?

She sat down on one of the high-backed chairs, let the outrageous new image of the most mysterious of the mystery dates sink into her brain. Someone—she suspected Larissa—had taken a Sharpie and blackened in every part of the mutant porn man's body, except the elephant trunk between his legs. Sick enough. But what corked it completely was the embellishment that went from there. As in the extended black wings, the birdlike head, the beak, and, at the bottom of the blackened legs, the claws.

A Goddamn ugly-ass raven. With a freak show appendage.

FIFTY

All the ducks are asleep. There is no activity whatsoever on the pond. On the shore, however, just down from the stone walking bridge, Special Agent Elizabeth Hewitt sits in the middle of the wooden bench along with one of her closest but most difficult friends.

Her name is Betsy, Little Lizzy, Angel, Sweetheart, Pumpkin, Dolly, Precious, Princess, or, the sum of them all, My Baby Girl. This child doesn't know the grown-up lady sitting next to her on the bench. She doesn't know jazz. Nor does she have any comprehension of how or why one human being would take the life of another or, when the world went really bad, the lives of many.

What she does know is that her daddy loves her, her daddy will protect her, her daddy will always be there. She knows because he told her so.

Betsy Hewitt sits with the older lady in the dark. But she does not see a dark pond in front of her. She sees a warm sunny day. She sees a day with dad. She sees them together by the pond, throwing bread crumbs to the ducks, like they always do after visiting mom at the hospital. They feed the ducks and they talk. They talk a lot. Now that mommy can't talk anymore, dad says they have to talk extra.

The little girl smiles for her daddy, even though with her mommy how she is now, she doesn't always feel like smiling. So she closes her eyes and turns her face into the body of the big lady next to her who puts an arm around her and hugs her. This makes the big lady start to cry. She doesn't want to cry in front of the little girl. But there is nothing in her experience, her training to draw from in order to stop the tears. There is nothing she can imagine in the universe that could hold it back, short of God's own hand. But God, if he was ever paying attention to begin with, has turned his back to her now. How else do you explain how he could just let her father die alone on the dining room floor like that?

Couldn't there at least have been some kind of sign? A dream premonition the night before. A dove in the window when she woke up that morning. A cloud formation that resembled her dad's face while she ate her lunch at a picnic table on the Illinois State Police grounds. Or maybe some skywriting over the freeway as she drove home that night. Like the wicked witch did in *The Wizard of Oz*. Except instead of "Surrender Dorothy," her message would've read: "Hey Hewitt, your dad just had a heart attack." And when the wind blew that away, the follow-up: "If you hurry, your CPR training could save him."

Hell, even the wicked witch had been decent enough to give Dorothy a heads-up and a chance to wave the white flag. But God, with the only relationship in her life worth living for, had just sat there and let it happen.

Blame. Sure, she could blame an invisible being with omnipotent power. But what about herself? She, who in the line of duty, had so often been credited with having an intuitive nature that had led her to the top of her field. Where the hell was she when her dad looked up suddenly from the bills and the check writing at the dining room table and grabbed his chest and called out.

It would haunt her, gall her, that in the midst of this cataclysmic event, this personal apocalypse, she hadn't heard or felt or sensed anything. She'd been in her car on the freeway, with the windows down and "The Girl From Ipanema" cranked up and set to repeat in a loop until she got tired of singing along with it.

That's where she had been. While her dad was rolling off the chair and falling to the floor and looking at the old chandelier above the table and mistaking it for the bejeweled light of heaven and calling— yes, he had to have called didn't he?—calling for her. But instead of getting his Betsy, Little Lizzy, Angel, Sweetheart, Pumpkin, Dolly, Precious, or Princess, he got The Girl from Ipanema.

That bawdy mellow tune was still sashaying through her mind when she pulled into her dad's driveway half an hour later. It was Tuesday night. Spaghetti Night. The all-you-could-eat special at Marino's, a favorite of theirs going back, like one long unbroken string of semolina, to her childhood, when they were forced to start eating their meals together, just the two of them.

Right away at the front door, she knew something was wrong. It was a nice fall night. And on such a night, he would have left the front door open for her. Inside, the unthinkable was already hanging in the air. The absolutely unthinkable. And when her calm voice went unanswered, her frantic voice preceded her into the dining room.

And so she cries on this night, just as she did then. When she'd followed the coroner's van to the morgue of the same hospital where her mother had laid in the coma for three weeks after ingesting the bottle of sedatives.

As the years since her father's death trickled by, her top-of-mind awareness of such dates, such commemorations of her father's life, good and bad, had begun to diminish commensurately. In the first year, of course, it had been pretty brutal. Not just the pain on the days when they finally came, but the psychological buildup, the way her mind anticipated, even feared the birthdays, holidays, the events he loved. The Kentucky Derby. The World Series. The Rose Bowl.

But today, five years gone, this darkest of anniversaries had nearly slipped past her unnoticed. In fact, if she had gotten past midnight without the thought finally hitting her, she would have felt it as a relief, as a sign of healing, of letting go, if only a little.

But leaving Samantha Griggs' body at the state crime lab morgue and stepping into the October night had set off the chain reaction that had landed her at the duck pond on the grounds of Good Samaritan Hospital in Wheaton.

And now in the final hour before midnight on the official anniversary, it only made sense that she would need the right company to observe the occasion. Without inviting her, the little girl had appeared. Betsy. To join the older one, Elizabeth, who had been there at the worst time, the night when it all happened. Spaghetti Night.

Maybe someday she would actually be able to eat a plate of

spaghetti again. Maybe that would be the watershed, the sign, not from God, but from herself, that she had made it out of the river basin of grief and reached the other side.

She reaches out, takes hold of the little girl's hand, looks up through the clear night sky and its infinitude of stars. Since her father's death, she has been the head of the family. And like it or not, the child she once was still needs her to be strong, to protect her, to keep her from harm in a world where harm falls like starlight on an almost forgotten pond.

FIFTY-ONE

"Stella By Starlight" ran through the basement jazz club of her mind as she slept. It was all those stars, reflected in the pond as she'd finally said her good night, her good-bye. Leaving the hospital grounds, she hadn't even waited to get to her car before checking her messages. In fact, by the time her eyes made contact with the Mazda, she had already gotten the predictable but still disappointing update. It came from Pete Megna whose picking and grinning with the Mount Prospect detective assigned to the Gabriel Rafferty disappearance had yielded nothing substantive in terms of his current whereabouts, but had coughed up some highly interesting information from his past.

Megna also had news from his interview of Samantha Griggs' estranged husband. Two items, both as Hewitt had anticipated. One, his business-trip alibi was solid. And two, his estranged wife was no stranger to karaoke clubs.

By 6:21 the next morning, Hewitt had already showed up at work, albeit on the microwave shift. While "Stella By Starlight" continued to play just above the surface of the microwave hum, Hewitt's inner ear had returned to the most interesting of the words Pete Megna had left her the night before. It was the information about Rafferty's parents, his *deceased* parents. The father, as Dr. Burton Willis had already informed her, had died of natural causes when Rafferty was fourteen. The mother had purchased her shroud several years later in what was termed a household accident. Some kind of fall.

A fall. What kind of freaking fall? Was that the beginning of it? Or was that the end of one terrible chapter and the beginning of another with an even more apalling ending?

Inside the microwave, the light was off, the mug had stopped turning. The reminder beeper was offering its insistent prompting: *Come on, you're staring right at it. Open the freaking door. Take out your damn mug. What the hell's wrong with you?*

Hewitt heeded the electronic chirp, put together the rest of her Swiss Miss eye-opener, her brain sipping on the notion that if Rafferty was The Raven, his flight into darkness may well have started earlier than the last few years or months. She took her first sip. Too hot. But she didn't care.

Jeffrey Dahmer, the serial psycho from just up the interstate in Milwaukee, had murdered his first victim in high school. But it wasn't until years later, breathing the sweet sick fumes at a chocolate factory that he went on his spree. This was probably the last thing she needed. Four girls dead at the hand of a black-winged monster who was accelerating like there was no tomorrow. And now here she was getting caught up in her panties over a household accident from twenty years ago.

Eyes on the prize, babe. Eyes on the prize.

She took another sip, lapped at the marshmallow coating with her tongue.

The scream thing.

Was the mother a screamer? A screaming abuser? Did she scream at him while she hurt him? Or, did the mother scream while her husband or, later, other men abused her? Did she scream when she fell in the purported accident? Did the scream echo through the house as he watched her fall? Did the scream continue to resound after she hit the ground? Did it live on in his memory after she was gone?

Was he trying to recreate the sick twisted thrill of the screams? No, that again would be too linear. The truth, whatever it was, would be much more convoluted. Inside out. Multilayered. In the history of the bad brain, this one was right up there at the top of the trophy case.

The screams.

The mother.

Poe.

Poe's mother. Shit. Poe's parents were actors. His mother had performed roles in which she died on stage. As a way of babysitting the very young Edgar, he had been seated in the first row. Night after night he had witnessed his mother's death from the best seat in the house.

To make them scream. To make them die. Just like mother. But why the transference? And what was the ultimate gratification?

Another lick of marshmallow. It didn't matter. Trying to follow a brain this twisted was like trying to play three-dimensional chess on LSD. If Rafferty was the guy and they got him and he lived through the getting of him, they would have all the time they wanted to map the forensic psychology.

If he was the guy.

She skimmed the last of the marshmallow off the top of the chocolate. It was still premature to put the Rafferty information out to the media. All she had was some letters, insane and informed as they were. But still a flimsy indicator in a court of law. Circumstantial as hell.

Hewitt rose from the table, took her cup of chocolate to the kitchen window. There were two big, black, ugly, but apparently healthy, crows on the lawn. She didn't know it at the time, though it would cross her thoughts later, that the morning crow count would equal the number of critical developments that would come to her attention within an hour of her final sip of chocolate from the big mug. Developments that would put Gabriel Rafferty in the living rooms and on the kitchen tables of every home in America.

FIFTY-TWO

It has been a long night for Deborah Deverona. And she remembers none of it. Even now, coming out of the chemically induced somnambular haze, she is having trouble remembering the smallest of things. Like how to move her limbs. How to open her eyes.

What she hasn't forgotten, however, is how to hear. As the fog of her mind continues to swirl, continues to mask her other perceptions, her ears are decoding the sound of *groaning*.

But not the groan of a human being. Or of any living thing.

It is the groan of something not alive, yet something capable of movement. It is the groan of a machine. A groan rising over the sounds of metal moving against metal, with shifts, consistent shifts in the volume and pitch of the groaning.

The paralysis of her eyelids begins to recede. The lashes flutter, each against its partner. She can count the beats between the grinding and the groaning fluctuations. And even before her eyes can open sufficiently, she knows she is in a hospital, on a table, with this medical machine whirring above her.

She remembers. The night with her friends. Mystery Date. The big-dick guy. What one of her friends did to the picture. She remembers cleaning up. Going to bed.

Going to bed. And waking up in the hospital. And the full terror grips her now. Something has happened to her during the night. Something that has put her here. On the operating table. And she is waking up. Coming out of the anesthesia. Coming out of the anesthesia too soon.

Eyelids fluttering wildly. She tries to move her feet, but they are bound to the operating table. She tries to move her hands, but she feels them strapped down at her sides. The medical machine groaning, whining, breathing. But the voices . . . Where are the voices?

As the machine continues to breathe, her scream grows from a tap-root in the base of her abdomen, erupts from the body, the throat, and rises to an unmerciful bloom as her eyes finally open to the reality of the operating room.

But reality is wrong. Terribly wrong. And the thing that drives the scream to a previously unheard height is the realization that the machine above is not some modern medical marvel, but rather a terrible apparatus of wood beams, ropes, pulleys, counterweights, and, at its modulating center, a swinging metal scythe.

FIFTY-THREE

Between Zack and Emily Gelder of Boston and Ms. Kendall Chartoff of Atlanta was a much more curious entry in the Poe Museum visitor registry. The signature belonged to a Mr. Rod Rehsu of Chicago, Illinois. Unlike the entries above and below in the book, the Chicago visitor had opted not to provide a street address. That would have been asking too much, of course. What he had provided, however, appeared to be more than Hewitt could have hoped for.

The first of the morning's two big calls came from Val Patterson, reporting in from the ISP's temporary branch office at a Holiday Inn Express in Baltimore. Armed with the printout of the Gabriel Rafferty writing sample Hewitt had sent her, Val Patterson had conducted her own unscientific but well-educated search through the Poe Museum's visitor registry for a script that appeared to be a potential match with the Rafferty sample and which also matched the time frame for the disappearance of the Poe artifacts. And Mr. Rod Rehsu, or someone purporting to be him, had claimed first prize in both penmanship and timing.

Both samples had been forwarded to the Quantico office of Fred Leland, one of the FBI's top handwriting analysts. Val Patterson told Hewitt she was anticipating a confirmation of her own naked-eye analysis within the hour, to which Hewitt had simply replied, "At this point I don't even need it. I mean the frosting will be nice. But I'm already up to my face in the cake."

On her notepad Hewitt had written the name of the suspected bogus visitor in question. Mr. Rod Rehsu. While Val Patterson prattled away in her ear, Hewitt stared at that name until the word game revealed itself.

Rehsu reversed was Usher. As in "The Fall of the House of . . ."

And Rod was short for *ding-ding-ding-ding-ding* . . . Roderick. Roderick Usher, the ill-fated host to the narrator in the Poe story.

Roderick-freaking-Usher.

Whatever else Gabriel Rafferty had going for him, he definitely had a wickedly sick sense of humor. When Val Patterson called back twenty minutes later—Hewitt was in the shower—she offered Fred Leland's analysis that the match was a ninety-eight-percent certainty. That was as good as perfect for Hewitt. She now had Rafferty in the Poe Museum at a time that intersected with the theft. She had evidence of one of the stolen artifacts—the ankle boot—at one of The Raven's crime scenes. And she had the pile of Gabriel Rafferty's godforsaken writings that had washed up on the lonely beach of Christiane Mons.

In other words, she now had Gabriel Rafferty and The Raven together, not only in the same geographical locations, but in the bloodstream of the same bad brain.

And this was only the first of the morning's developments. Because within minutes of the second Val Patterson call—by now Hewitt was toweling off—she took a call from Dr. Burton Willis.

"There's no blood sample I can track down," he informed her. "But I got you the next best thing. A couple of months into his stay at Mount Prospect—before I was put in charge of the case—Gabriel Rafferty had a suspicious lesion shaved from his upper lip. It was precancerous. So the doctor who did it had a slide of it banked."

Hewitt dropped her towel to the floor. They had a piece of Rafferty. A microscopic piece. But it would be as big as the sun streaming through the bathroom window if the DNA squeezed from it matched the sample The Raven had squeezed from himself at the Samantha Griggs crime scene.

That would not only frost Hewitt's cake, but add those little sugar-paste roses to the top of it. As many as she wanted.

But DNA was days. The handwriting, she had now.

Hewitt had made her way down the hallway into her bedroom, thanking Willis for his help and immediately calling the state lab with instructions for transport and processing of that sweet little piece of

Gabriel Rafferty's face. That done, she turned around and was confronted with a more personal form of evidence in the vanity mirror. She could see the wear and tear. Not just in her face, but in her body. The way she held herself. The muscles tight, tense. The bones feeling the constant pull and pressure.

The good thing was she looked more tired than she felt. Her face was drawn, her eyes looked heavy. Getting her hands on The Raven and keeping his claws off any more women would help with that. The rest could be cured by a special evening or two with Professor Gregory. That was definitely a circled appointment on her calendar. She didn't know the date yet. But one date she did know with morning-sun clarity was that today would be the day when Gabriel "Satan" Rafferty would be served up to the hungry media like a big, greasy junket buffet.

FIFTY-FOUR

By his estimation, The Raven is a mile from the abandoned barn. He stands on the crest of a grassy hill, facing this perfectly remote place where he has worked so meticulously to create the ideal environment for his penultimate performance.

It is here, finally, at this approximate mile distance where the screams, despite their extreme vigor, begin to evade his capacity to hear, whenever the breeze blows behind him and kisses the sound waves with a wild, passionate mouth, swallowing them, smothering them.

He feels the wind at the back of his ears now, feels the hair on the back of his head parting like wild wheat in an abandoned field.

It is at this point, this precise aural intersection, that the present scream is supplanted by the scream in the distance of his memory. The one true sound he returns to again and again. The pure sound of love ripped out of itself and scattered to the wind. The maternal scream that gave birth to all its progeny.

Until now, the screaming has been for his ears alone. Today he will share it with all who will listen. Not in the most sonically clear manner possible. But clear enough. Definitely clear enough.

He returns his focus to the living screamer in the distance. The breeze freshens at his back, once again impeding his ability to hear her. Yet it occurs to him as the breeze lessens, that the voice has been quiet for some moments. Perhaps she has settled into a lull of her own, a temporary armistice with the forces that have placed her on the platform beneath the pendulum. Certainly her eyes will be on the device now, its cutting blade, the heartless mechanical swing of it, counting out the moments, the heartbeats, the relentless unfolding of the tale, in this version created especially for her.

His listening exercise completed, it is time to return to the barn. The pit. It is time to unveil the work.

FIFTY-FIVE

On the ride into headquarters, Hewitt had pulled out the first disc of a double jazz compilation and set it for *shuffle*. She'd ordered the compilation off cable late one night, and it had turned out to be quite good. A little too packaged. But the kind of thing that gave the jazz-curious an instant stake in the art form.

The last song the stereo shuffled out before Hewitt parked and headed inside was Ella Fitzgerald's "Something's Gotta Give." It was a big, brassy, pulse-quickening rendition—characteristics it shared with the strategy Hewitt had decided to employ once she got it past Spangler and ran it up the flagpole for the media in a little less than an hour.

At the conference table, with Minerva Vann proofing Spangler's prepared comments, the captain took his time digesting the concept while he nibbled on a glazed donut.

"I expect you've heard the saying 'You can't argue with a sick mind'," Spangler said. He appeared about to lick his donut-handling fingers when Minerva Vann looked up from her proofreading and preempted him.

"I'm not looking to engage him in the Platonic dialogues," Hewitt said. "I just want to get his attention, see if we can get him to stick his head out of the hole long enough to see the color of his eyes."

"Hazel," Minerva Vann interjected. "According to the description, they're hazel."

Hewitt blew a breath into her fist, wasting it that way rather than responding. Spangler took the last bite of his donut.

"Regardless of how you do it," he said, "you're putting yourself right in this guy's sightline."

"Somebody has to be the window dressing," Hewitt said. "Here's another famous saying for you. 'Truth is a snare. You cannot catch the truth. The truth is what catches you.' "

"Who said that?" Spangler questioned.

"Kierkegaard," Minerva Vann supplied.

Hewitt confirmed it with a nod and gave Minerva Vann a curled-lip acknowledgment.

"And the truth shall set you free of the case from hell," Spangler added. "Jesus Christ. If he'd been a homicide detective instead of a messiah."

For her part, Hewitt hadn't scripted her lines for the direct appeal to Rafferty. Scripted always felt scripted. Off the cuff at least had a chance of coming across as believable.

Walking down the chilly block-and-tile corridor to the media room, Hewitt knew a packed house with all her favorite network and cable faces would be a hell of a time and place to debut her evangelical skills. But before she had a chance to reload and fill that little pocket of doubt, she was in the room, hearing the clicks and whirs of the tools of the trade, smelling the olfactory cacophony of too many overpriced and over-applied body fragrances.

Spangler's remarks were another series of clicks and whirs. And when the podium was handed over, Hewitt's initial commentary was as cacophonous in State Police–speak as the B.O. blockers in the media pool.

Thank God this time she had the big visual—to get all their little information-crazed eyes off her face and onto the face of the man whose coming-out party they were there to chronicle.

Seeing Rafferty's face on the official State of Illinois big-screen TV at the same time it was being fed to the world gave Hewitt a buzz in the front of her head. If Rafferty was watching, she could only hope he was feeling a reciprocal buzz. Once the picture of the monster had bloomed for several seconds, Hewitt heard her extemporaneous voice breathe into the sound system.

"His name is Gabriel Phillip Rafferty. He is a white male, thirty-nine years old. He is six-feet-one-and-one-half inches tall and weighs approximately one-hundred-ninety pounds. He is known to have two distinguishing marks on his body. A large dark mole on his outer right shoulder and a prominent scar on his right forearm. Although for our purposes today, the most distinguishing feature is the face you see on the screen."

This brought a little gallows-humor murmur from the assemblage.

"Is this the face of The Raven?" a voice she immediately recognized blurted out.

She looked, made eye contact with the questioner, the guy from FOX. The best-looking of the male reporters in the room. So the little shit was used to getting away with it.

"I'll remind you all to please hold your questions until Agent Hewitt has completed her remarks," Captain Spangler intervened, leaning in to the microphone. He definitely wasn't wearing overpriced cologne. Some good old dad-like Brut. And the whiff of it gave Hewitt a little grounding.

"Gabriel Rafferty is considered the primary suspect at this time," Hewitt said, looking to make eye contact now with the cameras in the room. "What we are asking today is for any information anyone may have related to the whereabouts of Mr. Rafferty. His last known residence was the Mount Prospect psychiatric hospital, where he was a patient. We believe he is currently living in north central or northeastern Illinois."

On one of the TV monitors, Hewitt could see Rafferty's face boxed in the upper left corner while she spoke to the camera in the main picture. So there they were, the two of them, almost cheek to cheek in the electronic ether.

"If anyone has any information about Mr. Rafferty, please call the Illinois State Police number you see on your screen."

On the monitor she could see the number superimposed with her own talking head and the serial-killer-in-a-box.

"And now, if I may . . ."—she focused into the main feed camera— "I would like to say a few words directly to Mr. Rafferty."

Another little murmur rippled through the room. Hewitt would keep her eyes on the camera lens as she spoke, as if it was itself an eye looking back at her—the dominant eye of Gabriel Rafferty. Talking to her Cyclops-cat had prepared her.

Hewitt drew a breath, the tension of it rearing upward from the podium like a dancing cobra. And not unlike a cobra in the instant before a strike, Hewitt's hard facial muscles smiled almost imperceptibly.

"Gabriel Rafferty, we would like to hear from you," she said calmly, evenly. "If we are seeking you under false pretense, we want to know that. If there is anything we can do in assisting you in airing any ideas you wish to be made known, please call this same number and use the House of Usher pseudonym you've used before, and you will be connected directly with me."

Her pre-strike inner cobra smiled benignly again.

"Again, Mr. Rafferty, we want to hear from you."

She had done it, thrown down the gauntlet live and for an endless cycle of replays if The Raven wasn't catching her live. She and Spangler took a smattering of questions at that point. All of them predictable. All of them answered with the official ISP thoughtful grimace and with only as much information as they were willing to disseminate. And all the while, buzzing in a brassy timbre in the orchestra pit of Hewitt's mind, Ella and the band continued kicking it out up-tempo.

Something's gotta give. Something's gotta give. Something's gotta give.

FIFTY-SIX

Between her cries there is no silence. There is no respite. There is no mercy. There is only the rhythmic hum, hiss, and clank of the device. It won't go away. It will not stop. No matter how loud she yells. No matter how much she contorts her spine. No matter how tightly she closes her eyes.

It is not just inarticulate sounds she is making with her voice now. It is words, phrases, promises, pleas.

"I have to go to the bathroom!"

It is becoming harder for her to recognize her own voice.

"Please! I really have to go!"

No response. Just the continued ticking of the death clock.

She listens to the fluttery beat. Not just of the apparatus above, but of the fleshy, blood-filled muscle that beats wildly inside her chest. And at the pulse points on her body, it is as if dozens of invisible fingertips are poking her skin and flesh, as if trying to awaken her from a coma.

What she would give to be in a coma. To be lost in a sea of black nothing. To feel none of this, experience none of this, only to wake up at some later time, dead but free of this cold slab, these monstrous sounds, and the screaming of the swinging blade. She would accept death now. Without any future review.

This is the balloon bouncing on a string in the wind near the vanishing point of her rational thoughts. Her body, however, that visceral animal now unleashed, continues to seethe and rage against the straps, against the slab, against the heaving machine that will cut her in two.

"Please! I have to go. Please. I'm going to wet my pants!"

"Then for God's sake wet them."

She feels the soft warmth of her bladder emptying well before her mind plays back the sharp, raspy voice she has just heard, well before her animal body and her higher brain agree that the voice has come not from inside her mind, but from inside the barn. And just a few feet behind her. And even closer now as it speaks again.

"See that wasn't so difficult, was it?"

The piercing laugh she hears next is the laugh of The Raven. It is not the laugh of a man. The man is in the laugh. But there is something more. Something predatory. Something that takes delight in predation.

"How can you . . . how can you do this . . . to someone?"

Her voice fills the barn with its bitter disbelief. She struggles, trying to turn her head in the direction of the presence, the voice, but she is unable to.

*"I am not just doing this to some*one," the voice tells her. *"I am doing it to you."*

From the pit of her being, the two words erupt.

"Why . . . me?"

The outcry rings out against the barn boards. After that, there is nothing but the incessant labor of the pendulum. Her next words are not consciously conceived but expectorated. "Answer me! Answer me! Goddammit, answer meeeeee!"

Nothing, but the pendulum, which also refuses to answer. Again, from her, an upheaval, a reflux over which she has no control.

"I will be there in hell to testify!" she cries. "I will be there to witness your burning!"

Eight swings of the pendulum. It is within a body's length of her. Not a big body. *Her body.*

Before the ninth swing of the blade commences, the voice of The Raven returns. From the same angle above her head. At its closest point yet.

"You will have a chance to redress your grievances well in advance of that pretty scenario. In fact, you will have a chance to tell your story any way you wish to tell it. But tell it well, tell it well. And above all, tell it succinctly."

She hears the sound of another kind of mechanical activity above her head. Metal turning against metal. A high squeal. And then, a new device swings into place above her head. Above her head, but clear of the path of the descending blade.

Breathless, bloodless, she listens as the voice delivers its last words and, as she decodes them, her final instructions.

FIFTY-SEVEN

Jenna Nordgaard was hired as a fall intern in the news division of Chicago's highest-rated network affiliate on the basis of her degree credits in Northwestern University's communications department. And as she knew, because it had been a factor all her life, her Nordic good looks. Apparently there was something life-affirming to a news department about having a six-foot-tall Scandinavian princess with a brain walking the aisles and doing the grunt work with only a modest amount of grunting.

The grunt work was fine for a college senior. And the hours were good. She only worked mornings—to allow for afternoon classes. And she would do whatever they asked. It was one of those positions. In one of those businesses. When she wasn't running the floor, she would sit in her interior office cube, the blonde crown of her head visible over the dividers, which made her an obvious target for on-the-spot call-outs for assistance. Tall as she was already, she made herself an even more visible underling by setting her chair seat to the highest possible position.

It was a long way from an interior cubicle to the news anchor desk. And anything that would expedite the advancement—short of actual sexual favors for the upper-dog males and, it was pretty clear, one senior VP female—Jenna Nordgaard would do. And she wouldn't even rule out a future tryst, if it came to that, looks and height being more or less compatible.

On what would turn out to be, by an astounding margin, the most dramatic day of her internship, and the single greatest advancement move of her career, Jenna Nordgaard had smilingly agreed to hold down the fort while the higher-ups—pretty much everyone—gathered for a quick staff meeting in the wake of the news conference they had just aired from State Police Headquarters.

The call came in at 10:18 to the breaking news Live Line. The Live Line phone tracking system immediately sought out the first live body in the department that would pick up the call. That live body, at 10:18 in the newsroom, belonged to a Scandinavian princess.

Jenna Nordgaard took the call at her desk, sitting up even straighter than usual as she answered, the blonde crown of her head more visible than ever inside the warren of gray cubicles.

When she heard the hysterical female voice gasping without intelligible words, her first thought was prank, and she came within seconds of hanging up. But in the next burst of deranged gibberish, she heard the word *Raven*. And in the next volley, twice, the word *Pendulum*.

FIFTY-EIGHT

Hewitt was in her office, humming Ella Fitzgerald under her breath when Spangler called and told her, in the most serious of his serious tones, to come to his office. He didn't spell out why, saying simply, "We've got a little situation here."

At a half-run, Hewitt could already hear the bizarre sounds coming from Spangler's office TV a good twenty-five steps before she arrived at the room. Once inside, she didn't know which was more unnerving—what was on TV or the look on Spangler's face.

"Rafferty's got a new victim on some kind of pit and pendulum device. He's also rigged up a phone and called Channel Eight. And the woman . . ."—he glanced at his legal pad—"Deborah Deverona. She claims he'll cut off the connection if the call isn't kept on the air."

"Does she have any sense of her location?" Hewitt called above the din.

"No. She told them she's in some kind of barn. But beyond that, she doesn't know."

Hewitt had zoomed in on a second voice amidst the panicked gasps and cries from the TV speakers. A woman, a Channel Eight reporter who covered the crime beat from the victim's personal perspective in most of her stuff.

"That's Heidi Gill."

"She's the one who got on the line after some intern took the incoming call," Spangler said.

"I've gotta get on that fucking line," Hewitt told him. "I think I've got a better chance of talking our way to the victim than Heidi Gill has."

"I know that," Spangler said. "But you'll be putting yourself right in the cage with this guy."

"Okay, fine," Hewitt said. "Let's just let Heidi Gill handle it. She'll do a great job. Just fucking listen to her."

In the ensuing moments, with Deborah Deverona continuing to spill the contents of her ruptured mind over the airwaves, they both picked up the phone voice of Heidi Gill. There was a photo of the reporter on the screen, with a crawl of type at the bottom describing the situation.

"Deborah, Deborah. Now stay with us. You're going to be okay. Deborah . . . God, I can't imagine what it must be like for you."

"See, that's it right there," Hewitt punched through. "She can't imagine. I can."

"Okay," Spangler said, " I'll get you conferenced in."

"No. This is no three-way. When I get on, she gets off."

With Hewitt's she-wolf scent in the air, Spangler negotiated the arrangement with the Channel Eight station manager. Hewitt would be patched in from Spangler's office. Heidi Gill would step aside. While that discussion was going down, Hewitt was on her own call with Rob Windsor, the department's tech guru who was monitoring the effort to track the call. Tracing the cell phone was doable, but only to a point. They could track this cell only as far as the closest transmitter tower. That would narrow the geographic area considerably, but hardly to a pinpoint.

Great, Hewitt thought to herself. *Now if only I was Supergirl, I could fly over the area and use my X-ray vision.* And with that negative thought out of its box, Supergirl hit on a more actionable idea.

"We need a chopper in the air," she told Spangler. "As soon as we get the tower location, we need to get a chopper over the area."

"One chopper?" Spangler questioned, the phone pressed to his ear, his eyes fixed in anticipation.

"One chopper," Hewitt confirmed. "She can't see out. But she has her ears. When she hears the chopper, she can guide us closer by the sound."

The fix of Spangler's eyes didn't shift. "It'll be a pretty Goddamn wide area. That'll take time. It'll come down to how much time Rafferty has factored into this machine he's set up."

The fix in Spangler's eyes went through a couple of clicks, like the tumblers on a safe.

"Has she given any indication of how close the pendulum is?" Hewitt said.

"I don't know," Spangler answered in a quieter voice as he handed her the phone. "Why don't you ask her?"

FIFTY-NINE

There is a new voice in the barn, crackling from the speakerphone that hangs over her head. Another woman.

Another woman who, she can only hope, won't keep telling her: *You're going to be okay. You're going to be okay. You're going to be okay.*

There was a steel blade swinging less than five feet from her body. How was that going to be okay?

Her back was burning in pain from arching against the restraints. Her lungs felt like she'd been inhaling fire. She couldn't catch her breath, couldn't remember how to do it.

"Deborah, my name is Elizabeth Hewitt. I'm a special agent with the state police."

It is the second, maybe the third time she has heard the voice say this. She wants to respond to the voice, but the burn in her back, the fire in her lungs won't let her. So she does the only thing that makes the fire go away.

She screams.

She screams as if the steel blade is already cutting into her breasts. That's the line of it. The way it's coming. The place where it will come down.

It Keeps Coming Down.

She hears her voice scream the words.

"It keeps coming down!"

And as soon as she says this, she hears the new voice in the phone calling back to her.

"Yes, that's right. It keeps coming down. So you have to *calm down*, Deborah. *You have to calm down.* We have a plan to help you, Deborah. But the only way it will happen is if you calm down first!"

Fuck you, bitch. I'm about to die, and your way to make it better is to yell at me. Fuck you.

"Deborah . . . Deborah, we have a plan to help you. We can talk, Deborah. We can talk, and we can help. But you have to talk to us. You have to talk to me. My name is Elizabeth. Elizabeth. You can call me Liz. What can I call you, Deborah?"

The voice from the phone is far away, surreal. Like the voice that comes from an old beat-up pull-string doll. But right now the beat-up doll is the only doll she has.

"Deb," she hears herself say in a heaving, crying voice that can't really be hers. "Deb. Deb. My name is Deb."

"Deb," the pull-string voice says from the other side of the world. "Deb, I'm Liz. And from right here, right now, Deb and Liz are going to work together, okay? Okay?"

She knows the right answer, but can't say it. She closes her eyes, hears the sound of the pendulum. And then, the sound of her own voice.

"Okay."

SIXTY

They had turned the sound off on Spangler's TV because of the delay between Hewitt's live voice and the television transmission. But even with that confusion abated, there was plenty left over. While Hewitt kept her ear to the receiver and her mind on the pulse of the woman and the pendulum, Spangler was on a second line with Rob Windsor as he worked with the phone techs to isolate the transmission tower. A state chopper was already in the air, awaiting instructions. Although Hewitt was speaking directly with the victim, the signal was also being run through a speakerphone so Spangler could monitor it. Spangler was on his own line with the chopper pilot.

To Hewitt, the only thing that mattered was keeping Deb Deverona live on the phone and alive in the flesh until a state trooper confirmed that he had her in his official state hands.

"Deb, I need you to look around and describe the place you're in."

A pause on the other end of the line. Hewitt could feel Deb Deverona struggling to move her hypnotized eyes off the pendulum.

"Deb, you have to make your eyes look around the room. Come on, Deb. Look around. Tell me what you see."

Hewitt heard a hard breath being forced in and, with even more force, out.

"I told them. It's a barn. With a high ceiling."

The detective in Hewitt was dying to jump into a line of questions about Rafferty. Had she gotten a look at him? Could she describe his voice? But the special agent in Hewitt knew she had to roll the dice at the other end of the table. Despite his threat to cut off the phone transmission if they took the call off the air, Hewitt figured there was a good chance he was off the premises by now. But she couldn't assume that. Couldn't take that risk.

Rafferty had set up the call for a reason. His amusement, his pleasure, to fuck with their minds. And there was a certain way he would envision the rest of the game unfolding. It was on that side of the table, in that game, that Hewitt decided to roll the dice. The game where Cat and Mouse met Pit and the Pendulum. If it got too personal—about him—he might get edgy, get mad, or just lose interest. And from there, from any of those reactions, it was a very short walk to the end of Deb Deverona's life.

"Deb, can you look to the ceiling or the walls and see any light coming in?"

"There's light . . . There's light coming in a lot places."

"Deb, can you see which way the sun is coming from?"

"It's . . . it's coming from the side I think."

"Which side—your left or your right?"

Hewitt had her sketchbook open, pen ready to do the schematic. At the top, bottom, and sides, she had already written the compass marks.

"My right side."

"You're sure."

"Yes, I can see it through the cracks."

Hewitt's pen was sketching, in the middle of the page, a stick figure of Deb Deverona, her arms out to the sides, her right arm pointing east. Which put her upside-down from Hewitt's perspective. Now Hewitt knew she had to ask the more difficult question about position.

"Deb, can you give me an idea of how far the pendulum is away from you?"

"I . . . I don't know . . . Four feet maybe. But it keeps coming down. *It keeps coming down!*"

That was it. Enough with the distance. But it was information Hewitt had to know. She had to have some sense of what they were up against. Some picture of how much sand Dorothy had left in the witch's hourglass.

"Deb, Deb. That's fine. That's great. That's what I was hoping to hear."

Lying not only to the girl beneath the pendulum but to herself, and with such a straight face. But it was either that or lose Deb Deverona right there.

It was precisely then, like manna from heaven, that the coordinates of the transmission tower landed on the war room table.

SIXTY-ONE

The bad news was it was a pretty wide swath of McHenry County they were going to have to cover. And for a moment, Hewitt considered putting up more than one chopper. Such a plan, however, ran the risk of sending conflicting chopper sounds that would only confuse the woman in the barn even more. Deb Deverona's ears had to receive one signal and only one signal for her to have a chance, through the Spangler-Hewitt-pilot team, to guide the chopper into a position where instructions could be given to on-the-ground troopers.

The image kept washing up against the side of Hewitt's mental dock. The image of what they would find if they got to Deb Deverona too late. If it broke that way, they had to keep the media out at all costs. Already, a directive had been issued to the news departments to keep their own choppers the hell out of the skies over McHenry County.

On the ground, twenty state trooper vehicles had been mobilized to spread out through that section of McHenry County, to be at the ready when the coordinates were determined. In Spangler's office, Hewitt had the map of McHenry County and was poised to begin the process of finding the woman in the haystack. She had just finished explaining to Deb Deverona that the helicopter would soon be over the area and that she had to listen very closely for the sound to help the pilot locate her position.

In order to give herself the best chance of hearing the chopper's approach, she needed to keep herself as calm and as quiet as possible. As soon as Hewitt gave her the instructions, she did quiet down precipitously. To Hewitt's ears, too much so.

"Deb?"

It was a hard silence now.

"Deb, what's going on? Talk to me, Deb."

Her ear pressing hard into the receiver, Hewitt heard for the first time the background clank and sweep of the pendulum. It was a sickening sound. And she counted four sweeps of the thing before she heard Deb Deverona's voice.

"What if he hears it, too? What if he's still here, and he hears it coming?"

She stopped there, the sharp, uneven breathing returning.

"We don't think he's there, Deb," Hewitt said in her most assertive voice. "We think he's moved on."

"But what if you're wrong?"

Now it was Hewitt's turn to fall into a cold silence. The point was she didn't know. Her sense was that Rafferty wasn't there. This was a game to him. A carefully planned game. Her instincts told her he would derive the most pleasure from watching the game unfold from a safe vantage point. But still she couldn't know that. The one thing she did know was that she had to answer Deb Deverona.

"If I'm wrong, you can kick my butt right after we kick his," she said into the phone.

With relief, Hewitt could feel that her ballsy assertion had succeeded in providing some reassurance to Deb Deverona.

"Okay, I'm listening for it," she told Hewitt. "Just tell the pilot to hurry. Please hurry."

"He's an expert at hurrying," Hewitt said.

It was only then, with the plan fully operational, that Hewitt felt the first cage of butterflies release into her solar plexus. For the first time since she'd gotten on the phone line with Deb Deverona, all she could do was wait and hope.

Seconds were minutes. And she knew if too many minutes accrued, they would have only one decision to make. When exactly to shut off the broadcast.

A couple of years out of school, Hewitt had been drafted by one of her unmarried college friends to coach her through a labor and delivery which the father of the baby had no interest in attending. While there had been no way of knowing it at the time, that experience had come back to serve Hewitt.

The entire sound package coming from Deb Deverona was a clear enough link to the birthing experience. But Hewitt, in her role of being calm when she needed to be calm, quiet when she needed to be quiet, and improvising the right words of encouragement when they were called for was the other parallel.

It was three minutes into the chopper search when Deb Deverona let out a sudden burst of sound that thrilled and terrified her coach.

"Do you hear something?" Hewitt said.

The response came in one long multi-syllabic moan.

"No. The thing just dropped. It just came down. *It's coming down!*"

SIXTY-TWO

"How close is it, Deb?"

She knows she should answer. She knows Liz is trying to help. She trusts her. But she can't answer. She doesn't want to give the answer. Because she doesn't want the answer to be true.

With her eyes closed, at least she doesn't have to see it. She could be asleep. For an impossible moment she actually feels like she could be asleep. And the sound of the thing is just the wind and a tree banging against the house.

"Deb, what's happening? Deb?"

Even the voice is just a voice from the TV left on in the next room. And the sound of the mourning dove cooing isn't a mourning dove, but her mother humming a song to her.

"Deb, you have to stay with me. Deb? Deb!"

Her eyes unseal themselves and open to the hissing of the death swing. She hears herself shriek, feels herself recoil. She pushes herself upward again with her back as a long, sustained scream fills the barn. And she sees, in that moment, that the arching of her back and the lifting of her chest has brought her breasts to within a foot of the pendulum blade.

Her body falls back to the slab. She forces the air out of her lungs and turns her next shriek into words.

"It's really fucking close!"

"If you raised your arm, how far away would it be?"

"I could touch it."

A cold silence grips the phone connection. And immediately Deb Deverona knows what it means. The thing is closer than they expected. So their plan has gone bad. The time it will take the helicopter . . . The time it will take . . .

"Deb, you have to hang in there with me," Liz calls to her. "At the end of this, you've gotta be there for me. Because I'm gonna be there for you."

But Deb Deverona is already entrapped, like a kitten in a burlap bag, inside the thought of finding a way out before the blade begins to take her.

She is totally still now as she contemplates the action. And the barn, except for the sound of the pendulum and the mourning dove, falls into stillness around her. The slab is her way out. What the motherfucker who put her here didn't figure. The hardness of the slab is exactly the thing she needs. The slab is her way out. The slab is her escape.

"Deb, you've gotta be there. Deb! Goddammit Deb! Wherever you're going, you're not going without me. Deb. Deb!"

But Deb is going there anyway. Her legs push hard against the ankle restraints. The muscles of her legs and her back join forces to lift her shoulders as high as the restraints allow them to lift. Until her head, in the interval between pendulum swings, is as high as possible above the slab.

It is with everything she has left inside her that she suddenly drives herself, her head, downward. She hears the sound of the back of her skull striking the slab an instant before the lights of the outside world go black.

SIXTY-THREE

Like a Coltrane explosion of thirty-second notes, Hewitt's mind was racing to interpret the silence that followed the single kick-drum thud of a living human body against something totally dead.

She squeezed it down to three possibilities.

One. Rafferty, still lurking on the premises, had struck her and knocked her unconscious. Or, and there was no avoiding this, worse.

Two. The pendulum had made another sudden drop, this time hitting her and opening a wound that had made her lose consciousness instantly.

Three. She had cashed in, given up, found the way and the means to take herself out.

For the next minute and a half, Hewitt continued her attempts to call Deb Deverona back to the world.

With the line still open and no response coming from the victim, Hewitt couldn't keep her thoughts from wrapping around Possibility one. That Rafferty was still there, that he was the causal force behind the silence.

Looking around the room, it was still Hewitt's table, the dice were still in her moist hand.

She could see him. Gabriel Rafferty. *The Raven.* Standing there in the invisible barn. Back erect. Chest puffed. Eyes serene. On his mouth, the smirk of victory. But only . . . only if an opponent failed to show up

"Gabriel Rafferty . . ."

Once spoken, his name left a bilious taste trail in her mouth.

"Gabriel Rafferty, if you're there, if you can hear me, please respond. This is a chance to speak with us, Mr. Rafferty. To tell us what you want."

She waited. For the sound of The Raven. Ten seconds went by. Ten more. And Hewitt had just opened her mouth to reissue the challenge when the voice of the carrion bird called across the electrified sky.

It was exactly that, a primitive call, a cry. Not an articulation. But when the primitive voice called out again, Hewitt suddenly changed her species identification from avian to human.

It wasn't The Raven. It wasn't Gabriel Rafferty. It was Deb Deverona. The girl in the barn, crying in the voice not of a woman surrendering to outrageous death, but of a fetus awakening for the first time to an outrageous outer world.

SIXTY-FOUR

The first thing is the taste of blood in her mouth where she has bitten her tongue. If the slamming of her head against the slab had worked, she would have never tasted the blood. But she is alive. And the blood is fresh. And the barn is still bright with the infiltration of sunlight. And the mourning dove is cooing.

The blade of the pendulum swings past, no more than six inches from the surface of her blouse.

From the phone, she hears the woman calling to her. The swing of the blade is so close now she can feel the concussion of air against her face with each passing. Her head hurts where she hit it, hurts terribly, and her body is using her wooziness like a child's comforting blanket.

Above her, above it all, the unseen mourning dove continues to call. Is it calling to her? Could it know? Could it sense what is happening? When the blade would begin to hit her, when the worst screams came, would it stop its cooing? Or would it just sing on?

She listens to the cooing. It is a beautiful sound really. A lovely sound. Somewhere in it, she hears the sound of a mother singing. Her mother.

A wave of wooziness washes through her head. So strange the feeling now. Could her brain be bleeding? Her head, hurting in the back, feeling heavy in the front.

The mourning dove . . .
The pendulum . . .
The voice on the phone . . .

The pendulum . . .
The voice . . .
The mourning dove . . .

All of them bleeding together.

> *The voice . . .*
> *The mourning dove . . .*
> *The pendulum . . .*

All flowing together in a quiet red pool. . . .

Then the sound of something else. Of something falling toward the red pool. Rippling through the air. Falling . . .

Her head so heavy on the slab. So heavy, her eyes feel the downward pull, dropping into the sockets. Dropping into the red pool. But they are not dropping alone. The sound of the other thing. The thing in the air. Or is it things? Birds? Wings beating frantically. A hundred wings. A thousand. Coming to the red pool. To meet her there. To meet her . . .

She feels a hit against her body, from the inside out. And it is enough, this signal from within, to force her to open her eyes. Still deep in the sockets. She sees the flight of one of the dark birds over her body, hears the rush of it, feather and bone, against her face. Another bird powers past from the opposite side as her eyes fight for focus. Focus . . . Focus . . .

The pendulum swings again. She feels the concussion of air, not from feather and bone, but from steel.

As her mind rushes back to her, as the red pool vanishes behind it, the sound of the thousand wings is still there.

"I hear it," she says, using the push of her lungs, her mouth to direct the words toward the telephone. "I hear the helicopter."

SIXTY-FIVE

Her voice sounded different. Spacey, wobbly, *injured*.

"Deb? Deb, are you hurt?"

"I . . . I hit my head."

"You hit your head or someone hit you?"

"I . . . I did it."

Scenario three. But no one was counting scenarios. The only thing they were counting was the grains of sand in the witch's hourglass.

At the conference table, next to Hewitt, Spangler was on a radio patch with the chopper pilot, Reed Charbonneau. Hewitt was quickly fitted with a headset to the radio patch as well. So she had Deb Deverona in her left ear and the rescue bird in her right. All she had to do now was get those two parties together in the same vertical plane above a barn in McHenry County. But she had two huge problems. Deb Deverona was sliding toward unconsciousness again. And in a slurred voice that proved just how close to a blackout she was, Deb Deverona articulated the even bigger problem.

"It's really, really close," she managed. "I can feel it. I can feel what it's going to do. Help me, Liz. Help me."

"I'll help you, Deb. But you've gotta help me, too. You have to stay with my voice and focus on the sound of the helicopter. Can you do that?"

"Yes. Yes . . ."

"Okay, Deb. Now listen closely. There are four directions we're going to use. Four directions. There's the direction your head is pointing. Then there's the direction your feet are pointing. And then there's your right. And your left. Are you clear on that?"

"Yes. Yes, I think so."

"Okay, from those four points—which direction do you hear the helicopter coming from?"

A foggy, fractured pause. The amount of time it had taken for Marilyn Monroe to slide from her last conscious thought to the point of no return.

Deb Deverona did return, but not with the answer Hewitt wanted. "I don't know. It's just out there. It's just kind of everywhere."

"Reed, you're going to need to get down," Hewitt said into the headset mike. "If you're too high she can't distinguish direction."

"I'll take it down to two hundred feet," Charbonneau said in her ear, in his relaxed, drawly voice.

"Deb, listen closely now," Hewitt said into the phone. "The pilot is going to come down a little. So that'll make it easier for you to tell the direction. Okay?"

Marilyn Monroe had closed her eyes and started drooling on the pillow.

"Deb!"

"Okay, say it again. No, wait. I can hear it. It's . . . It's coming from my feet. But a little to the right side."

Hewitt checked the inverted figure of Deb Deverona on her notepad.

"Reed," she said into the headset, "you're north and a little east. That means you need to go south and west."

"I'm already there," Charbonneau volleyed back. "Just tell her to say when."

"Okay, Deb," Hewitt directed. "You have to really focus now and tell me if the helicopter is getting louder. In other words, does it seem like it's coming toward you?"

Hewitt paused to let her listen, mindful not to wait too long, to keep the encouragement as relentless as the pendulum.

"Deb?"

The voice spilled out of the phone. "I hear it . . . I hear it . . . It's coming. Keep coming. But he has to come really soon. *Really soon!*"

Hewitt could hear it now, too. The gorgeous sound of the chopper rattling distantly in her ear. Then, an even more exquisite sound from the chopper pilot.

"Okay, I see it," Charbonneau drawled in the headset. "An old barn. Some outbuildings. Looks abandoned. No vehicles visible in the area. If there's a drive going in, it's long grown over. Nearest paved road is at least a half-mile. County Q. Best bet is to put her down right here and send the four-wheelers in behind me."

Hewitt looked up at Spangler who was on the horn with the ground troops, working the coordinates from the paper map and the zoom-in look on his laptop. He gave Hewitt a double nod.

"Okay, that's a go," Hewitt called into the headset. And in the static echo of that came the words she'd been dreading.

"It touched," Deb Deverona said in the hunched voice of a child awakened from a nightmare. And from there, sitting up in bed, eyes and voice wildly awake. "It touched my shirt . . ."—a thin, breathless scream—*"It's hitting me!"*

SIXTY-SIX

Reed Charbonneau has put down choppers in more harrowing places than this forgotten farm field. The Persian Gulf, for starters. But never has he felt the urgency he feels now, to get down, get out, and get to the objective.

In the service, the training forced you, always, to keep the objective front and center. He remembered being in the dark, dusty sky the night of the Apache friendly fire disaster in the first Iraq war. He remembered with utter clarity the voice from the Apache a hundred yards away from him, the voice of absolute dread. And he remembered even more clearly the prompt response of the C.O. in their headsets.

"Stay with me here, men. We have a mission to complete."

This mission is radically different. It isn't just the rolling Midwestern greenery replacing the Middle Eastern desert. This is a mission where he'd been able to get inside the objective like never before. To hear every word, to feel every feeling. And the damn awful thing of it is that this girl is about the same age as his only daughter. Since the time his chopper first lifted off the pad, his mind has been all over this parallel to his own world, the connection only intensifying the longer he searched the countryside, until the two girls crossed through the reflection and became one.

She could be his daughter.

And it is absolutely maddening to hear, in his headset, her cries, her terror as he utilizes everything in his skill set, everything in his power to get to her. But the one thing he can't do is hurry to put the chopper down. These are big delicate birds. And if he messes up here, it won't do any of them a rat's ass of good.

Fifty feet . . . Forty . . . Thirty . . .

The girl has stopped using words with the special agent. And there is a distressing change in the quality of her cries as he hears them in the headset.

Twenty-five . . . Twenty . . . Fifteen . . .

It is a red-hot saber stuck into his belly, searing his guts. To hear what he is hearing.

Ten . . . Five . . .

Down.

It is now as he powers down, abandons the headset, and begins to exit the chopper that his military hormones begin to flood his tissues. In his solar plexus, the thousands of sit-ups, the punishments, the insults, coiled in stored rage. His boots hit the tall grass. He activates his shoulder radio. He draws his service revolver.

The beat of his boots against the hard ground. The hiss of leather through the high grass. The buzzing of cicadas. The coo of a mourning dove.

All of it bullshit. All of it piss in the ocean of the mission.

Charbonneau scans the brush around the barn for signs of life. Fifteen yards from the entrance, his eyes iris-down. There will be no outside fight. The engagement will be inside.

Bursting through the door, his face is instantly hit with a rain of fluid. Between his lips he tastes the human blood at the same time his eyes locate its source. The blade of the pendulum, its cruel edge blood-coated, leaving a spattering trail as it reaches its apex and swings toward its next incursion into the body of the girl on the concrete block.

SIXTY-SEVEN

Hewitt took the news hard. With her hands on the wheel of the Mazda and her foot on the accelerator, it was hard to feel either, hard to feel much of anything other than rage at her failure.

Eighty miles an hour on the expressway. Ninety. What the hell did it matter? She was a Special Fucking Agent. She was special. Wasn't she? Yeah, she was so fucking special she'd allowed Deb Deverona to become a special victim.

Though she knew she had to have done it, she didn't feel like she hit the brakes once before encountering the speed bumps in the parking lot of Mercy Medical Center. Mercy. Yeah that was pretty fucking funny, too. Another serving of God's Famous Irony.

A couple of minutes after the last speed bump, her eyes hit the wall as they encountered the damage done to Deb Deverona's chest, her breasts. The cuts ran horizontally, above the nipples. A bad time to have big tits. As Hewitt knew, they were a blessing and a curse. In this case, your worst enemy.

There was really no reason for Hewitt to be there, no way to talk to Deb Deverona now. She wasn't even family. But as with the other women, Hewitt was an honorary sister. And it killed her now, looking down at this little sister, that she hadn't taken better care of her.

Another couple of minutes was all she would have needed. It always came down to a couple of minutes. The universe was fourteen billion years old, but human lives were made or broken in these ridiculously tiny intervals.

Deb Deverona's breasts. Her father's heart. And in her own chest now, Hewitt felt the deep tolling bell of separation, of loss.

She was so tired of losing. Of being a couple minutes late. With the bell of loss continuing to toll in her chest, it was joined by the sonorous chant of second-guessing. Had she pushed Charbonneau hard enough? Hell, he was a decorated combat pilot, doing everything by the book, with the ultimate experience. What would have been the other option? That she would fly the chopper herself?

Given a chance, she would've tried. Because Supergirls can do anything. Because sometimes Supergirls have to do everything. When her mom had finally succumbed to the suicide attempt and her dad had dwindled into the pathetic mess at home after the breakdown, she had done pretty damn well for a kid who had to do it all. She had figured out how to use the washing machine, hadn't she? So she could wash his over-worn shirts and his pee-stained underwear.

It was exactly because of things like that—such upside-down victories—that Supergirls hated to lose. Ever.

She looked down at the evidence of her latest loss. There would be no *Girls Gone Wild* appearances for Deb Deverona. At least not unless she came out of the additional surgeries that awaited her with a much prettier picture than this.

Yeah, she was alive. And that was all hugs and kisses and great and everything. Who knew—maybe when she came out of her post-op stupor, she could provide them with the kind of information that would help them get Rafferty. But for now, the best Hewitt could do was stand there and hate the claw marks The Raven had put on her little sister's body.

One thing she knew with moral certitude. If the fates gave her even the slightest opening, she would put a hole in that monster.

Deb Deverona was alive. And maybe someday she'd thank her for that. Hell, it was better to be alive with your tits cut up by a psychopath than dead with a perfect rack, wasn't it? Sure. With the proper passage of time, and the thousand hours of body-image and emotional-wholeness counseling.

With enough time and enough brain massaging, anything was possible. Look at what the decades had done for her father's memory. It had raised that fallen Ozymandias from the urine-smelling sands of the Nervous Breakdown Desert, raised a new king and granted him a second chance at earthly reign.

But kings were born of the parents of failure and redemption. That was kings. Female superheroes were cut a far less generous length of rope, especially by themselves.

"Sleep, baby girl, sleep," Hewitt whispered to the peaceful face on the pillow. "And don't be in a big hurry to come back."

SIXTY-EIGHT

The Raven sees everything. He has seen it for hours. From his carefully chosen perch a mile away, his keen eyes follow the frenzy in the sky above his latest and most ambitious staging. Whereas earlier in the day he had observed the movements of the lone helicopter, now he tracks the movement of half a dozen.

From his position, elevated as it is, he is also able to observe the movements of the ground vehicles that come and go. So much fuss over one little woman.

He knows she has escaped with her life, or at least some aspect of it. Perhaps this explains, in part, the extra degree of fascination the event has generated. The living victim, so much more engaging than the departed.

Let them have their little moral victory, their happy ending. If that's what it is. But only this time. Before the sun would set twice more, the final and most adventurous chapter would unfold. There would be no shortage of wild discussion then, no absence of outlandish conjecture. And that was all he would ultimately leave them with. Discussion and conjecture. For as long as the story would be told.

His next heroine, his final heroine, would not meet with such a fortunate fate as the most recent, the woman for whom the convocation in the sky is being held. No, the heroine in the next tale would join the others in the ultimate dénouement. And this one would take not just the story but the entire book with her.

He stands on the limestone ridge, in the late afternoon sun. He is, of course, the prize they so covetously seek. No doubt they have imagined him to be hidden away in some cloistered place, to evade their scrutiny. But here he is, standing in the sun. All they would need do is look his way. But they are unable. What they see is what has already been. What they cannot see is the screaming truth of the present.

He decides to make it even easier for them. His dark clothing is almost certainly working as camouflage against the pines behind him on the ridge. So he calmly sheds his clothing, and stands out at the very lip of the ridge. His body lit by the sun and glowing bright white, like the filament of a lantern in the dead of night. But this is broad screaming daylight. On the precipice of the final day. And still they do not see him.

The Raven hears himself laugh. With his throat arched against the sky. A predatory echo follows in the wake of the bemused call. He raises his arms, his hands skyward. He laughs again, this time the predatory nature of the vocalization more pronounced.

The surge of excitement begins in his feet, climbing through his legs, his pelvis, pushing higher. Another surge at the station of his heart, his chest expanding gloriously. The infusion of power engorging his arms. To the tips of his fingers he feels it now, as the arms begin to move from the shoulders. And the faux wings begin a slow flapping. Upward. Downward. Exquisitely slow at the onset, then building.

More rapid now, the movement of the wings—as the legs become integrated into the dance. A little hop to one side, a matching hop to the other. Avian legs exploding with power.

In full dance now. The wings whipping audibly. The feathered feet pounding the petrified bone of the limestone ridge. Until there is only one thing left to do.

And the cry goes out from the dancing beacon on the dark green hill. A cry of equal parts predatory incantation and wild joy.

SIXTY-NINE

Hewitt hears a small cry come from Deb Deverona, from somewhere deep inside. Her mouth hasn't moved. Nor was there any discernible movement in the throat. It had come from the chest. *Through* the chest. As if some incredibly tiny version of Deb Deverona had suddenly awakened from a nightmare on the soft pink pillow of her heart and had let out a miniature cry.

Small as it was, it was Hewitt's best moment in the hospital room so far. The staff—the lead physician herself—had suggested more than once that she leave and come back at a time when the taking of a statement would be a little more plausible.

Hewitt, of course, didn't or couldn't tell them she wasn't just there to represent the criminal justice system. It wasn't the big-time detective who needed to be there when Deb Deverona opened her eyes and looked around and started to remember. It was the big sister.

The rest of Deb Deverona's immediate family was en route from their native Baltimore. Damn the irony there again. Thank you, God. What a funny guy.

There was a sudden flutter of Deb Deverona's eyes. And then, *bink,* shit—the eyes were open, looking at Hewitt from miles away, having trouble focusing, but looking for the first person she could find, to ask if the nightmare was really over.

"I'm here, Deb," Hewitt said softly. "I'm here. Liz is here."

The eyes of The Raven's only living victim continued to peer through the anesthetic distance.

"It hurts," she whisper-cried. And then, in a voice that seemed to swallow itself before it finished, "Why? Why did they do this to me?"

Now it was Hewitt's turn to look through the fog for an answer. "You say 'they', Deb. What do you mean 'they'? Who are they?"

The eyes remained set back in their sockets, between an ugly past and a hideous present. "The boys. The bad boys. The boys who did it. They lied. But they did it. They know they did it."

Hewitt felt a woozy coldness run through her body. As if she was the one hooked to an IV freshly infused with a full syringe of dread.

"Who are the boys, Deb?'

Now the eyes pulled back even deeper into their caves. Fear riddled her voice. "I don't . . . I can't see them anymore. Their faces. I can't . . . Please, I can't . . ."

Hewitt reached across the sheets, took Deb Deverona's hand.

"You don't have to see them. Just tell me what they did."

The cold hand tried to pull away from Hewitt's grip. But Hewitt cupped her free hand around it, reassuringly. And the cold hand squeezed back suddenly, as hard as Hewitt's hand had ever been held.

"The boys from the team. The runners. They pulled off my shirt . . . my bra. They put the cream on them. And they stuck it between. Each boy. Stuck it between. Each one . . . Each one . . ."

"It's okay, Deb. They're gone," Hewitt said, squeezing the hand in return, trying to pump something into it as an antidote to the confusion, the transference.

The eyes of the living victim went sleepy again. Not peaceful sleepy. Narcotized. Her chest drew in a breath and let it all out, without a fight. Her face let go its mask of bewilderment, and she was out again.

Through Hewitt's eyes, just as well.

It would have been challenge enough getting her to replay the events of the last twenty-four hours. But now that those events had been wrapped and coiled with some pearl-necklace gang bang in her adolescence, she didn't know if she had the time, the patience, or the professional training to make it through all the layers.

She shared her observations of what had just happened with the attending psych nurse. The nurse thanked her curtly, advised her that members of the patient's family would be arriving within the half hour. So it was a good time for the pretend family—Hewitt's editorial now—to get the hell off the wing.

SEVENTY

"So how was your day?" the voice in the phone message asked, with no scintilla of sardonic or humorous intent. Which made it infinitely more sardonic and, even with the circumstances, humorous, than if he had unloaded a full cannonade of each in the initial asking. *"I just thought it might be nice to hear one non-crazy voice today. Although based on some of the reaction to my last book, you might get some argument in certain dyspeptic academic circles."*

The soothing quality of Scott's voice, the way he offered his psychological balloon ride above it all, actually made Hewitt forget the immediate pursuit of the Swiss Miss and mini-marshmallows she'd been craving all day.

"I don't know what exactly to tell you beyond that. Other than— I'm here for you."

Hearing his voice tiptoe self-consciously around the cliché had the surprise effect of actually making her a little wet. Or maybe it wasn't so surprising.

"Wow," the voice continued. *"I've become a greeting card with one of those pictures of the beach at sunset and two friends walking and talking. Well, I can't guarantee the beach and the sunset, but the walking or talking I can offer. Let me know. Bye."*

It was what she needed. Not that there was any way she could take him up on the offer, given the extreme circumstances of one of the worst days in her life, the night version of it now. She put the phone down, stood there just breathing in the bright kitchen light, letting herself have a hold of the moment. Then it was off to the pantry for the packet of sweet sensuality she'd promised herself during the day from hell.

At the microwave window, she had fully intended to process the mental review of the sorry state of the case—the dearth of useable tips on Rafferty, the recommendation to let Deb Deverona sort through her psychological junk drawer without her fake sister's help, the registration of the Pit and Pendulum farm property to an absentee landowner who hadn't been seen for several weeks. The information was there in her head. But the bits and facts were like Chinese lanterns above a garden-party dance. There. Glowing. But not necessarily worth staring at. Especially if you were already locked on the eyes of the one who had made his way through the rose bushes and crossed the lawn to ask you to dance.

The microwave beeped out the final countdown. On cue, Shorty showed up in the kitchen, looking for a treat of his own. Maybe a little Reddi-wip in his bowl if mama cat was giving.

Indulgence was indulgence. Human, feline. Lives defined by itches that needed scratching. Backs that needed rubbing. Secrets spots that needed touching.

"Fresh whipped cream from a can, baby," Hewitt said as she sprayed it into the bowl. "If kitty heaven is any better than this, in my next life I'm gonna be a dead cat."

THE SECOND SHIFT at the department was on to sift through any new information. If there was anything that really bumped in the night, Hewitt would be called immediately on the cell. She had offered to stay on and work into the night, but Spangler had convinced her to go home, to take a load off, and to hit the case hard in the morning. She knew Spangler could see she was starting to press too hard. Who wouldn't have seen that? But Hewitt was also honest enough with herself to know that an exhausted prospector could miss the shimmer of the magic dust when it finally showed up in the pan.

A few years earlier she might have fought Spangler. Now she was seasoned enough to save the fight for the time and place when she was locked and loaded on the real enemy. And if she could also tap into some of that fighting energy from her own internal wars, then she might really have something.

The extent of her exhaustion was obvious when, after the Swiss Miss and a microwaved chicken Provençal dinner, she conked out on the couch in a seated position with the TV tuned to an A&E *Biography* of Eleanor Roosevelt. Anything to stay off the cable news cycles and the news-conference images of herself from earlier in the day. Over and over and over.

When Hewitt awoke, she was still on the couch, but lying on her side—she had no recall of a head-to-couch drop—and Eleanor Roosevelt was long gone. As often happened after one of her hitting-the-wall pass-outs, she was reenergized enough to make it difficult to get back to sleep. She realized this after five minutes of lying on her back in the bed in the dark. She didn't do anything about it, however, until another forty-five minutes had elapsed.

It was a simple enough deal she made with herself. The way she saw it, she could spend her next few hours staring at the ceiling. Or she could spend the same stretch of time staring at the ceiling with Scott Gregory riding shotgun.

It was 12:24 A.M. when he took her call on the second ring.

SEVENTY-ONE

He was either so aloof, so engrossed in his reading or writing, or so close to sleep, that his voice revealed absolutely no surprise, pleasant or otherwise. As to the call's contents, he was more than amenable. He had volunteered to make the midnight ride to her place. Hewitt, however, had already offered herself the jazz-accompanied sortie in the Mazda as one of the perks of returning his phone call. She already had her music picked out—a repeater she would stay with for the duration of the drive.

"Darn That Dream." From Miles Davis' *Birth Of The Cool*. With vocals and testimonial to the bewitching powers of somnambular desire by Kenny Hagood. There was something utterly comforting and safe about being in her car and speeding through the Illinois night, regardless of the circumstances that existed in the outer world. This was her pod. Her remote little capsule in the coursing arteries of reality. Especially with the music up. And if her personal night nurse saw fit to spike a vein with a dose of the real, well, her freaking cell phone was always listening.

Darn that dream, I dream each night . . .

There was really no need to rationalize or justify the actions she was taking. Her life had been squeezed into a foxhole, that last outpost on earth where fantastic acts of the body and soul were known to transpire while all hell was breaking all around.

Maybe that was the body-and-soul deliverance of the blue Mazda. A taste of it anyway. The rest of it to come on the wings of cotton sheets, in the starlight of a votive candle.

She pulled into his driveway at a few minutes before one. The porch light was off and the interior of the house was dark, which only made the butterflies in her heart beat their wings all the harder. On the stone walk leading to his front door, Hewitt noticed a soft glow coming from the bedroom. With her mind blinded by this single source of light, Hewitt failed to notice her host already waiting for her on the front porch, sitting in the Adirondack chair, silent as a statue.

When the statue moved, it startled her. But her recognition was instant, as was her acquiescence. For all the words that flowed between them in their original incarnation, for all the words written and spoken in their separate worlds in the years since, there were no words offered here as he rose and stepped forward in the dark and she stepped into the incandescence of his arms.

Nor were words a tradable commodity as they crossed through a house lit only by the sporadic presence of small appliance clocks and indicators, each like a single glowing eye placed there to capture their escapade for the amusement of a voyeuristic God.

Down the hallway they proceeded, in a deeper dark, allied spies coming together in a rendezvous planned not by them but by a higher organizational structure, some network rumored to exist but never actually assembled. He, always a single step ahead, leading her by the hand, impossible to judge now where the anxious perspiring of one palm ended and the other began.

At the closed bedroom door, no pause for affirmation or final permission. Just an almost imperceptible squeeze of her hand as he opened the door and their bodies, already merging, spilled into the transmigratory light of the lone candle.

They removed their own clothing. This had been a ritual element of their past, and it had continued with subsequent lovers, despite the not-infrequent attempts by other players to break the flow of their irrepressible history.

Naked, they stepped into one another like bodies into a perfect equatorial waterfall, each stepping through to the other side, then turning and moving back into the cascade and staying there, one.

They fucked standing for several minutes, then went to the bed without disuniting. Again, despite the passion circulating furiously between them, there was, dancing at the edge of their respective horizons, a wondrous satisfaction in knowing the needs and wants of the other and articulating them before the need or want had bubbled to the surface.

In the hatha yoga each had dabbled with periodically in their original time together and in the intervening years, there was a position or a state of the body known as a baddha. It was a holding, a locking, a physical—and some would say metaphysical—binding of a part or parts of the body in the maintaining of a posture. Their flesh and bones and whatever prismatic energy flow existed inside them remained in such a baddha through the course of their lovemaking.

But as with all yoga practice, the baddha, the binding, is only transitory. No matter how adept the practitioner. His was the first half of the baddha to release. Hers followed within moments. And in the space of several seismic breaths, they were no longer Hindu deities on a temple wall in a lightning storm, but the perfectly real human beings they had tried so desperately to transcend.

SEVENTY-TWO

"Christ," he said, his voice low, thick, saturated. "I can't believe I forgot."

"Seems to me you didn't," Hewitt said, her own voice reedy, but equally sated.

They were lying on the bed, on their usual post-sex sides of the mattress. Usual, even after a fifteen-year interlude. His face was turned toward her. She continued to look up at the ceiling. Without turning away or taking his eyes off her face, Scott Gregory reached to the nightstand.

"No," he said as he picked up a remote. *"This."*

After a sweet, sad piano intro, sixty-five years of human history disappeared into the golden throat of a single saxophone.

Lying there naked, it was as if Hewitt could actually feel the breathing of Coleman Hawkins against her skin, and in some phrases, inside it. With her sensitivity exposed in such raw form, the notes, the passages touched, nudged, caressed and settled into her physical form.

The Body.

The Soul aspect was inextricably conjoined to the response of the body. But discernible only in those places where the body held one of its invisible trapdoors to the soul. The eyes. The throat. The brain stem. The spine. The sacrum. The palms of the hands. The soles of the feet.

She had never felt the song—any song—the way she felt this. And in her veins, her glands, far away from the higher brain functions, there were forming even then little crystals of panic. Coleman Hawkins was all over her. On top of her. Inside her. And she loved and feared it mortally at the same time. She knew exactly what it was, this feeling, exactly as she had experienced it once before, as every girl can experience it for the one and only first time. And she knew, from that moment on, just as she had known as a high school girl in her canopy bed, on a Friday after school when her daddy was working, that her body and soul would never be the same again.

While Hewitt navigated these thoughts, with her eyes still pressed to the ceiling, she had registered, peripherally, that her bedmate had finally drawn his eyes away from her and had, she could only assume, withdrawn into his own response to the song. When she turned to look at him, she could see, even in profile, that something had changed. Now it was his turn to feel her eyes on him. And when he looked at her, the haunted caves of his eyes made her suspect that this song didn't just belong to the two of them.

"There's a reason for this," he said, his bravado gone, replaced by a fuming exasperation. "I don't know how I can even bring this about . . . to explain. But the explanation exists."

He rolled his face away from her, returned to his own ceiling watch.

"If I'm your editor," Hewitt said, "right now I'm writing *just make your fucking point* in the margin."

"I couldn't agree more," he said. "Okay. But heads up."

This, she didn't like the sound of. Which made it a perfect fit with the reaction she felt when his face turned toward her again.

"A few years into my marriage, I fell into the pattern. I returned to the habit of . . ."

Out of words, the only thing left was a musical reference. So he nodded in the direction of the final bars of the Hawkins track as it continued to suffuse the air all around them.

Hewitt had a pretty good idea of where he was going. And though it was flattering in an inside-out way, her gut told her she didn't want to go there with him.

"To quote another song," he said. *"I thought about you."*

He had actually put a sense of music to the lyrics as he'd spoken them. And he did it again. *"I thought about you."*

He turned away momentarily, uttered his next words to the ceiling, or perhaps the sky. "You're the only other woman I would have ever married."

When he flipped his focus back to her, the face of the troubled adult had been replaced by a shy adolescent.

"Did you ever think about me?" the shy boy asked. And just like that she knew he had found the entrance to her *Cave of Deepest Secrets.*

"Why are we talking about this?" she stalled.

"Because we're here. We just made love. And it could have been you. It could have been us all along."

Hewitt answered with the only right answer there was. "Yes, I thought about you. I thought about you all the fucking time."

Waiting for his response, she felt regret over her decision to come to his place. What she would have given for a one-eyed cat to come slinking into the room to shift the energy, alter the mood, if even a little. But this was Scott's time to spill. He'd been through the death of a spouse. He'd just fucked an old flame. Now, in the pounding aftermath of his guilt, he was going to lay a wreath of contrition at his wife's grave.

"This is the first time," he said. "Since she died, this is the first time for me."

Naked in the cemetery with him, she figured the truth should be just as undressed. "If you want to talk about it," she said, "I don't have anything on my agenda until the sun comes up."

She felt his body give a little start. Somewhere in his nervous system, a train had jumped the tracks.

"If I'm going to get into this, I need a fucking smoke," he said.

He rolled onto his side, reached to the nightstand drawer and procured a pack and a lighter. He laid his head back on the pillow, mouthed a cigarette and, with an unsteady hand, lit it.

SEVENTY-THREE

Gabriel is dreaming, in the great green mortified fields of the sleep he loves, in his moments of lucidity, as a relief, a safe harbor, from the nightmares of his waking state. In his dreams there is no time, no pressure, no voice controlling him.

The voice cannot follow him here. In the great green field there is silence. But even in the dream, Gabriel knows the silence is only temporary. He has dreamed in this place before. And he knows that the sound of his mother's voice is out there. The bad voice. The terrible voice. The voice of the end of the world.

In the dream he is a little boy. His little-boy body is moving quickly through the green field, through the stalks and leaves of a plant that doesn't exist anywhere but inside the dream.

At first the cries are distant. So far away he can't even be sure they belong to his mother. The little boy in the dream doesn't know whose cries they are. The dreamer already knows.

Moving faster through the verdant growth. The crying growing louder. And he, the boy, like some lower mammal, some separated cub, loping across the wilderness in search of his mother's cries.

But this is not quite right. He is not the one in trouble. Alone, separated out as he is, there are no hyenas, no jackals, no carrion in this field. He is not the one in danger.

The crying intensifying, filling his ears, coating his face.

Traversing the great green field, ascending, no longer feeling his feet on the ground.

At the horizon now, in the center of his sharpening vision, he catches the first glimpse of the tall thin object with the circular top.

The feeling of his body is of flight now. Low, juvenile flight through and then just above the earthbound plants. Fixing his more powerful eyes on the thin form with the misshapen head, his flying becoming stronger, more confident. Yet inside the little-boy mind, the fear growing commensurately with the rising wind of flight.

He has become bird again. So many times in his waking state, the voice has told him, insisted upon the identity. *You are The Raven. Whether you wish it or not, you are The Raven.*

His body free of contact with the green field, he feels his arms, his wings, propelling him forward. His eyes, striking in their clarity now, focused on the thin crying entity at the far end of the field.

And now, approaching full freedom from the earth, he is able to make out the true identity of the screaming specter.

A sunflower. A lone sunflower standing against the pink-red sky. With the bonnet of petals to mimic a face, an idiot flower crying out in the voice of his mother.

It is several desperate snaps of his wings later when he sees the inconceivable union his dream, *his mind,* has created. On the face of the sunflower. Yes, there is no mistaking it now. The human features . . .

The eyes, half his, the nose as well. And the mouth, fully open and shrieking in a voice to which he can claim half-ownership.

His mother's living image. On the face of the sunflower.

Approaching it, her, at such a speed now. He fans the wings to slow his approach. And with a final tuck of his tail, he alights on the head of the sunflower, pulling with him the stalk and bending the entire plant sunward. Feeling then the spine of the plant springing back to its original disposition, and stopping, holding, with a shudder, not unlike a death shudder, and with not a single warble in the pitch and volume of the cry.

He perches here now. His claws buried in the top of the face, the cellulose brow. Feeling the vibrations, the meaning of the cries. Until he feels no other course than to open his own lungs and join her.

SEVENTY-FOUR

"Can a ghost make you feel guilty?"

A plume of exhaled cigarette accompanied *guilty,* and for a moment it seemed as if the swirling smoke was actually conspiring to spell the word in the sagging air above the bed.

"As far as I know that's one of the main reasons ghosts hang around," Hewitt said. "Is that what you're feeling. Guilty?"

"You're supposed to be the expert at reading people. What do my face-and-body language say to you?"

Hewitt reached over to him, touched the side of his face with her fingers, completed the gesture by brushing her index finger across his lips.

"My reading of that tells me you look like a guy who just got laid. And maybe you've got a little buyer's remorse."

"Do *you?*"

"No, I'm quite happy with my merchandise," Hewitt said. She reached out, did the index-finger-and-lip-thing again. "Now I guess I'm wondering if that comes with a warranty."

He drew on the cigarette, let the smoke inhabit his chest a while before releasing it. "That's one thing none of us gets, I'm afraid. A chance to trade in the people in our lives for a brand-new model that performs to our specifications."

Until then, the closest Rose Gregory had gotten to the recombinant lovers was the hallway outside the bedroom. Now she had not only infiltrated the room, but had come to sit at the foot of the bed.

"Sometimes a single flaw in the design can cause the whole thing to crash."

Scott Gregory looked at his cigarette quizzically, as if it had been the one that had uttered the statement rather than himself.

"I can only hope you're planning to explicate whatever the hell you're talking about," Hewitt told him.

He was up to the task, instantly.

"There were other men. Through the years. She didn't exactly make a secret of it. And when she fell ill, I stayed on. I stayed with her. And none of them ever came around for so much as a sniff of her dying."

Hewitt felt his body sag into the bed even more, felt her own body being pulled in the direction of that heaviness.

"I can understand your staying with her once she was sick," she offered. "But why didn't you leave earlier? Why did you stay?"

He turned, looked at her as if the reason should have been as obvious to her as the red hot burn of the tobacco at the tip of his inhalation. "Why do we remain in any difficult or painful situation? Why do you continue doing what you're doing? This business of death?"

"Because I believe in justice," Hewitt told him, her voice cutting through the smoke but having no influence in purifying it.

"Who's to say, in staying with her, I wasn't pursuing a form of justice myself?"

"What kind of justice is that?"

"Turnabout. It being fair play—as history often reminds us."

His eyes looked at her patiently while his mouth continued to pursue the nicotine aggressively.

"My own indiscretions," he said. "Back when indiscretion was the rule of law in my life."

Hewitt sat up in the bed, her body tensing for the first time since the last of the sexual releases. "What the hell are you talking about? Are you talking about me?"

"I'm talking about everyone. Everything. I'm talking about the pages of my fucking life. All the ones I can't ever go back and revise."

His cigarette was down to the end. He tried to draw one more hit from it anyway. Unsuccessful, he finally put the thing in the nightstand ashtray.

"I guess upon reflection I'd have to give you a resounding *fuck, yes,*" Hewitt said.

"To what?"

"Your initial question. Can a ghost make you feel guilty?"

To this he added nothing but smoky silence. Which left Hewitt alone with the one thought she didn't want to be thinking. That their crossing the line into intimacy had pushed him over the edge into all this—this dark foreign territory of his psyche.

"I loved you," he said, turning his face to her. "For that sweet sad season, that lovely year and a half. *I loved you*. And if I could have found a way to take that, to hold onto it. It might have been something else entirely. Something good. And real. And human."

The sound of his voice, the depth of his regret sent a reciprocal chill of regret through Hewitt.

"But it happened, didn't it?" she heard his low voice continue. "She had to go off that Goddamn roof. That crazy, impetuous little girl had to jump off that roof and take you with her."

"I knew Sarah Lee," Hewitt said. "Impetuous, I'll buy. But Sarah Lee wasn't crazy. I know the university, the media painted her that way. But I never bought it. Maybe I should have. But I couldn't."

"You believe someone pushed her, don't you?"

"Maybe. Or something went wrong in some kind of fucked-up prank. I don't know. The one thing I'm clear on is that she didn't jump with her own free will. You know I see her? Sometimes when I'm lying in bed. You know how people have that startle—that falling startle— as they're releasing into sleep. Well, my version of it, my falling startle, is seeing Sarah Lee falling, in that stupid witch costume. Falling. Never landing. Never hitting the ground. Just falling. Forever."

She'd been looking up at the ceiling, seeing it play out in her mind's eye one more time. When she took her eyes from the ceiling, she turned to look at her bedmate, saw he was regarding her with concern.

"When you see her, does she say anything? Does she call out to you?"

"Not in words," Hewitt answered. "But unspoken. There's a message. There's definitely a message."

"What does the message tell you?"

"It's a cry. A cry not to be forgotten. A cry for justice. I don't know any other way to interpret it."

"Are you sure it isn't God crying for justice through Sarah Lee's voice? The taking of one's own life being his one unforgivable sin?"

"Why do you refuse to accept my opinion that it wasn't a suicide?"

He turned, his eyes tightening. *Pain.*

"Because of that. That one incredible leap. And your leap of faith— to believing she died for your sins. That's what interjected—what did we decide it was—four thousand years between our last dalliance and this one."

Hewitt ran her hand across his midriff, stopped, pinched a curl of hair just below his navel and pulled it in a way that wasn't exactly playful.

"And how many millennia do you think will pass between Sarah Lee's last dalliance and her next one?"

Now it was his turn to apply the principles of finger-painting to her body. In this case her left nipple.

"You're right," he said. "At least we're still here. With our love to keep us warm, if nothing else."

"If Sarah Lee hadn't died," Hewitt posed, "how do know our thing would've survived? How do you know you wouldn't have found your way to Rose anyway?"

"I don't know that. All I know, Elizabeth, is that I'm sorry."

"For what?"

"For you being the only one I ever loved more than her."

His eyes drifted to the end of the bed, to the place where Hewitt had already positioned Rose Gregory on the down-turned quilt.

SEVENTY-FIVE

She had fallen asleep listening to him talk—listening, actually, to the sound of him talking to himself. It was the writer in him, the purveyor of this internal dialogue. That, and the stunned, remorseful husband. His response to his wife's sudden death could be described in a multitude of ways. And the sequence of events that night, while a matter of public record, could also be recounted via any number of literary interpretations. And for a time, lying next to him there in his crowded bed, without question feeling for him, his loss, his regret, she had done her best to hang in there.

But the bottom line was that she had just gotten laid, and quite well, and her nervous system was pulling her deeper into the sleep she craved. She kept telling herself not to let sleep happen. Though the sex had been everything she could have asked for, the post-sex stuff had gotten a little too weird—or at least too weird, too soon—for her to feel comfortable sleeping there for the night. So she made a deal with herself. With her consciousness lolling like a hopelessly drunken tongue at bar time, Hewitt made a deal with herself.

She would let herself have a little catnap. In a strange bed, she never slept long anyway before her mind sent her a warning flare that things didn't feel quite right. And Scott Gregory, worked up as he was, and hypnotized as he seemed by the sound of his own words, probably wouldn't even know she'd been gone. If he did notice, if she fell into heavy breathing to tip him off, then he would know it was time to give the story of his life a rest and give himself to the psychological salve of sleep.

Forty-two minutes later, a white streak of flame sketched itself across the backs of her retinas. Her eyes opened to the dark. And the silence. Which meant two things. The candle was no longer burning, and neither was Scott. Asleep beside her, with his mind mercifully detached from all of it, an unseen flame still seemed to burn in the room. And with him asleep, she was the only conscious attendant to the junta of grief that continued to rule the Gregory house.

She had to get out of there. Beneath the sheet, her hand walked the distance that separated it from his own hand.

If you were the only one with unfinished business I'd stay, she heard her inner voice tell him.

She located his sleeping hand, gently stroked the side of it. Sitting up, she turned toward him and her lips found his forehead. She left him with that. And he left her with a low, contented murmur, which told her he still had the tip of one oar in the sea of the senses.

She got out of the bed. He didn't stir. Before she went to retrieve her clothes, she surveyed for signs of any glowing embers left from his ridiculously rekindled habit of smoking in bed. She sniffed the air for any scent of smoldering. She detected neither. But she figured if she was going to do any of this again—and she was pretty much signed on now—it would be a good idea to keep him alive.

In the kitchen, she switched on a light, located some note cards and, on the lined side of one of them, wrote her message to him, excusing herself for stealing away into the night, blaming it on the conspiracy of madness in her life. She closed with a little joke—not easy to summon in the middle of the night: "Thanks for a smoking good time." She made no reference to the post-sex conversation. That, she figured, wouldn't help.

She finished with what, in a bad greeting card way, would have to pass for a positive sign-off. "Let's talk soon. Liz."

She placed the note card on the counter in front of his coffeemaker and let herself out of the house.

SEVENTY-SIX

Back in her own bed, Hewitt didn't think sleep would be possible. On the drive home, she had processed heavily—on both sides of her brain. On the one, her wild ride of an evening with Scott Gregory. On the other, the entirety of the case of Gabriel Rafferty, looming like a Thanksgiving parade balloon in a rainstorm, where the rain was blood-red and the balloon raven-black.

All of it, accompanied by the CD in the Mazda. *Birth Of The Cool.* She'd let "Boplicity" repeat a couple of times. The laid-back contra-puntal arrangements of Miles Davis and the octet. Offbeat West Coast cool in the middle of an insane Midwestern night.

So with all that swirling in her head when she finally laid down on her pillow, the idea of actually sleeping was the furthest thing from her mind. But that was mind talking. Her body, her *après*-orgasm body, had other ideas. And after twenty or so minutes of doing the whole world's thinking, body hit mind with a big cool wave and knocked down every last sand castle on Hewitt's beach.

She woke up twice during the night, with whirling thoughts of falling friends, wounded breasts, dead loved ones, and the very much alive one she'd just slept with. Each time she managed to stumble through the maze and return to the flat white beach of sleep. Her clock-radio woke her at 6:30.

She had a briefing with Spangler at HQ at 8:30, but she gave her-self a couple of eight-minute snooze cycles. And then she was up for good and into the next day of the nightmare. While she watched the water heating in the microwave, she could hear Shorty moving around in the living room. But with something different. Did he sound *heavier*? Was she feeding him too much?

With that notion and thoughts of the original dark bird flitting through her mind, she left the mug of hot water in the microwave and went to put on a warm-up and her walking shoes for her first morning excursion in days.

At the front door, she began to step outside when she had to catch herself to avoid stepping on a tissue-wrapped parcel of flowers that had been placed neatly in the center of her welcome mat. She picked them up, saw there was no note, no card.

She took the flowers inside, set them on the kitchen table, felt a little rush of sweetness at the scent of them. Roses. She would unwrap them and put them in a vase and call Scott and thank him when she returned from the walk. For now she was really craving the air, the exercise, the escape from reality, no matter how temporary.

The walk went off without incident. No new dead birds to report. The old one was still there. In its current state of decomposition. It would be some weeks before the steady march of microscopic nature would fully remove the thing. And then, magically, it would be as if it had never been there. No one else would know. And once Hewitt herself was subjected to the same march of nature, the only thing left would be the sands of time covering all of it in ever deepening layers.

Christ, that was some cheery thinking. Top-of-the-morning to you, too, Agent Hewitt. She had taken the walk for some physical exercise and ended up on a detour of fatalistic thinking. The last quarter mile, she managed to shed it, let her mind freshen, her thoughts clear, allowed her body to enjoy its warmth, gave her face, her eyes permission to relax.

At the front door, her softer eyes found the doormat, sketched the outline of the position of the tissue-wrapped roses. She had just enough time to get them in water, finish the Swiss Miss, make a piece of toast, eat, shower, groom, and hustle her ass to HQ.

And she had to call Scott, had to call him from home. It was flowers. A very special delivery. A call from the car wouldn't get it done. With that thought, she unlocked the door and entered the house, figuring Shorty would be there to greet her. To her mild surprise, he was not.

With the hum of the microwave reheating the water, she went to the kitchen table and unwrapped the flowers. It surprised her only mildly when she saw they were white. But that was cool, that was fine. White roses. A dozen white roses.

The microwave was chirping its final countdown at the same time her phone beeped the numbers to Scott Gregory's cell phone.

In the middle of the third ring, he picked up.

"Paradise Hotel," his mostly awake voice said into her ear.

"The only thing I'm not clear on is how you had them delivered so bright and early," Hewitt said. "But I don't give a shit. They're lovely. Thank you."

The pause that ensued was long enough to have given the sands of time enough time to bury them both. Unnerved as she was, Hewitt's eyes went for grounding to the flowers in the faceted green glass vase she'd put them in.

"Scott?"

She was counting the flowers.

"I'm afraid I don't know"—Scott's voice fading into the distance.

Eleven. Eleven white roses. One less than the full dozen she would have had if the white rose in Samantha Griggs' bedroom was added to the vase.

Hewitt felt the phone slipping from her hand, heard Scott's voice falling off the edge of the world.

She regained her grip on the phone, set it down soundlessly. Her ears froze against the silence of the house. Dead silence. Too dead.

Shit. The bathroom window. She'd left it partially open. To the right set of deranged eyes, a free pass to the funhouse.

Her service revolver was in the bedroom. Under the nightstand. She'd been smart enough to have done that. After practically inviting Rafferty over for pie and coffee in her on-camera tease.

If she bolted from the house, he might be waiting outside. He could've tailed her on the walk. If she tried for the bedroom, he might be waiting for her there.

She could hear Scott's voice calling to her from the abandoned phone, tiny electronic blips a million miles away.

She was moving through the kitchen, grabbing one of the carvers from the cutlery stand.

She was in the hallway, moving. Sleek. Slinky. Like the cat that was suddenly missing from her life.

At the door to the bedroom, she assumed the entry position, holding the carving knife like something that could actually fire a round of bullets.

She slipped into the room, her back finding the near wall. And then she felt herself in flight, rolling across the bed, hitting the floor, feeling under the nightstand, securing the weapon. Releasing the safety.

A noise.

From the closet.

The slightly cracked door beginning to swing open.

Zing-pop.

The bullet had blown a hole in the closet door. But it kept swinging open.

Opening . . .

Poised to fire at the body if it was still standing. But, Christ, no body. Just her fucking clothes hanging there. Already she was hoping she hadn't hit anything good.

She rose above the edge of the bed, saw, finally, the only thing that was there to be seen.

On the wood floor, in a puddle of its own pee, a shell-shocked one-eyed cat.

SEVENTY-SEVEN

Room by room she secured the condo. In every corner, in every shadow, she found the same thing. No Rafferty. No monster. No Raven.

On the grounds outside she did the same. With the same results. No imminent danger. But she knew in her rattled heart that the concept of imminence was purely relative now. Gabriel Philip Rafferty had not only set foot in her personal world, he had laid flowers at her feet. And the problem was that she was the one standing still. He was the one moving. And she was relegated to waiting for his next move.

Back inside, the service revolver holstered to her now, she mentally mapped Rafferty's most recent movements. It was difficult not to embrace a scenario in which Rafferty had been following her, at least to some degree. At least, she figured, to the previous night.

Shit. *Scott.*

She called his cell phone. Waited. Waited to freak until she absolutely knew it was the only response left.

No answer. No Goddamn answer. Which, of course, was the answer she feared most.

She threw her car coat on over her warm-ups, left the condo, locking it this time. In the car the only music she opted for was the drum kit in her brain, syncopating Elvin Jones–style around the downbeat of the thought that Scott was already in big trouble.

The parallels were screaming out over the whine of the Mazda engine. Starting with the white roses. But turning immediately to "The Rue Morgue." The Rafferty-Raven version of it. The one scenario that didn't fit with the others. The one with two victims. One of each sex. And sexual function had been the theme of the party. A two-way at first. Samantha Griggs and Kevin Kell. With the *ménage à trois* completed by an interloping psychopath.

Hewitt figured there had to have been a voyeuristic component to it. And something about what Rafferty had seen had pushed the creative intensity of his violence beyond any imagination. Except, of course, his.

The Elvin Jones drum solo filled her gallery of thoughts for the entire twenty-two minutes it took before her Mazda pulled into Scott Gregory's driveway. At the front door, she drew her revolver.

Bad news, straight-up. The door. Unlocked. Cracked open a couple of inches.

Again, the entry position, though her sinking heart kept her adrenaline from pushing to the level she'd felt in securing her own dwelling. And it was in securing Scott's kitchen that her heart hit the floor of the ocean.

On the table of the breakfast nook he'd once shared with his wife, Rose, a floral arrangement left for neither of them.

Lying flat on a red dinner napkin, the twelfth white rose. And an envelope. With her name on it. In the bold grandiloquent script she knew too well.

She opened the envelope, extracted the contents. A piece of inexpensive stationery, with more of the grandiloquent etchings, in black.

Welcome to the next outrageous chapter in your sweet story of public servitude, Agent Hewitt. It is a chapter you yourself have conceived and outlined. Now you shall compose the precious words and fantastic phrases. Or, shall I say, we will compose them together?

You should be proud to know that your lover did not allow himself to be taken without an admirable struggle. And in his protestations, your name was invoked more than once. Yes, Elizabeth, you should be proud of such a potent paramour.

Yet despite his most noble efforts, he has been taken. With my abiding admiration for true love in all its forms, I will offer you one final opportunity to look into his eyes and see his eyes looking back into yours.

You shall pay us both a visit today, at a residence on the outskirts of the lovely hamlet of Ringwood in the county of McHenry. Your travel instructions may be found below. Our appointment is scheduled for twelve noon. There is but one stipulation for your attendance. Attend alone. Any effort on your part to include uninvited guests will be met with the instant demise of your gallant gentleman friend. Again, I cannot underscore enough the need for you to be on your very best behavior.

We look forward to your arrival.

Gabriel

It was the worst-case scenario. Rafferty not only controlled the game; he could make up the rules as he went. All Hewitt could do was dance with him now, follow his lead. She could use every scintilla of her intelligence and intuition to anticipate his actions, his decision-making. But she would be the reactive one. And reacting even the slightest bit askew with this brutally unforgiving entity would mean *game over*.

Worst-case scenario. Well, actually it was second worst. Absolute worst would have been if Rafferty had killed them both while they dozed in Scott's bed the night before.

He was planning to do it now, of course. Making this sick game of it to challenge, to amuse himself. Since the moment she had taken the case, but especially since she had offered herself as a prize to him, the notion had been crawling up and down the back wall of her skull.

What if?

What if Rafferty did take the bait? What if he did decide to look her way, to feast his eyes on her?

There were any number of Poe scenarios still untapped in the anthology of atrocity. It wasn't a question of whether he would attempt to make her a character in one of those remaining tales. It was only a question of which one.

SEVENTY-EIGHT

It is not quiet in the hovel. By no human measurement can it be considered quiet. Yet a quiet has come to him, a sense of stately peace, of having influenced the unfolding of events to the point of utter predictability. It is not quiet in the hovel. The persistent yelling of the other voice has precluded any possibility of that.

Sitting at the writing desk, he is unperturbed by this. He watches the drops of anisette as they fall from the spoon.

One.

Two.

Three.

Four.

Five.

Six.

And, with a gentle tap on the handle, seven.

Who is The Raven? It is a question he has been posing to himself for some time now.

He allows himself the first sip of the anisette coffee. Appreciative of its proper balance, he awards himself a second sip.

Who is The Raven? Were the beverage in his cup reflective, he would be staring at the answer right now. Or, he would be staring at the visage of the answer. But the coffee is opaque. And his face is not reflected in its surface. And the voice continues to call from the adjacent room. And the hovel is not quiet. It is nowhere near quiet.

I am The Raven.

He sees the words on the black slate board of his mind. But by the time his mind's voice articulates them, he hears the words not in his voice alone but in the voice of the other who is also alone inside, abjectly so.

If any being understands what it is like to be truly alone, it is him. It is *them*.

He is writing now, writing these words on a new page of the journal.

We are The Raven. We are the only souls who possess the inner peace to perch impassively above the madness, above the cacophony, to observe, to bear silent witness to what we see, to all we unwittingly hear.

Our mothers were good souls. Angelic souls. They were corrupted by the forces of earth that corrupt even the angelic with the power to debase, to pervert angelic song into the howls of demons, forces with such power as to rupture the umbilical bond between mother and son, forces that render the sons of such mothers forsaken, relinquished, alone.

Alone . . .

Alone . . .

He sees the hateful-beautiful title of the composition in his mind. He hears his own voice beginning the recitation.

From childhood's hour I have not been

The next line has scarcely begun when he hears the other voice join him in the recitation. The slightly stilted, scholarly voice with its veneer of darkness, its waver of worldly detachment. *Edgar's voice.*

As others were—I have not seen
As others saw—I could not bring
My passions from a common spring—

They are, at the first, a bit uneven in their vocal union, clearly the sound of two voices speaking. Yet as they continue to bring forth the phrases, the voices begin to find a common rhythm, a common tone and, increasingly, a common purpose.

From the same source I have not taken
My sorrow—I could not awaken

My heart to joy at the same tone—
And all I lov'd—I lov'd alone—

They are falling into place now, the way they have fallen into place before, each time, synchronizing as if by grand design.

Then—in my childhood—in the dawn
Of a most stormy life—was drawn
From ev'ry depth of good and ill
The mystery which binds me still—

The union perfecting, purifying itself now, syllable by syllable. The voice of the writer and the one for whom the words were truly written.

From the torrent, or the fountain—
From the red cliff of the mountain—
From the sun that round me roll'd
In its autumn tint of gold—

Impossible to shine even the most brilliant light between the seams of the voices now. For they are no longer voices. They are one voice.

From the lightning in the sky
As it pass'd me flying by—
From the thunder, and the storm—
And the cloud that took the form
When the rest of heaven was blue
Of a demon in my view.

And as the single voice recedes and evanesces into the undulating wake of the poem, the hovel is filled with the sounds which emanate from the next room, the sounds that have been passing through the wall throughout the recitation.

But the reciters of the poem are together now as one. Alone together in the body, the personage of *The Raven*. And as such, they are
above it all, looking down from a stately perch with utter detachment,
eyes gleaming in repose, mouth offering just the slightest suggestion of
a grin.

SEVENTY-NINE

It was quiet in the car. As quiet as a life could be. The rational cop inside her kept peppering her with the same message. *This is a tough call. This is a tough call. This is a tough call.*

All other aspects of her mind were telling her there was no decision at all. The call had already been made. She could arrange a stealth backup. But only if stealth meant actually invisible. Anything less than actually invisible ran the risk she knew she couldn't afford to run.

Rafferty had Scott. Her rekindling of the relationship had given Rafferty access to Scott. If Rafferty killed Scott, it was on her. If she followed Rafferty's instructions and he ended up killing Scott, well at least she'd done everything in her capacity to stop it. If it went down with Rafferty killing them both, then she and Scott would pass through the turnstiles together.

On the McHenry County map she found Ringwood and followed the yellow brick road of her directions until they squeezed down and petered out at the end of Jonquil Road and what appeared to be an unnamed, unpaved road after that. For a moment her mind speculated on what she might find there, what kind of Edgar Allan Poe scenario Rafferty had in store for her. For the first time, her thinking entered the box she knew had been waiting there all along.

The Premature Burial.

She felt the panic run up her back like a million cold spiders. It was the thing she feared most. The thing she couldn't let herself think about. Staring at the map, it was the one thing she couldn't get away from.

She took out her phone, turned it on, checked her messages. Among them, three from an increasingly angry and then anxious Ed Spangler. The eight-thirty briefing. It was a thousand miles in her rearview mirror now.

Among the other messages was one from the state crime lab. The confirmation of what, in her mind, had been a foregone conclusion from day one. The semen from Samantha Griggs' eye cavity—a DNA match with the Rafferty tissue sample.

Not that it mattered. Not that it helped. Not that sitting there in the Mazda, looking at the map of the next hours of her life, it changed a Goddamn thing. In a way, it only made it worse. A reminder of what he was capable of, what the species she still belonged to was capable of.

She had to take him out. She had to cleanse the species of him. She'd been given this opportunity for a reason. It was down to this. One on one against The Raven. Right now it was the best chance the species had.

She had to take him out.

The cell phone went off. Spangler. She took the call. Not because she wanted to hear what he had to say. She just wanted to hear his voice. No matter what it said.

"Hewitt, what the fuck is going on?"

"Could you please rephrase the question into one I can answer?"

"We had an eight-thirty today. After our public offering yesterday, we've had a hell of a lot of responses. But apparently that isn't—-"

"None of them matter," Hewitt cut him off. "He communicated with me this morning."

"You talked to Rafferty?"

"I received a message from him. With an offer."

"Christ, Hewitt. Don't tell me you're even considering doing something without backup."

"I made a deal with myself," she said.

"You don't make deals with people like this, Hewitt!"

"What can I say—I did."

"Well, then you can just break your fucking deal!" Spangler detonated. "God almighty, how long do you think it would take Rafferty to break a deal? Try a nanosecond. One twitch of his brain the minute he doesn't like the way things are going."

"I've thought about that," Hewitt said calmly. "And I'm willing to put my ass out there. These other girls have sacrificed more."

She heard him suck in all the air in his office.

"Jee-Zus Christ, Hewitt! You've made the cardinal mistake. You've let it get personal. You, Rafferty, what he did to those women. It's not your job to avenge them. Your job is to deliver justice, Hewitt. Justice is the best you can do. The rest is up to God."

"Maybe just this once," Hewitt heard herself say, "God could use some help."

EIGHTY

The Raven sits calmly at the writing desk, the slight suggestion of a grin permanently fixed now. In a moment or two he will cross the hovel to the closet and begin to dress for the reception. He will don the ruffled shirt, the breeches, the shoulder cape. When all is in place, he will turn his attention to the facial adornment.

In the next room, the ballroom, his first guest of honor has already been prepared. He is standing on his chair, the rope tight around his neck, a bag over his head to spare his keeper from his pathetic facial expressions. The bag, however, does not mask the pathetic cries.

He knows now, knows what is coming. He knows there is nothing he can do to stop it. He knows that tomorrow the world will go on, but he will not be going on with it. Nor will he receive word from the world the following day. Or any of the days that will fall from the sky like the leaves of autumn are falling in the winds that whistle now against the outer walls of the dwelling.

Of course, he could silence the cries at any time. The temptation is swirling all around, utterly pervasive, curling into his ears, his nostrils, tapping against the meat of his face, pulling on the skin around his eyes. He could quell the disturbance prematurely. Certainly, the world would be an improved place without this belabored bellowing.

Yet belabored bellowing is a small price to pay for a first-row seat to the performance of a lifetime. Besides, who can blame the poor fool? Now that the noose is around his neck, the dark bag over his head. Now that the delicate Victorian chair beneath his feet is all he has left of the terra firma of earthly existence.

The Raven knows he would do the same. Were the tables turned, were it him, his visions, his dreams of moral recompense that were about to be expunged from the world. He would bellow in protest too. But his visions, his dreams are alive and well.

It is the best way to consider one's life and living in the world. As a dream. Perceived in this manner, life becomes so much more challenging, stimulating, alive. In our dreams we are much more likely to take the bold actions we crave. We are much more likely to confront our demons, to stare our fears deep in their dark dismal eyes.

The world is my dream, and I its dreamer. May all who encounter these words know the truth or the truthfulness of the teller.

The Raven sets down his pen and reads the last of what he has written in the journal. Pleased, he turns to the beginning of the volume, to the first page, the page he has left blank through the many weeks of his composing.

In a robust, antique script he pens the title.

For Edgar.

EIGHTY-ONE

She'd had no choice but to hang up on Spangler. She had never hung up on a superior in her career. But her career had never taken her here before. To this precipice. To this thin ribbon of highway, with life's vanishing point up ahead and death riding in the backseat, dozing, for the moment, in a bumpy sleep.

She was on the road, and that was the only place she could be now. She couldn't go home. Knowing Spangler, he would stake out not only her condo but every coffee and hot chocolate dispensary within a ten-mile radius. She couldn't go home. And it hit her then, like a glockenspiel strike against her bones, that she might never go home again.

She couldn't go there, either. Not that thought. She checked the backseat. Death was still dozing.

Fuck him. Fuck death.

It was an hour and a half until the rendezvous—if she adhered to Rafferty's schedule. What if she showed up early? It would give her the element of surprise. Or would Rafferty flip the tables on her? Would he have a surprise waiting for her if she failed to follow the program? He was a super-achiever when it came to realizing his ambitions, acting out his fantasies. He had no doubt planned this one down to the last detail, too. Screwing with his raging dreams at this point ran the risk of making things worse. For Scott. For her. For the species.

She forced herself to squeeze her thoughts into a semblance of perspective. She had put herself on public display, shopped herself to a killer for one reason. To flush Rafferty out of his nineteenth-century fantasy hole long enough for just one shot at him. One face-to-face shot at him. If someone—God, for example—had offered her that deal a week ago, she would have signed on the dotted line. In great big cursive letters. In her own blood. The only pisser, and it was as big as it got, was the collateral she'd been forced to give up. If Scott Fitzgerald Gregory, in hostage form, had been part of the deal, she would have walked away. But there was no walking now. There was only the hour drive to Ringwood. And the half hour to kill in between. A half hour to kill, without attracting the attention of any of her mobile trooper colleagues from ISP.

How the hell had it come to this? And how the hell had it come to the truck stop she was eyeing up the road as the place where she could kill two of the three things she needed to kill that day in order to hang on to her own life? One, they would have hot water and some form of powdered chocolate. So she could eliminate her craving for that. Two, the truck stop would have a sticky table and crummy plastic chair where she could park herself for the amount of time she needed to kill.

For the third killing, the truck stop couldn't help. But she already had everything she needed for that. Her brain. Her body. Her service revolver. And any luck the forces of goodness could send her way, she'd be happy to take that along, too.

It wasn't until she walked into the truck stop that the magnitude of her undertaking hit her. There they were, the best of the brawniest, sitting there, eating, reading, sucking coffee, coming down off speed, or ramping up on more. Eyeing her like a French poodle stepping into a dog pound. And Hewitt knew that not a one of them, maybe not even the best tag team in the bunch would have had a chance in hell against The Raven in a head-to-head.

He would skin them, butcher them, and turn them into truck stop chili before they knew what hit them.

The son of a bitch had Scott. *The son of a bitch had Scott.*

She made her way to a table against the far wall in the back, a table that she quickly understood was open because of its proximity to the rest room. But she was a desperate woman in a truck stop. In no position to be choosy.

She sipped hot chocolate, nibbled at something resembling an American cheese sandwich and ate the two bananas she'd procured from the food-mart area.

She was down to the dregs of the hot chocolate and considering getting another when the truck driver at the next wall-table down from the bathroom swirled his ice water and addressed her.

"You're the one from the state police. The one chasing this son-of-a-bitch lunatic."

"I'd be lying if I said I wasn't," Hewitt told him. "And state officials aren't supposed to lie to the people who pay our salaries."

That got a sarcastic laugh from the guy, and from a couple of the others who were also within earshot.

The original guy lost his amused look then all at once, as if a wiper blade had made a pass over his face. "So how the hell is it going?"

"You want the truth there, too?"

"That's up to you."

"I'm close," Hewitt told him. "I'm getting real close."

EIGHTY-TWO

Hewitt's conversation with the trucker, though brief, had created enough interest among the gathered brethren that she had gotten out of there, quickly, quietly.

A thought had occurred to her, asinine as it probably was, but plausible enough to have spooked her. What if Spangler had put out an interdepartmental version of an Amber Alert—a *That Stupid Bitch Hewitt* Alert. Who was to say a trucker might not have caught wind of that? Truckers. Troopers. They were shipmen on the same sea.

She was in that same briny sea now. She had her coordinates. She knew where she was going. She wasn't going there at ninety miles an hour, though. That was the damn irony again. After speeding through her life in the pursuit of truth and justice since the day Sarah Lee Hooker died, in this, her ultimate pursuit, she had all the time in the freaking world.

The speed of her driving, the pace, this normal way reminded her of someone else, the way he drove. She glanced in the rearview mirror, saw him sitting there. On the passenger side of the backseat. He gave her his smile, the smile her dad always offered when things were shitty but somehow you had to keep going.

Her father hadn't replaced death in the backseat. Death was still there, sitting right behind her now. But with her dad back there, too, she felt a little better about it. Maybe her dad could get death's attention with one of his long rambling stories. Maybe he could get death into a debate over the greatest game in Rose Bowl history. Throw in a cheese plate and a pitcher of beer, and the old man could keep death occupied for hours.

No music on the stereo. She had impulses during the drive. But she couldn't settle on anything. Until it struck her. The only track that qualified.

"Little Girl Blue." The Joplin version.

Sit there counting your fingers. What else is there to do?

At five miles under the speed limit on Highway 120 West, with Dad and Death riding shotgun, with her mind in a deadly *ménage à trois* with Scott Gregory and Gabriel Rafferty, Hewitt began to dream of how she would kill the one and save the other. And in so doing she became, for the rest of the drive, the dreamer and not the dreamed.

EIGHTY-THREE

There is wondrous irony in the fact that his guest has abandoned his unintelligible hollering and has rallied his mind and voice around the words of Poe. And of all things to choose to recite by rote in that quivering, quavering voice, "The Bells."

Brilliantly apropos for a man standing at the edge of the abyss, at the final hour. This is his announcement. This is how he proclaims himself. This pitiable attempt to impress his keeper.

Yet The Raven is impressed. Dressing himself in front of the mirror, he pauses now to listen to the words that come from the next room, from a reciter already halfway to the next world.

The doomed soul has just entered the second section of the poem.

"Hear the mellow wedding bells. Golden bells. What a world of happiness their harmony foretells . . ."

Does his guest conjure some such wedding event within the darkness of his bagged head? In the voice, there is the glimmer of wistfulness.

"Through the balmy air of night. How they ring of their delight! From the molten-golden notes and all in tune. What a liquid ditty floats, to the turtle-dove that listens while she gloats, on the moon!"

The voice has moved from wistfulness to a tone on the edges of warmth.

"Oh, from out the sounding cells, what a gush of euphony voluminously wells! How it swells! How it dwells, on the future, how it tells of the rapture that impels . . ."

Yes, there, upon the reference, rapturous overtones infusing the voice.

"To the swinging and the ringing of the bells, bells, bells! Of the bells, bells, bells, bells, bells, bells, bells. To the rhyming and the chiming of the bells!"

At this, the end of section two, the recitation ceases. The Raven is left to wonder if, in the dark confinement of the head bag, this sudden explosion of rapture has been too much.

Yet just at the moment a melancholia begins to sweep over The Raven, a sense of loss over the cessation of the poem, the voice rises again.

"Hear the loud alarum bells, brazen bells! What a tale of terror, now, their turbulency tells!"

What is at first a small comfort in the return of the reciter becomes a disquieting rumor in The Raven's thoughts. He must complete his dressing. The costume has already been three-quarters applied. His second special guest will be arriving soon.

He does not have time to tarry over the mad oratory of this false professor. Yet imagining the completed costume on his person is all The Raven can do as he looks at his image in the mirror and listens to the voice on the other side of the wall.

The pitch, the timbre, the quality of the voice so steadfast now, so confident, so very nearly boastful in its conviction. He must complete his preparation. His next guest must be mere minutes away. But the voice from the parlor compels him to pay heed with his burning ears.

"Of the bells, bells, bells, bells, bells, bells, bells. In the clamor and the clangor of the bells."

Here again, at section's end, the reciter pauses. To reflect upon the words? Or, to allow his listener to reflect. He will resume the poem, of course. Surely he will continue. To leave Poe's final poem three-quarters finished would be a pity.

He absorbs his image in the mirror. He is but moments away from completing his preparations. His next guest is en route. Yet the completion of the poem will take precious little time. Once it begins again. When it begins. Surely it will begin.

An awful thought moils up from his heart. Perhaps by some calamitous intervention the reciter has lost his footing and slipped from the chair prematurely. With the stage so exquisitely set, what a tragedy this would be. With a voice so rare in its interpretation, its empathy, its belief in the words of the poet. He turns from the mirror, begins to step toward the parlor door.

He hears a throat clear. An unconstricted throat. Ah! Section three.

"Hear the tolling of the bells, iron bells. What a world of solemn thought their monody compels! In the silence of the night, how we shiver with affright at the melancholy menace of the tone."

Rhapsodic now the voice. Deepening in tone, conviction, truth. The mouth and throat widening. The mind arcing between the century and a half gone by and this rendering in the absolute moment, in the parlor, in the darkness of the black silk bag.

"They are neither man nor woman. They are neither brute nor human. They are ghouls. And their kind it is who tolls."

Behold, yes, how he embodies it now. The voice itself—neither brute nor human. But the voice of the ghoul. The king of ghouls.

"And he rolls, rolls, rolls, rolls, a paean from the bells! And his merry bosom swells with the paean of the bells! And he dances and he yells, keeping time, time, time, in a sort of Runic rhyme—to the paean of the bells, of the bells."

The throat of the reciter nothing less than gaping now. The resonance shaking the oak door that separates the rooms, creating prismatic radiation within the glass of the faceted doorknob. The voice, lowing, throbbing like some diaphanous creature of long-buried myth now come to life. Some man-beast. With human face. Leonine throat. Poet's heart.

The Raven listens, thrills to the recitation of the final lines.

"Keeping time, time, time, as he knells, knells, knells, in a happy Runic rhyme, to the tolling of the bells. Of the bells, bells, bells. To the tolling of the bells. Of the bells, bells, bells, bells, bells, bells, bells. To the moaning and the groaning of the bells."

Silence from the parlor. Silence in the composition room. Silence returned to the century and a half of reticulated memory.

The Raven considers what he has just heard, doubts that in the years since the words of the poem dripped from Poe's pen, has anyone delivered a more inspired recitation. As if, he thinks, as if some phantasmagoric aspect of Poe himself has visited the inner core of the doomed man in the black hood.

Did Poe know "The Bells" was his final poem? A voice inside The Raven says yes. Does the doomed soul in the black hood know these are his own last words? He knows there is no alternative. There will be no last-minute reprieve from the voice that governs this narrative. No hands of benevolence to reach out and lift the dark veil of eternity from his face.

No, the poem is over, and so, too, the life of its purveyor.

Yet no sooner has the narrator crystallized this notion when its subject initiates a defiant rebuttal.

"Of the bells, bells, bells, bells, bells, bells, bells."

The voice of the doomed soul calling desperately from the other side.

"To the moaning and the groaning of the bells."

Repeating with greater fervor, in a tone almost mocking. The Raven, concentrating in the mirror, pulling the cape over his shoulders.

"Of the bells, bells, bells, bells, bells, bells, bells. To the moaning and the groaning of the bells!"

The voice of the reciter has gone beyond the sphere of earth and its creatures. The Raven adjusts the collar of his shirt. His hands tremble. The cloth laughs at his clumsy attempt to control it.

The voice from the other side of the wall thunders anew.

EIGHTY-FOUR

The blue Mazda has taken Hewitt as far into the rural acreage as it will be able to. A white pine tree is down on the overgrown dirt road, freshly fallen. Hewitt assumes, freshly cut.

She will have to make the rest of the way on foot. She must also make one final tactical decision, a decision which she has left to herself, but one which Captain Spangler influenced in their parting conversation. The part where he insisted that she contact them with her coordinates if and when she reached The Raven's nest. The part where she had implied she would.

Hewitt shuts off the car. Before the engine fan completes its last revolution, the Spangler contact question is gone, eclipsed by the sound coming from the distance and gripping Hewitt's ears through the open car window.

It is a howling human voice, pushed beyond human capacity. A voice she cannot recognize from its sound, but which she knows intimately from its source. A yelling male voice, repeating words she doesn't understand as she steps from the car and adds her own running feet and pounding breath to the cacophony.

What white disc of sun may have still been cutting through the clouds is lost to the great volume of trees and underbrush that threaten now to absorb Hewitt. She runs what feels like a hundred yards, probably more. When she reaches the place where the walls of vegetation begin to recede, she has already informed herself that Rafferty felled the pine tree to make her do exactly this. To approach on foot, in the open.

At the clearing that exposes the vestige of a Victorian country house, Hewitt pauses. Out of the valence of her own labored sounds of approach, she is assaulted once more by the monstrous voice that cries out from the dwelling. The nausea that hits her at the sound of it is so strong it pushes tears from the ducts of her eyes.

She scans the terrain for a route by which she can approach the house without being seen. But the house sits naked in nothing more than high grass and dying goldenrod. Hewitt strains to decipher the tortured bellowing. It is the rhythm of the words she recognizes first. An eternity of a moment later, she recognizes the words themselves. The words that confirm what her guts and her tears already know.

"Of the bells, bells, bells, bells, bells, bells, bells . . .

To the moaning and the groaning of the bells . . ."

Hewitt shudders at the honking madness of the voice. She fights through the revulsion, knowing that under the incalculable duress, Scott's mind has already been ruptured, bled. The voice tells her that. She knows the one responsible for the vocal mutations is watching for her through one of the windows. But she sees no other action to take than a sprint across the tall grass and an assault on the building.

She draws her gun, takes a moment to find her center, to steady her breath.

From the hell house, the terrible voice continues its deranged tolling.

"Of the bells, bells, bells, bells, bells, bells, bells . . .

To the moaning and the groaning of the—"

Hewitt's heart begins to plummet into the abyss as the voice is suddenly swallowed by its own throat. The tongue flapping against the walls of the mouth. The sounds of asphyxiation. Of strangulation.

Of hanging.

Hewitt feels the whipping of the tall grass against her legs. Seconds more and the Victorian house greets her with the sound of her shoes against the planks of the porch steps.

She stops. Checks the door. Open. He wants her to come in. Anticipating an assault the moment she steps inside, Hewitt slams the door inward with all her force, brandishing the weapon. Her eyes absorbing everything. But seeing nothing.

The downstairs is an empty, gutted shell. The thought streaks through her mind that the interior decorating has been saved for the second floor. In the brief interval in which she freezes to listen, she can no longer hear the gasping, strangling sounds. But she hears the sound of weight pulling, struggling, against a support beam upstairs, the creaking of old wood freshly disturbed.

And then, the rolling thud of an object against the floor above her.

A shoe kicked off in the struggle, she tells herself as she moves to the staircase. At the top of the stairs, another door, unlocked. Leading with her firearm, Hewitt enters the upstairs, enters another century.

In a camera flash she absorbs the contents of the room. The writing desk. The chest of drawers. The dressing mirror. The photos on the wall. The five victims. In two rows. Three on top. Two on the bottom. With a space for another.

In the last photons of the visual flash, Hewitt registers the door to another room. The floor creaks abominably as she crosses the room. This last door, also left unlocked.

Assuming the entry pose.

Entering.

In her next heartbeat, the outside world is vaporized and she is inside the crimson bag, looking out through the eyeholes of her own skull at a red world illuminated by a single translucent membrane at the far wall, a membrane the seeming texture of skin.

And she is not alone. The red world is populated by human figures standing erect, unmoving. Costumed entities from another time. Each in its own period costume and topped with its own garish mask. The bodies are turned to face the center of the room, the center of the masquerade, where a man she has loved hangs by a rope from the ceiling, his feet offering their last twitches as Hewitt churns through the lane that has been left open by the guests for her approach, stowing her gun as she does.

From the corner of her eye, she sees the chair kicked over, swings down to grab it with one hand while she uses her free arm to grab Scott Gregory by the legs and lift him, raise him in the vestments he has been placed in, to lift his windpipe free of it all, to displace the tongue of death that has snaked past his own and slithered halfway to his soul.

His feet on the chair now, she is climbing onto the chair with him, their feet intermingling as if in drunken dancing, holding one another up at the last dance of humankind. She is face-to-face with him. His face covered by this hideous veneer. His hands are tied behind him. And his lifeless shoulders sag into Hewitt's upper body.

She absorbs his weight with her left arm and the entire left side of her body. With her right arm, she pulls the gun from her side pocket. She raises the gun, presses the barrel against the taut length of rope, fires.

The first blast kills only half the rope. She fires again, taking out a second piece of ceiling directly beside the first one. In the slow-motion mode into which her fight-or-flight mind has shifted, the plaster falls like confetti in the bloody light.

The rope turns, pulls, the last of its threads separating under the weight of Scott Gregory's body. And as the heaviness of the unconscious body hits Hewitt, her dancer's feet fight to hold the chair, her gun spills from her hand. With his full weight bearing down on her, her ankles wobble, the collective weight of the dance team shifts, and the couple falls in slow-motion to the floor, the male by gentlemanly fate landing on his back to cushion the female who falls face-down on top of him.

Before their bodies have come to a rest, Hewitt knows something in her reading of reality is horribly flawed. She pushes herself up from the masquerading body and lifts the blood-streaked mask from the face of the man she had been willing to die for.

In the grievous light, the condition of the face makes her gasp. The identity of it implodes her mind.

Rafferty.

She feels The Raven's neck for a pulse. Finding none, she feels no compulsion to attempt to regenerate one. Moments earlier she would have blown his brains out at the drop of a hat. Now, shit . . .

He is already dead. A victim of his own twisted interpretation of "The Masque of the Red Death."

On his face are the bloody red lines created to mimic the symptoms of the plague in Poe's tale. As to whether the blood is real or faked, she has no interest. The Red Death is real. Real enough to have killed The Raven.

But why, Hewitt asks herself, why would he make this his exit, his ending? She speed-reads through her recollection of the story. The Prince Prospero had cloistered himself and his courtiers away at an endless gala in order to seal themselves off from the ravages of the Red Death. In the end, the prince himself falls victim to the disguised infiltration of the plague in the person of a masked stranger. He falls dead in a blood-illumed room, with his party guests all around.

Hewitt has returned to standing. She has retrieved her service revolver and returned it to the shoulder rig. Gabriel Rafferty continues to lie dead at her feet, surrounded by the contingent of mask-wearing mannequins, each in its own garish period costume.

The bad brain had been busy. It had been a hell of a production, only to close with this shocker of a finale.

Maybe that was it. The ultimate surprise ending. Or maybe it was the ultimate in the paying of homage. Perhaps later, under the bright white lights of the coroner, they would find the words *For Edgar* carved on the dead killer's heart.

She would love to have some of the coroner's bright white light with her now in this dismal red room. Dismal, yet with enough crimson glow to illuminate the mannequins and their grotesque masks. With Rafferty dead on the floor, it was Hewitt who had unwittingly become the focus of their interest, positioned as they had been to witness the final act of their beloved prince.

Now it was the princess upon whom their eyes were trained. If they had eyes. If dead souls were granted eyes by their creator. With the masks obscuring whatever faces were behind them, it was impossible to tell.

Yet with or without eyes, she felt the gaze of them. These bizarre, spectral creations. Together, all of them, in their animated poses, the cocking of an arm here, the turning of a neck there. Like the impressive but grotesque countenance of carousel horses at rest. At rest, yet poised to leap into exaggerated gallop the moment the music began to play, their world to turn, their wooden hearts to beat.

As dead as The Raven lies at her feet, these subjects of his seem as if to have acquired life, or at least the breath of it.

Breath. Yes. As if she can feel the unmistakable presence of it.

Of breathing.

In her mammalian core, there is a firing of signals to her nervous system. The sluice to her adrenaline is thrown open. The impulse of flight careens along her spine and the bones of her limbs. But even as her muscles begin to respond, there is a physical response from an entity in the room.

A movement of a torso, a turning of a mask.

A mannequin, springing to life. Hewitt grabs for her service revolver from the inner holster. She fumbles, her fingers slipping against the colder-than-the-rest-of-the-world metal. She feels the first contact of the entity's clothing against her own. In the same instant she draws her gun and fires and blows the head off the attacker, the mask flying loose and spinning through the red air in the slow-motion registry of her mind.

The rest of the attacker crashes into her. And it is all horribly wrong, horribly artificial. Desperately, she pushes the false entity off of her at the same time she feels the pull of a length of rope against her side hip.

She realizes, in screaming detail, the gravity of her error as, from behind, a pair of costumed but very much alive and very much familiar arms grab her, and a gloved hand presses a chloroform rag through the openings of her face and into her brain.

EIGHTY-FIVE

Sarah Lee is falling. In the endless ether. Toward a bottomless death. A death without an ending.

Sarah Lee is falling through the glowing black fog of Hewitt's mind. She can see her, see her face. Her eyes are open, but they do not call out. The mouth of the falling witch opens, and Hewitt's inner ears brace for the scream she knows is coming.

But the scream does not come. And in its place is a sound Hewitt has not heard since the night Sarah Lee first began to tumble through her dreams.

Sarah Lee Hooker is singing. She is singing something Hewitt heard her sing only once, drunk at the Halloween party at their apartment, on a dare from her. It was a piece she'd sung numerous times as a solo in her youth choir back home in Black Earth. It was the last thing Sarah Lee would ever sing.

As she falls inside the great, black velvet tunnel, Sarah Lee Hooker is singing the "Ave Maria." Sarah Lee is singing the "Ave Maria" to her. And the sense of it is that she is not singing it for her roommate's pleasure. She is singing it for her roommate's enlightenment.

The first bubbles of Hewitt's consciousness effervesce up and out of the chemical darkness. A blanket of absolute dread opens, billows, and covers her completely. She struggles to open her eyes, struggles more to move her arms and legs.

There is darkness on the other side of her eyelids. Slowly, with concentrated effort, her eyes open to what at first appears to be the dark ether of death. But there are stars in the sky of the dead. Familiar stars.

Her mind starting to clear now, she begins to connect the light of those multitudinous glowing bodies. And by so doing, she connects the dots into the inconceivable pattern that has led her to be here, in this oblong box, in the middle of a nightmare, looking up at the night sky.

At the edges of her peripheral vision, she senses the shape of an earthly constellation. *The Great Dark Bird.*

"You killed Sarah Lee," she hears a voice say, a voice that could be hers if it wasn't so fractured, so dry, so close to its own death. "You killed Sarah Lee. You took her up to the roof. To hear it. To hear her scream."

The Raven's refusal to move from the peripheral shadows makes the shadows even darker, colder, more inconceivably real.

"You heard her sing that night. At our party. She was drunk. She was singing "Ave Maria." You heard her voice. And hearing her sing made you want to hear her voice pushed all the way out of her. It was screaming, Sarah Lee's screaming you wanted to hear. To satisfy whatever the hell you're trying to satisfy."

Silence from The Raven. Hewitt's eyes detect a slight movement in the shadows. She hears a heavy sigh from him, a long grace note before he speaks.

But it is not words that articulate his response. It is a series of sighs. With intervals. Pitch. With a rhythm. Humming. In the range of a tenor sax. Humming. Humming . . .

She lets him have this, lets him have the melody. But she refuses to let him have the music.

"You killed Sarah Lee while I was asleep in your bed. You went back to the apartment. You knew she had a thing for you. And you lured her up to the roof."

The soloist pauses briefly at the end of the accusation, but continues undeterred.

"Is that when it started? Was Sarah Lee the first? Or were there others? Others before this spree of yours. What set you off? Was it Rose? Did she scream for you, too? Did you make Rose scream?"

He is into the Hawkins solo now, humming it by rote at about half-speed, the notes swimming lazily in the pool of shadows.

"That's what you were talking about when you quoted Dupin.

Don't look for what has happened. Look for what has happened that has never happened before. You were talking about yourself. You were talking about me. And all the women. All the other women."

The soloist slithers through a glissando as if Hewitt, the oblong box, the night, the stars no longer exist. A sustained run of historic sixteenth notes, with no hint of verbal capitulation.

"The thing that had never happened before. The thing that couldn't possibly happen. That you, The Raven—the two of you—that you were both lying next to me the whole fucking time."

In his humming of the solo, there is a shift, a more insistent tone.

"And these women, these girls. You auditioned them for their voices. You were looking for similar voices. Whose voice was it? Whose voice were you trying to match? Was it Rose?"

He has completed the solo and has returned to the theme. The tempo has quickened, to match the original Hawkins.

"And now there's me," Hewitt says. "Right here. Right where you wanted me all along. As long as you were playing the game, fooling the world, why not have a little fun with an old friend? You knew I'd be assigned to the case. You picked a state park where the state police have jurisdiction. Once I had the gold bug, you knew you had me. You marched me around like a marionette. You rubbed my back. You listened to me talk about my life. Last night you fucked me. Tonight you kill me. Your kept man, your zombie slave—Rafferty—he gets the blame. For all of it. The circumstantial evidence. The DNA in his semen. That's one I don't want to know how you pulled off. But it doesn't matter, does it? None of it does. Because Gabriel Rafferty kills himself at the end of his spree. And by the time they find me, there'll be no way to know that Rafferty died before I did. End of story. Case closed. Did I leave anything out?"

The Raven continues his humming rendition of "Body and Soul" until it reaches its conclusion. She still cannot see him. But the shadow that contains him moves in her direction, cutting the original distance between them by half.

"Yes, you did leave out one thing," the shadow says. "The part where you use everything in your repertoire to change my mind."

It shocks her to hear The Raven speaking in Scott Gregory's voice. If this is Scott speaking, he might actually be leaving the door open for her. If it is The Raven, it is just one last pull on the marionette strings.

With Professor Gregory, she could reason. With The Raven, she could not.

"I won't plead with you not to hurt me," she says firmly, almost calmly. "I won't beg you not to kill me. If that's what you've decided, there's nothing I can do to convince you otherwise. You're the one who knows the questions on the test. All I can do is guess."

"For someone as intelligent as you, there's no such thing as a pure guess."

Hewitt looks at the stars, sees an infinity of glittering dice tumbling through the cosmos.

"Then my guess is you're leaving the door open," she says, her voice so whispery thin now he has to strain to hear it.

He laughs, closer to her again. In the laugh, inside it, there is the overtone of a voice she doesn't know.

"Leaving the door open? Or leaving the lid off?" he asks in a voice even less his own.

"You play to my greatest fear," she says. "Does that make you my inquisitor or my liberator?"

"I am not the one who does either. I empathize with your fears. It is the character who takes advantage of it—who has no choice but to take advantage of it."

The stars wink at Hewitt, wink with an accompanying laugh.

"And do you condone the actions of the character?"

"No. But this is the beauty of creating a character. The character and the creator are separate entities, with distinctly separate lives."

"And yet you share information with the character. Information a young woman told you fifteen years ago. In a conversation over white wine and grilled cheese sandwiches. How, of all the Poe stories, it was

'The Premature Burial' that terrified her the most," Hewitt says, fighting off a gag response on the last of the words, the thought.

Silence from him. Silence, too, from the stars. When the silence is broken, it is by him. Not by his voice, but by his hand, the back of it, gently stroking the side of her face. Once. Twice. Again. The back of his soft hand against her cheek. The way an ex-lover touches a face. The way a father touches the face of an adolescent daughter.

"Elizabeth Taylor Hewitt," he says, petting her face again, this time with his open palm and fingertips. He is next to her now. She sees his face, sees not the face of The Raven, but the face of the man she has loved.

"You lie here, more vulnerable to your deepest fears than you have ever been. And yet you build this moat around yourself, to keep it out. You ensconce yourself in the highest room of your castle with thoughts of white wine and grilled cheese."

Hewitt turns her head, moves her face to conform more intelligently with the shape of his palm. She knows she has no choice but to use the truth as she has come to know it. "Rose must have had a beautiful voice. A special voice. You've heard me try to sing, Scott. I could only disappoint you. I know you loved me, too, Scott. Like you loved Rose. But you killed her, Scott. You killed Rose. And I can't give you her voice back. I can't sound like her. I can't be Rose. No matter how much you want it."

She feels his hand pressing hard against her face.

"I didn't kill her," he whispers. "The other men killed Rose. All the other men. They broke her. Broke her heart. When her mind was no longer strong enough to fight them off."

"I can't be Rose, Scott. I can only be me. Elizabeth. The one who loved you more than she did. The one who always will."

The stars disappear. His face is over hers. His body climbs into the box with her, on top of her. On his breath, she smells something she has never before detected from him. A fermented licorice smell.

"Sing to me," he breathes into her eyes. "Sing to me. In the good voice. In the pretty voice."

She tells herself she can love him. She can love him. She can love her teacher.

His tongue is inside her mouth, his teeth butting against hers. She feels his hands at her pelvis, fumbling for an opening through her clothing. She feels him pulling things open.

She feels him hardening against her as the opening appears, the opening opens and the opening closes around him.

She can love him.

She can love him.

She can love him.

"I love you, Eliza," she hears him say. But it is not eloquent. It is not poetic. It is broken up by his hard breathing and the thudding of his bones against hers.

No viable words come to her mouth. Yet it is from this place that her favored response is generated as she slips away from his mouth and begins to work across his face. Moving. Licking the earlobe. The skin behind the ear. Her tongue flicking down under his jaw line. The tongue receding. Her lips, fishlike against his neck.

Tasting the taste of him, she kisses his neck.

She kisses his neck.

She kisses his neck.

And when she has him so he desires nothing but the continued lingual worship of his body, this is when she opens her mouth, draws in the flesh of his neck and bites.

And bites.

And bites.

And bites.

His scream comes from a depth he has coveted in his women. It is prodigious. It is horrific. It is the cry of The Raven leaving his body.

Ventilated of the scream, he grabs at his neck with one hand, grabs her throat with the other.

And she, with her tongue, analyzes the contents of her bite, finds what feels like a piece of a night-crawling annelid lolling inside her mouth. And she celebrates, knowing that among the other tissue she has exacted, this section of his carotid artery has also been exacted.

He pulls his hand away from his raging neck, adds it to the hold of the other upon her throat. She feels the wetness of his hand, smells the ferric content.

His hands, not professing to strangle her now, but to hold on to some last warmth of earth as his body temperature falls.

It is this final picture of Professor Scott Fitzgerald Gregory that Hewitt will carry with her forever. Of his torso lifting upward, his neck craning skyward, his eyes looking into infinity as his blood disperses in rhythmic arcs of flight across the starry sky.

EIGHTY-SIX

Hewitt woke up in heaven to the feeling of her father's hand stroking her forehead. This was heaven with her eyes closed. When she looked at heaven with her eyes open, it was in the guise of a hospital room with Captain Spangler doing the forehead touching.

"Welcome back," the stand-in dad said.

"Where did I go?" she managed in a voice that sounded like it had been asleep for days.

"According to the punches on your ticket, hell. And back."

For several seconds her memory attempted to retrace the route. The trip backward ended when The Raven had fallen on top of her, bleeding his way into death and, she had been convinced at the time, carrying out his goal of her premature burial. Instead of a lid, he had used his own fresh cadaver. With her hands and feet bound, and his weight on top of her, it was as effective as any nail-driven cover.

His blood against her clothes and skin had cooled to the temperature of the October night by the time her mind had steered its way to the escape route laid out a century and a half earlier by Poe himself. She was bound, her body covered by dead weight. But there was still the potential for motion in her body and, to make it that much more compelling, her soul.

So, like the prematurely interred wife of the Baltimore congressman in Poe's story, she began to move her body within its confines—with every chemical, every fiber, every muscle. And the rocking went on for what might have been an eternity had she not finally succeeded in forcing his weight off of her, following its outward pitch with a centrifugal thrust of her own body. At which point, the box and its contents had tipped on its platform and spilled onto the cold ground.

Hewitt swung her hand out over the sheets of the hospital bed, found her forehead and the dressing beneath which she assumed were several stitches. These, from hitting her head on the shovel he had left on the ground for filling the hole in the earth he had already opened for her.

"Is it coming back, or not quite?" Spangler asked.

"To the part where I got this," she said, gently fingering the head wound, her voice a flat low tone, her mouth and jaw as tired as they'd ever been. "I remember crawling, wiggling on my belly. Back to the car. It must've taken an hour. I know I was bleeding from up here."

Hewitt's mind lifted away from the blood, focused on a much more pleasant liquid, the scent of which her nostrils had located but her mind had been unable to fully embrace until that moment. On the rolling tray table, behind the chair where Spangler sat, she saw the Styrofoam cup with its plastic cover.

"It's the third one," Spangler told her. The first two went cold. It's just the cafeteria blend. But I figured under the circumstances you'd be okay with it."

Hewitt sat up a little, made one of those rolling head gestures a person in a hospital bed can get away with when they want something. Especially on the day they killed the monster.

Spangler got up, wheeled the tray table into place for her. He let Hewitt sip in peace until half the cup had been emptied. She knew the questions and concerns were lined up in his brain like jets on an O'Hare runway in a thunderstorm.

"Did you take any pictures of me at the scene?" she asked between sips. "I wouldn't mind having one for my mantle."

"It wasn't your prettiest moment," Spangler said. "After you made it to your car and called in, you passed out again. But from what I saw, from your face, all that blood, you looked about as dead as a living person would ever want to."

"You had no way of knowing the blood wasn't all mine."

The empathetic look on Spangler's face gave way to something more serious. It was time. "Who the hell was this guy, Elizabeth?"

"I'll tell you about that," Hewitt said, holding up the empty cup. "But it'll cost the state at least one more of these."

"I've already spoken to the governor. He's agreed to pick up the tab."

Spangler paged the nurse's station and put through the request. Hewitt felt her mouth trying to smile as he finished. When it didn't quite get there, she opened it instead and began to tell him what she knew. She would come to know much more. She would come to know things about the man who became The Raven that she could have never imagined. But for now, she told Captain Spangler everything as she knew everything to be.

She managed to squeeze that version of everything into less than ten minutes. And she was grateful when Spangler took the cue at that point that she was one very tired monster killer. He thanked her, kissed her on the forehead, withdrew from the room like a quiet, efficient orderly. Hewitt had actually succeeded in dozing for a warm sweet oblivious half hour when a nurse appeared at her bedside, loud enough in her mere standing there to pull Hewitt from sleep.

"Excuse me, Agent Hewitt. There's a detective here to see you. He said I should tell you he heard a siren and followed it to your room."

Groggy as she was, the siren didn't rationalize out right away. But once her mind got out of an ambulance, out of Illinois and floated over the Mediterranean Sea and farther east and back to the time of Homer, she got it.

"You can send him in," Hewitt said.

She pulled her blanket up a little. Because she was cold, she told herself. And when she looked up, there he was, dropped into the room from another galaxy.

The Luke Skywalker sound-alike. The Odysseus of Wilmette. Brady Freaking Richter.

"When I heard they had you here, I told myself no way in hell should I come tonight," he said with a smile that showed hurt because he could see how much she was hurting. "I tried my ass off not to, but no go."

First her surrogate dad. Now this brother from another dimension. She was a lucky girl. Psychologically shredded. But with each drop of the saline IV above her, it was time to count her blessings.

"I know it probably isn't proper," Brady Richter said. "With the circumstances what they are."

"I don't think there's an etiquette to follow for this," Hewitt said. "But thanks. If you hadn't come, I would've been alone with my thoughts. And that's probably not the best place for me to be right now."

"Would it be all right?"—he bounced his eyes off the visitor's chair. Hewitt nodded that it would be. He sat down.

"I know there probably isn't much of anything I can do," he offered. "But if you think of something, you'll tell me, right?"

"I'll tell you right now," Hewitt said. "I have two hands. I want you to take the one without the IV needle and hold it."

EIGHTY-SEVEN

The Raven lies awake in his childhood bed, his eyes tightly closed but his ears wide open to the sound that has brought him out of sleep to full, gleaming consciousness again.

It is the sound of his Madonna, his queen, his wife, his sister, his protector, his temptress, his life-giver, his executioner. It is the sound of his mother—as only he has been permitted to hear her. It is not a single sound, but of many, in bawdy chorus. The sound of laughter, crying, fear, fearlessness, lauding, derision, pleasure, pain, love, hate. In the one voice, hers, the one that comes to him from the other side of the wall.

It is the voice that sings to him in the darkness. The voice that sings. The voice that will continue to sing, even when the sound has changed, inexorably, to the other voice.

He could cover his ears, but that would require both hands. This is not possible. Because he needs his dominant hand to help do the one thing he has left to protect his mind from the truth of the screaming. And so he does it. Again and again and again. As only a boy who has metamorphosed into a man can do.

SCOTT GREGORY'S PRIVATE journal closes in Hewitt's lap. Doing this part of the post-mortem has been helping her. Reading the journals, hearing him speak from memory of earlier times.

Monsters like Scott Fitzgerald Gregory weren't born that way. Hewitt was convinced of that. She was also convinced that such creatures were born with a seed that, with the right amount of perverse nourishment, would produce the transmogrification.

The alchemy that resulted in the potent nourishing of The Raven's demon seed had, as its key element, the extreme schizophrenic episodes of the mother. Hewitt has been thinking about this. Trying to put it together. Not as part of any official investigation. But as part of her own personal inquiry, which she now knew had no official beginning and, in all likelihood, would have no official ending.

She had been processing it heavily in the days since she put The Raven down. And this wasn't the first time she had taken her contemplation to the grounds of the Mount Prospect psychiatric hospital. It was weird being there, of course. But it was Halloween. So sitting outside on an unseasonably temperate end-of-October afternoon, like just any other mental patient on the grounds wasn't much of a masquerade.

On this afternoon, the grounds were quiet. A handful of residents out for some exercise with their attendants. One of the patients, a younger man with badly uncombed bangs, had given Hewitt the eye upon passing the spot where she sat. As if the wooden bench she occupied was on personal loan from him.

This was her third visit to the grounds. Her first had occurred within hours of her release from the hospital, when she'd returned to the office of Dr. Burton Willis, sitting in the presence of his insane dart board again while he retrieved the file on a past resident of Mount Prospect. A patient named Rose Camilla Gregory. A patient who had passed away in the facility more than a year earlier.

There would be a number of revelations in the contents of Rose Gregory's case file. But the first one was the real beauty. It was right there on the first page of the file. The patient's personal profile. Specifically, the date of birth.

If the date was accurate, Scott Gregory had married a much older woman. At the time of her death, Rose Gregory had been seventy-two years old. She had also been, as she had been all her life, Scott Gregory's mother. There had never been a wife. Realistically, there had never been the potential of a wife. Not given the relationship of mother and son. Not given the sad, twisted, bizarre valences of history that surrounded and held the relationship together.

The most enduring of these connections, on a psychological time-line, had been an appreciation of a specialized form of American music. Rose Camilla Gregory had been a singer, a professional singer. A jazz vocalist. Her husband had been her manager. And a dismal failure at that. A drinker. A philanderer. Who drank and philandered his way to an early heart attack.

But Rose Gregory had sung on. As her own mental illness wors-ened. Paranoid schizophrenia and a singing career could hold hands only so long. But while they did, Rose Gregory held nightly sessions with an ever-changing lineup of male accompanists. In her bedroom. In her bedroom, but by carriage, in the room of her son, thin walls being one of the staples of the jazz lifestyle.

The screaming had started there. Seeming at first to have been a slightly more out-of-control response to the gesticulations of the suit-ors. But advancing into the unsettling, the shocking, the ungodly. And yet the men had kept coming. Like carnival patrons at the end of the night with one last ticket to spend in The House Of The Bizarre.

Scott Gregory had written extensively about that charmed adoles-cent world in the journals. He never referred to his mother's screaming as screaming. He always alluded to it as his mother's *other voice*. And he never alluded to his compulsion to re-create that voice for the twisted gratification it gave him once his giver of life and the keeper of the voice had left his world.

Rose Gregory had spent the last eight years of her life at Mount Prospect. She had been institutionalized at other venues, on and off, since her son's late adolescence. Leaving the burden on the shoulders of a fatherless son whose mind had already reached a divergence in the yellow wood and had created a means by which to take both roads at the same time.

And maybe that was it. Maybe that would have changed it enough to change what happened to the world. If Scott Gregory hadn't become a child of Poe. If he had, instead, become enamoured of someone like Robert Frost, the keeper of the yellow wood. Maybe that would have made all the difference. The markers weren't there in the life of Frost, the markers that would pull Scott Gregory in, grab his mind and, in time, his soul as well.

Robert Frost did not have an actress mother named Eliza, a mother who died before her young son's eyes on a grimly lit stage in performance after performance. Robert Frost did not have a mother who was ripped away from her son by the fates at a tender, impressionable age. Robert Frost did not wander through a short, stricken life in an effort to replace his lost Eliza, a road that would be traveled in vain as the fates again delivered death blow upon death blow to his mother-replacing quest. No, these sparkling bubbles of life had been reserved for the lips and tongue of Edgar Allan Poe.

The great doomed teller of tales had never sired a child in his lifetime. Yet there were children strewn about his literary wake. The types of young minds that were drawn to the grotesque tales as adolescents in an otherwise sleepy English class. These children of Poe who felt the visceral thrill, the intellectual tingling at the darkness, the madness, the admission of the unthinkable.

Scott Fitzgerald Gregory was one such child—in his mind, a very special child. In the journal, Hewitt had found the brief but telling self-evaluation that would come as close to a face-to-face explanation as she would ever have. The psycho-sexual desire to re-create the mother's voice. The way in which he equated the quality of the singing voices of his victims to the quality of the wailing that would come later. While never spelled out precisely, the case for the auto-erotic nature of his attachment to the screams was easy enough to advance. And at an equal if not deeper level of the psyche, there was his affinity, his connection, his conjoining with the mind of Poe. It was his way of marrying the one with the other. His mother, Rose, the tormented. And Poe, his surrogate father, the tormentor by proxy. It was his way of re-creating the genesis of the screams he reviled, feared and, ultimately, loved.

Scott Gregory's journals had revealed much of what she needed to know. Of course, they would never reveal enough. No process of human encoding and decoding could have.

Sitting there on the wooden bench, Hewitt drifted on the thought that these were the same spruce, maple, and juniper-enshrouded grounds where Scott Gregory had walked with his mother. Being Halloween, it didn't take much for Hewitt to conjure up their ghosts and project them onto the path that wound past her bench and into a stand of trees fifty yards away. She could see Scott accompanying Rose, always, she assumed a half-step behind her, in quiet obeisance to her after all those years, all those monstrously raised voices of the past.

With the oddly balmy Halloween breeze lapping at her face, Hewitt opened the journal, took a moment to reread the one passage she considered the most telling, the most truthful, the most horrifying.

I will always remember the way my mother sang to me. I will recall with love her body warm and full and cradling me, her voice the most precious intonation of the maternal bond yet expressed. I will remember with greatest fondness her presence on the softly lit stages of my youth, her face abloom, her voice alive. I will live in abiding respect for the unavoidable process, the inevasible forces that created her change of voice. Yet even with the profundity of the transformation, I will remember the loveliness of the voice. I will admit only to her soul and my own how I came to love my mother's second voice.

Hewitt looked up from the page, left the journal open in her lap, left the writing to the Halloween breeze, as if the ink in which it was composed was still not entirely dry.

EIGHTY-EIGHT

The Day of the Dead. Hewitt has begun her observation with a four-hour drive to a town west of Madison, Wisconsin. A town called Black Earth. Four hours is a lot of windshield time. And Hewitt's eyes have found ways to occupy themselves beyond the slow, steady absorption of the Illinois and Wisconsin countryside. So, against that backdrop she begins to sketch with her eyes. Images that will find their way into her sketchbook. When that makes sense again.

She'll get to all of them eventually. A vignette of Scott Gregory ushering Gabriel Rafferty from the psychiatric facility. Another of the professor supervising Rafferty's writing of the letters to Anna Magdalena and Christiane Mons. The joint visit of Gregory and Rafferty to Baltimore, to the Poe Museum. Rafferty's holding cell, the infamous third room in the upstairs of the Victorian country house. All of it, eventually.

Again, when she is ready.

On the passenger seat beside her is an audio tape she's been saving for just such an excursion. It isn't a tape from her own music cache. It has come from a special collection. From what she knows, it is the only one of its kind.

Hewitt is more than two hours into the drive when she finally works up the nerve to put the thing on. More than once she'd thought of lowering the window and tossing the tape out for a proper highway burial. But that wouldn't have been fair. Not to the artist. And not to her listening public. Which, at this time, consists of those present in the Mazda and no on else.

It has been a while since Hewitt actually played a cassette tape in her car. But when she slides the thing in, the analog hiss greets her instantly, and they, the vocalist and her audience of one, are on their way.

There are no introductions. And the music itself begins several bars into a piano intro to a song Hewitt quickly identifies as Gershwin's "Someone To Watch Over Me."

The recording is rudimentary. Someone had hung a microphone above the stage of what sounds to Hewitt, from the background clinks and chatter, like any of the smoky little nightclubs that served up jazz back when Chicago served up such offerings on a nightly basis.

Following the piano intro, played with professional dexterity and a somewhat boozy articulation, a bass and drums enter. And, after a pause for dramatic effect, the vocalist begins to tell her story.

Hewitt has never heard this jazz vocalist before. But she knows the voice. She knows it through its descendents in the tragic universe to which the voice of Rose Camilla Gregory gave birth.

As haunting as the listening experience is, the jazz aficionado in Hewitt is still alive. And while she can never be truly objective in listening to the singing of Scott Gregory's mother, she finds herself slipping into a mode that actually comes close to that. As the Wisconsin fields roll by. As the distance from the events of September and October lengthen with every blink of her windshield eyes.

Rose Gregory could sing. She had a strong clean voice, very adept in her phrasing. And she could take it soft and soothing or hard and sultry as the mood of the music suggested.

The tape contained an entire set of music as performed on that otherwise forgotten evening. Hewitt listens to all of it, cataloguing the repertoire in her mind. Between songs the singer kept things simple. Expressing gratitude for the smatterings of applause. Succinctly identifying the pieces, the composers. Pretty much standard jazz fare. A couple of Ellingtons, Cole Porter, Harold Arlen among them. And to close it out, an equally moving and chilling rendition of Gershwin's "The Man I Love."

With the listening experiment completed, the last hour and a half of the drive passes in silence. But upon her final approach to Black Earth, Hewitt can't resist the thought of starting the tape again. So she does, the jazzy strains of "Someone To Watch Over Me" accompanying her through the wrought-iron gates of Black Earth Memorial Park.

It has been one full decade and more than half of another since Hewitt has been here. In a physical sense. In all other senses beyond the physical, she has been visiting here on a regular basis.

Sarah Lee Hooker is buried at the foot of a small rise in the cemetery tract, in the shadow of a solitary elm. Hewitt stands at the base of the rise, in the shadow cast by the old elm, even though the skies are a muddy gray and offering the earth below pulses of windswept mist, like exhalations, sighs, from a weary God.

On the monument that marks Sarah Lee's final landing place, there is a glass-covered photo embedded in the stone, just above her name. The yearbook photo. The idealized Sarah Lee Hooker. It is the one face, the perfect face that presented itself to the eyes of God, with maybe just a slightly quizzical skew to the eyes and brow, to ask, as all such victims ask their God, *why me?*

On earth, there will never be an answer to the question. Not a satisfactory one. The psychiatrists, the clergy, the grief counselors, the talk show gurus, the drunk at the bar, not a damn one of them would ever get there. The best any of them could hope for was that someone would come forward with a requisition form for atonement, a form with the name of the human actor who was responsible neatly filled into the blank space. What God did with such requisitions would always be a private matter.

Hewitt likes the feeling of the mist against her face. She can't escape the cleansing aspect of it, any more than she has been able to escape the form, the countenance and, especially, the color of the large bird that watches her from a low-hanging branch of the elm.

There is a sense Hewitt feels coming from the bird, a sense of expectation. Laughable as that seems to Hewitt's mind. But the damn thing just sits there, waiting, waiting for her to do or say or perform something. So Elizabeth Taylor Hewitt, the mist kissing her face, the picture of Sarah Lee Hooker filling her eyes, parts her lips and begins to sing, in a less-than-beautiful voice, the "Ave Maria."